GOLDEN RESISTANCE
BOOK ONE OF THE SIGNALBORN SERIES
A.O. GARNETTE

A.O. GARNETTE

For my readers:

For those who believe they can be more.
You already are.

CONTENT WARNING

Golden Resistance contains some themes and depictions that might be sensitive to certain readers—<u>your mental health matters</u>. Please use your own discretion when reading.

Themes and depictions include, but are not limited to: slavery, unwanted touching, death and dying, kidnapping, misshapen limbs and body parts, public execution, revenge, sexually explicit content, trauma, and grief.

CONTENTS

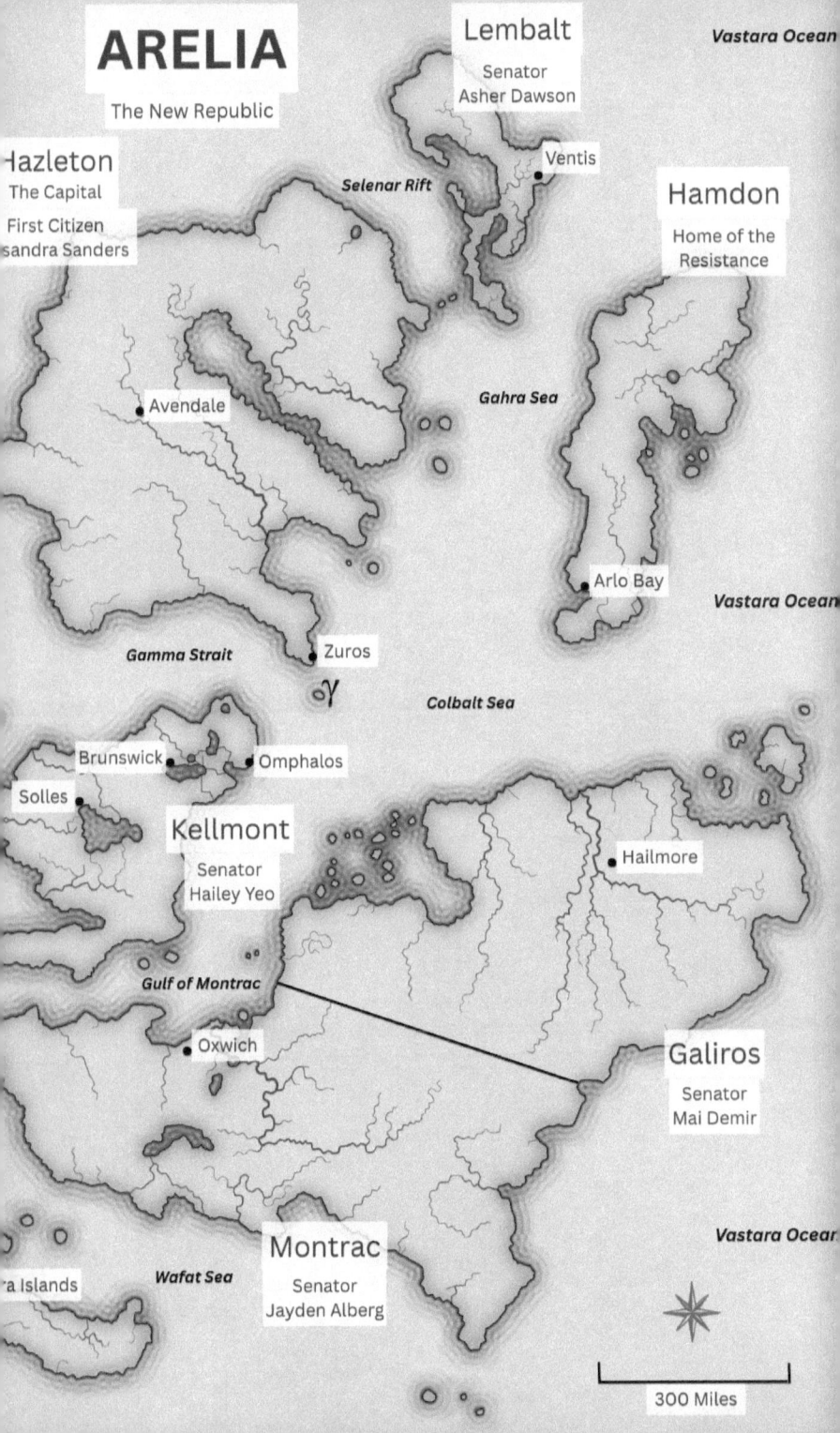

BEFORE THE NEW REPUBLIC

ARELIA WAS A DEMOCRACY in all ways a democracy should be—until it wasn't.

The news of the first explosion broke in the early hours of the morning. The government thought the blast was a fluke, an accident. Officials contained it within a water treatment facility nestled in the snow-capped mountains, just outside the city of Ventis, state of Lembalt. No injuries were reported, but within a day, Ventis saw an increase in hospitalizations, missing persons, and reports of individuals with strange new abilities.

Two days later, a second explosion occurred at a water treatment facility in the tropical region of Solles, Kellmont. The following day, Arlo Bay, in Hamdon, was targeted. Due to Hamdon's unforgiving coastline of uninterrupted sea cliffs and the violent surf from the Colbalt Sea, the State of Hamdon went silent within twenty-four hours of the explosion.

By the end of the week, the entire world of Arelia was in chaos. All major water treatment facilities were destroyed. The last to fall was the facility in the rainy city of Zuros, Arelia's capital, in Hazleton.

The government took too long to act. Too long for other water treatment facilities to receive adequate protection. Once the government realized the attacks were deliberate, the damage was irreparable. The entire potable water supply within the world of Arelia had been contaminated.

That was 146 years ago—before the New Republic, before the humans were enslaved—when the contamination forged a new race: the Behtari.

Official Edict

The New Republic is built on order, and order is built on truth.

The truth is this: The Behtari are not an accident. They are the future of Arelia. Their abilities are not a threat, but a foundation for growth. Behtari do not divide us, they define us. From this day forward, all Behtari will be recognized by their ability.

The Six are as follows:

1. Inflictor — Those who hold dominion over sensation itself, able to create pain or pleasure.
2. Mind Reader — Those who uncover deceit within the shadows, able to enter into the mind of others.
3. Illusionist — Those who shape others' perception with the ability to alter one's sight or reality.
4. Prophet — Those who sense future currents, possibilities, or outcomes.
5. Manipulator — Those who control the body of themselves or others, able to restrain or force.
6. Shielder — Those who conceal sound, smell, and mind, with the ability to create a barrier around the mind or body.

These six are not privileges. They are truths. They exist in blood and in bone, without question, without error. We are grateful for the Behtari's vast contributions to the New Republic.

As such, a human's purpose in the New Republic is in service. Their labor and their obedience are equally necessary for the New Republic's prosperity.

This is the Order of the New Republic.
By the authority of the First Citizen,
Leader of Arelia, Voice of the New Republic

PART 1

TREASON

1

LUNA

LUNA'S MOTHER GRIPPED HER clammy hand so fiercely it almost hurt.

Solles was one of the warmer cities in Arelia, but tonight it was the kind of cold that cut through Luna's clothes and straight to her core. It didn't help; it was the middle of the night, pitch-black. Luna couldn't even see the stars above as her mother pulled her into another alley. Her mom walked so quickly she was almost running, and Luna had to quicken her pace to keep up.

Earlier that night, Luna's mother had burst into her bedroom, waking her. She had a medium-sized, half-full black bag slung over her shoulder.

Luna sat up, disoriented until she recognized her mother's desperation. Her throat closed as she watched her mother pick up random items from the bookshelf, check them, and either return them or stuff the knick-knacks into the bag. Luna paused for a moment and watched, transfixed, as her mother picked up another item, studying it, and turning it over in her hand at least twice before setting it down. As if her mother were unaware Luna was awake, she continued moving around the small room. Frantically, she moved on to the drawers, opening and closing them as if she were looking for something vital.

All the while, her mother did not take her eyes away from the object she held in her hands.

"Do not ask questions right now," she ordered in a hushed tone, though she did not look at her daughter. "Get dressed. Pack comfortable, dark-colored, practical clothes. Here is a burner holo so you can contact your brother, or hopefully, your father. Pack anything personal you may need over the next few days."

Luna's father hadn't been home in the last two days. Her mother said it had been for business, which wasn't abnormal for her father to take a night or two at work, but now Luna's mind raced.

Had they been lying to her? How much of what they said was actually true?

Luna's thoughts were interrupted when she jumped as her mother hefted the bag onto her bed, now over three-quarters full of items and knick-knacks from around their house. Luna opened her mouth to argue, but her mom immediately put her finger to her own lips.

Her eyes were wide, the gold flecks in her blue irises seeming to burn from within. She put her hands on Luna's shoulders gently as she leaned forward and whispered into Luna's ear, "Say. Nothing."

Luna gave one sharp nod and stood. She quickly got into black cargo pants that were cinched at the ankles, a long-sleeve, form-fitting shirt, and a fitted jacket. Luna always had an easier time shielding herself when wearing form-fitting clothes, but she would have to work around the pants today.

She shifted her attention to packing the bag, careful to work around the knick-knacks. It was almost impossible with how haphazard and full the bag already was.

What is all this doing in here? Certainly the golden cat with its moving paw from the kitchen didn't need to come with them.

When Luna finished packing, she zipped the bag shut and grabbed the burner holo, stuffing it in the back pocket of her oversized cargo pants. With the bag over one shoulder, she turned to walk out of her bedroom, but not before she caught a glimpse of herself in her mirror. She noticed her green eyes, flecked with gold, were glowing particularly bright—almost as if they were lit from within. But they would only burn brightly like that if they were feeling any emotion with intensity, like fear. The flecks made it incredibly easy to determine whether someone was human or Behtari.

Luna had been born with gold flecks sprinkled through her green iris. The initial Behtari obtained their powers—as well as the gold flecks—through the contamination. However, children born to Behtari—referred to as Signalborn—inherited their powers genetically. Although the Signalborn are born with gold flecks in their eyes, their abilities emerge during adolescence, when the brain is developed enough to handle increased gamma waves. Even so, it is impossible to know what ability would manifest. While some inherit their parents' abilities, that wasn't always the case.

When the contamination was released 146 years ago, Arelia had been utterly human. Even after all this time, little was known about how the water contamination occurred. However, there was no question that the attacks on the water treatment facilities were targeted, planned, and well-orchestrated.

Once a human consumed the contaminated water, the foreign matter attempted to increase the human brain's threshold for gamma waves. If successful, the human would develop one of six known mental abilities of the Behtari: Mind Reader, Shielder, Manipulator, Inflictor, Illusionist, or the rarest and most coveted by the government—a Prophet. Unfortunately, the water only had a forty-one percent success rate. Thirty-six percent of those who drank the contaminated water died, and twenty-three percent remained human. At least that's what Luna read in her history books when she studied the formation of the New Republic in school.

From there, chaos ensued. The contamination allowed the Behtari, with their newfound powers, to form the New Republic and take over Arelia with ease. Consequently, this allowed the New Republic to implement the enslavement of humans with minimal to no resistance. It made Luna's stomach turn just thinking about it.

She hated the treatment of the enslaved. They were out of sight most of the time, assigned to posts no one else wanted to do, or no one wanted to be seen doing. They performed almost all factory work, including sanitation, maintenance, and back-of-house tasks in stores, such as restocking. It was rare to see any working amongst the Behtari.

She knew her family did not care for the New Republic leadership, but she had only learned recently of her mother and father's involvement with the resistance. Kent, her older brother, apparently knew for some time of their parents' involvement, but all three had kept it from her.

Luna grabbed a nearby hair tie and secured her hair into a low bun to contain her bright copper curls. Once Luna tamed her hair, well, most of her hair, she then constructed both a mental shield and physical shield, as she always did before leaving her home.

Luna's mother wasted no time teaching Luna how to shield, practicing with her repeatedly until it became second nature. Luna took one last look in the mirror before leaving her bedroom, walking down the hallway toward the living room.

Turning the corner into the living room, she found her mother standing in the dark by the door. Luna swung the pack's strap over her head, so it crossed in front of her body and rested on her right hip. The bag was heavy, cutting into her shoulder uncomfortably.

Though impatient, her mother took the time to silently help Luna adjust the bag, making it more bearable. She eyed her daughter and gave Luna a nod of approval. Her mother was dressed in what looked like dark green combat pants, a black band t-shirt with their shared favorite band's name, Infiniti's End, on the front. Additionally, she wore her lucky oversized black leather jacket, a black fitted hat with a curved brim, and, as always, her gold chain necklace.

The gold necklace was simple, but she never took it off. The chain was delicate, with thin, small links. Luna always thought the necklace was too long, as it always fell beneath her shirt's neckline. She and her father exchanged a necklace and a bracelet instead of rings.

Luna's mother made a final adjustment to the bag on her shoulder, then opened their apartment door, grabbed Luna's hand, and guided her into the hallway. Luna followed her out the back of the apartment building, keeping to back alleys and shadows of Solles.

Her mother picked up her pace more than once, as if she were late for an appointment. After several minutes, they ducked into a side alley. Once engulfed in the darkness of the alley, Luna's mom dropped her hand.

Luna felt a small crack inside her chest. It felt childish, but she couldn't remember the last time she held her mother's hand. Luna blew warm air from her lungs into the palms of her hands.

Luna looked up at her mom, who was slightly taller than her. She noticed how solemn her mother's face had become. Her blue irises flecked with gold didn't shine as brightly as they used to, and her hair had grown grayer than the deep black it once was. It was at that moment Luna realized how much her mother had aged in the last two years.

Suddenly, her mother went stiff next to her, pushing herself and Luna flat against the alley wall. Then Luna felt it against her shield, which surrounded her body like a glove. The feeling came from the frequency a fellow Behtari was emitting by using their ability.

It felt as if there was a light scratching against Luna's skin, making her hair stand on end. Luna could feel a Mind Reader using their ability, gently searching for them. She remained as still as stone, ensuring her shield was muffling all her sounds, her scent, and anything detectable. The shield didn't make Luna invisible, but it gave her an edge of stealth.

Luna's mother always taught her to shield before leaving the house. They'd even argued about it once. When

Luna stormed out, her mother yelled after her, "*Better safe than sorry!*"

Now, Luna was glad she listened. Her shields were strong, and when Luna's shield was in place, it fit almost like a bodysuit, covering her head to toe, making her nearly silent. When a Shielder has their ability in place, they are harder to hear, see, fight, and therefore, kill. It was one of the reasons her mother had become so valuable to the government—she was one of the strongest Shielders in Arelia.

Not only was she a fantastic scientist who worked alongside Luna's dad in one of the New Republic's labs, but she was also a powerhouse. Luna's mother could easily shield two hundred New Republic soldiers without flinching. Luna heard the story only once, told by her father. It was one of the small rebellions that had grown into a threat to the New Republic. Her mother's ability was used to help the New Republic soldiers conceal themselves before reaching the Resistance camp and slaughtering everyone.

That was when her parents agreed to help The Resistance as much as they could. They never signed up for slaughter. Luna hoped her mother would share her side of the story when Luna was older, but she never did. Now, Luna was worried if she had truly run out of time. Luna would turn nineteen tomorrow. The whole family was supposed to celebrate at home with her favorite treat: strawberry pound cake with cream cheese frosting.

Her mom turned back and took Luna's face in her hands. "You've got those shields as strong as you can, right?"

Luna nodded quickly, watching as tears rolled down her mother's face. Luna realized, very quickly, that her birthday celebration was becoming unlikely.

Avoiding as many street cameras as possible, they continued moving. Luna followed, keeping her head low and face covered. Suddenly, they slowed, as if her mother was waiting for something. Then Luna heard it. The distinct buzzing sound of a MAV—Micro Air Vehicle—a government drone the size of an insect that could record their every movement. They were usually used to keep watch over the enslaved in the slums, but one was here, watching them.

Luna kept her head down and hood up. "Mom..." she whispered tentatively.

Her mother grasped her hand again to hurry her along. She gave Luna's hand three squeezes—*I love you*—something she had done with Luna and Kent since they were children, when they needed reassurance.

"I know," her mother said, voice thick with exhaustion. "If we do not hurry, there will be more."

Luna understood then. She understood the knick-knacks in her bag, why her father hadn't been home, and why they were out in the middle of the night. The government turned on her parents, and now they were fleeing for their lives.

2

<u>LUNA</u>

Luna was determined. She would not let this MAV gather any usable footage. The MAVs were the latest invention from the New Republic, another way to watch everyone's waking move.

Luna and her mother were still out of the MAV's line of sight, but they had to time their next move just right. Luna inhaled deeply through her nose and out through her mouth. She was desperately trying to calm her nerves and failing. She felt like an electrical current just beneath the surface of her skin was about to catch fire. She would not let this robot take her family, and she would not be collateral damage.

Her mother moved first. She pulled down her hat, covering her face. Then, spinning to her right, she took her hand from her pocket, and threw a sticky-looking material at a camera Luna hadn't seen. She gathered more of the sticky material from her pocket before she opened three separate exits. The gate at the back of the alley, the door to a different apartment building, and the grate that led to the sewers.

All the while, Luna had been inching toward the edge of the alley to intercept the MAV. She was so close to the edge of the alley that she didn't dare move forward for fear of being seen. Her Shield was excellent for stealth, but it did not make her invisible.

While Luna waited for the opportune moment, she gently slid a black glove on her hand. The glove didn't look like anything spectacular; however, it would create an E.M.P.—electromagnetic pulse—surge immediately when it encountered the MAV, rendering it useless. All Luna had to do was catch it.

Suddenly, Luna leapt toward the MAV, immediately catching it in her gloved hand. The glove did the rest of the work, as the E.M.P. immediately fried the MAV's circuits. Then, she closed her fist as hard as she could, squashing the device. The thing looked like a fly but wasn't—just another robot.

Luna tossed it toward the sewer drain no more than two feet away, delighting in its *clink* on the way down. She turned to her mother with a broad smile, but it faded abruptly at the sight of the sadness in her mother's eyes.

"Lu..." She took Luna's hands. "You have to leave through one of these doors. We have a minute at most. I need you to listen and go now. You know nothing, so you are in no danger, I promise. I couldn't leave you, knowing they were coming. I love you more than all the stars, but I need you to do this for me, because I can't bear it if they take you, too." Tears spilled from her mother's eyes as she blinked.

Luna knew, deep in her being, that this would be the last time she would see her mother in person.

Her mother then grasped her fiercely, pulling her close and saying,

"I love you. You are everything. I am not going to look—you choose. I will count to fifteen and close them all, so ensure you are around the first bend by then. If they use a Mind Reader on me, they will never know, just as I won't know."

Luna nodded, hugging her mother as tightly as possible. Luna tried to control the shaking of her voice as she whispered back. "I love you, too." Luna released her mother, refusing to waste the gift she'd been given. Time. Luna walked behind her mother, and as they were back-to-back, Luna grabbed her mother's hand one final time. She couldn't say anything; she couldn't bear to. All Luna could manage were those three short squeezes.

I love you.

Her mother's reply was immediate: four short squeezes back. *I love you too.* Then, with a trembling voice, as if her mother was hanging on by a thread, she started to count.

Luna sprinted for the door on the left, doubling back at the last second, and went to the one on the far right. That way, if a Mind Reader used their ability on her mother, it would be almost impossible to pinpoint which door she had used by sound alone.

She ran up the first set of stairs, taking them two at a time, feeling the bag slamming against her side as she went. As she anticipated, there was a door at the top of the stairs that led to a store or nightclub. Judging by the stale smell of beer and thumping bass, it was the latter.

When Luna pushed through the door, she entered the back of a packed club. The bass was so intense every time it pulsed, it made the hair on the back of her neck stand on end. She made her way through the crowd, shoving past dancing people to get to the exit. When she burst through the door, she ran.

She ran until her lungs burned, and she couldn't continue. She ducked into an alley and put her hands on her knees to try to slow her heart rate. It took everything in her to breathe rather than break down and sob.

Luna continued to force her breathing to slow; she pulled out the burner holo and dialed Kent's number from memory. He picked up on the fourth ring. "Hey. Why—" His voice sounded gravely and raw, thick with sleep; she clearly had woken him. She didn't let him finish, as she said through panting—

"Sending... you... my... location. Please." She hung up before anyone could trace the call, or any MAVs would have detected her voice. Then, Luna tucked herself into the far back corner of the alley, behind a rancid-smelling, overflowing dumpster, and waited.

She could barely see the light from the alley. In another life, this might have been a night she could have gone out with her friends, celebrating her birthday. She didn't have many friends; if she wasn't working at the art museum, she was home with her parents. Would that even be her home anymore? Where would she go?

She knew she could live with Kent and his roommates, but she had been saving up for her own place. There was this beautiful loft above the art museum, and Luna had inquired with the owners about it since her first shift. It was a loft, but with enormous glass windows that looked out over a park which was full of her favorite flower, the delta lily.

The delta lily resulted from contamination and began to bloom shortly after the Behtari were created. Most of the delta lilies grew right near riverbanks and only opened at night. They had ivory-white petals with a deep

ocean-blue center. Like the Behtari, it was flecked with
luminous gold within its blue hue and along its tips and
edges, almost as if it had been painted.

Luna's mind raced, not unlike a wild pinwheel in a
gust of wind. She couldn't stop her mind from spinning,
each thought bringing her deeper down into her anxiety.
She pulled her knees so close to her chest that it was
almost painful as she tried to control her raging mind.
Luna forced herself to breathe in through her nose and
out through her mouth.

Ping!

Luna jumped at the notification on her holo.

Across.

She slowly rose from her hiding place, and sure
enough, Kent was on the other side of the street wearing
dark, loose sweats and an enormous gray hoodie,
pulled up around his head with a black baseball cap
underneath. It hadn't taken Kent more than twenty
minutes to find her. He was staring at his phone like
he couldn't be bothered by anything around him. The
world might as well have been burning.

Luna slowly emerged from the shadows of the alley.

Her brother quickly crossed the street to her. He
gently tugged her arm toward him and, in a jovial tone,
asked, "What is going on? Did you have too much fun?"

Luna shook him off in disbelief, but she fell in step
beside him. Kent was to the left of the walkway, next
to the street, and she was on the right, nearest to the
storefronts and shops. Kent was almost a half-foot taller;
Luna had to quicken her pace to keep up with him. She
caught his dark auburn waves peeking out from under
his hoodie and cap.

"Actually, no. Mom freaked out in the middle of the night, had me pack this bag—" She patted the bag still resting against her right hip. "—full of random items from the house, told me to pack some stuff for the next few days, and gave me the burner. Then we left." Luna stopped walking, looking down as if the ground would show her what had happened. Kent paused beside her, allowing her a moment to collect herself. She knew she was terrified, but she had to push through this and began walking again.

"Kent, someone was after her—or us. I don't know. Dad hasn't been home for two days. I didn't think anything of it until tonight. It isn't like he hasn't slept at the lab before."

Though Kent had not sped up, Luna was out of breath from the pace. He gave her a look that said *Really? This is too fast?* His green eyes were the same as hers.

Kent surprised her by slowing before he said, "Look. *I* have zero idea what is going on. *You* have zero idea what is going on. We will find someone within the New Republic to help us. I cannot risk my position as a LEO—Law Enforcement Officer—, and we don't need to add 'criminal record' to your file. We need information before we dive into...whatever *this* is."

Luna wanted to argue, but she knew he was right, even if she didn't want to say it out loud yet.

He took her silence as an agreement between them and continued the path to his apartment. They had at least nine blocks to go.

Luna had hoped they would take the underrail or a cab. She wasn't sure whether he wanted to avoid exposing themselves or if he was pissed she had called him. If she was being honest with herself, she knew it was both. She followed one step behind him the rest of the walk.

3

KENT

KENT DECIDED IT WAS best to break the news of his sister's situation to his roommates alone. The fact that it was only just into the next day meant his two roommates would either still be drunk from the party they had gone to, or they were passed out. Kent reasoned neither was suitable for retaining information, but he had little choice; he had to do this now.

As he opened the door, he could hear a distinct *clink* of glass as the front door met bottles Kent meant to recycle—two days ago—against the entryway wall. He cringed as each *tink* seemed louder than the last. When the door was finally open, he waved Luna inside, locking the door behind him. Once inside the dimly-lit living space, he sighed at the scattered clothes, mismatched furniture, and overall sense of chaos he knew she didn't care about. Still, he wished he had tidied up a little yesterday.

Kent ushered Luna into his room. He got the shower started, grabbed a clean towel, and some of his clothes for her. Once the shower was running with hot water, she closed the door to the bathroom, leaving him to contemplate the night's events.

Kent never wanted Luna to be forced into The Resistance; he told his parents as much. His parents agreed, but then they kept her in the dark about almost everything. Luna knew they were passing information to The Resistance, but she had no idea how deeply entrenched they were. Kent had been screaming at his father just two weeks ago.

"At least give her the choice! Don't keep putting her in situations she doesn't even understand because you won't let her. She deserves to know why everything is going to shit." His father stared at him, as if Kent were asking for something outrageous. He hadn't seen his dad since.

Kent had no idea how much Luna knew. How was he going to figure that out? Because, if he was being honest, how much did he actually want to tell her? How much did *he* actually know at this point? Kent was sure he knew far less than he should.

He hoped they didn't know enough to be a problem to the New Republic, but he couldn't be sure what knowledge the New Republic would find valuable. Realizing now that was how his dad had been protecting him, guilt crawled along his skin. He and Luna would have to discuss what they both knew, but that conversation would have to wait—Kent needed to inform his roommates that they were having a guest for at least a few days, and she might need some space right now.

He figured Wyatt would be the path of least resistance, at least that was what he hoped. Wyatt was passed out on the couch with several empty beer cans on the floor, as well as a recently-used purple glass bong.

Wyatt clearly had a great time tonight.

"Hey..." Kent said, shaking Wyatt gently. When Wyatt slowly opened his eyes, Kent noticed they were bloodshot, and the contrast intensified the gold in his eyes.

Wyatt ran his hand down his face, groaning.

Kent had to stop himself from chuckling at his friend, who was sometimes an enormous idiot. "I need you and Marcella. I only want to say this once. I'm going to get her; can you make coffee?"

Kent then knocked on Marcella's bedroom door and waited. She was an extremely private person, but he also knew she wouldn't have gone to bed completely blasted; she was never late for work. He knocked again, louder this time. "Marcella, I have to talk to you right now." It took a minute, but finally he heard feet shuffling toward the bedroom door.

She opened it a crack and stared at him, exhaustion lining her face. "Can I help you with something?" She raised an eyebrow.

Kent rolled his eyes and turned to walk back into the living space, saying over his shoulder, "Marcella, we all know you want to know what is going on. So, please get out here?" Kent couldn't help but feel grateful for his roommates, his friends; they had no idea what they were about to get themselves into. He knew the only way he could approach this without feeling guilty later would be to let them choose. Did they want to go with him down this path? Or did they want to be absolved entirely of it? He truly wasn't sure which way they would go. Wyatt was a musician and DJ who worked weekends at local clubs, and Marcella worked as a security detail for a private investigative service. They both loved their jobs, and he knew this information could cause both of them to lose their lives.

Kent and Marcella each took a seat in the two faded green armchairs on either side of the couch.

Wyatt lied back down on the brown leather couch, with two bottles of water, one sports drink, and a large, steaming cup of coffee. He clearly felt terrible. Marcella looked over at Wyatt and crossed her arms in exasperation.

There's a story here. Kent made a mental note to ask Marcella about it later, then he cleared his throat. "Okay, I know you guys trust me...but I am speculating at this point, so bear with me. Luna is going to have to stay with us for a while. Something has happened with our parents, and I think it is related to their jobs and the New Republic. My dad has been missing for two days, and Luna thinks LEOs are after my mom."

Wyatt stared at Kent, his mouth slack. "What?"

Marcella rubbed her fingers along her temples and looked at Wyatt, seething. "Wyatt, please, drink the coffee and focus. We are assuming the government took their parents, number one because they work for the government, and number two because Luna thinks it was LEOs after them."

Wyatt blinked once, but then his eyebrows pinched together as he looked at Kent again and asked. "What?"

"Go back to sleep, please, and come back to us when you are sober," Marcella quipped as she got off the couch and went back to her bedroom.

"Where are you going?" Kent asked, shocked at this reaction from her.

Marcella turned around, putting her hands on her hips as she said, "What are we going to do? Tell Luna to leave? Of course, she can stay, but the rest of this is a problem for the morning. I am going back to bed."

With that, Marcella went directly to her bedroom, shut her door loud enough to make Kent flinch. The light emanating from beneath her door went dark a moment later.

Kent turned back to the couch to say something, but Wyatt had already started snoring on the sofa.

Well... that did not go the way I expected.

By the time Kent was back in his bedroom, the shower had been turned off, and Luna was standing in his bedroom wearing one of his white shirts and boxers while she towel-dried her curly copper hair. Luna looked better, but she still had a haunted quality in her eyes, one he hoped she could return from.

"Did you tell them?" Luna whispered.

"Yeah. Everything is fine," he answered, but his ability was tingling at the corners of his vision, making him feel uneasy. Kent was an Inflictor, which unfortunately was extremely useful as a LEO. He was able to cause any sensation within someone's body without touching them. He didn't like to think about what the New Republic asked him to do in the cells below the State building. He made people feel like their bones were breaking, or as if they were drowning, or dying. But his other ability, the government didn't know about—couldn't know about. Kent was also a Prophet, and that ability allowed him to sense something was changing. He could feel it in the frequency of the air around him.

Luna must have sensed it as she took his hand. She gave him three squeezes and let go. "What do we do now?"

Kent squeezed Luna's arm back four times. "I'll go to work tomorrow—well, *today*—and see if I can dig up some information."

She nodded and turned toward the air mattress. It was still up from last weekend when she crashed here after a night bar hopping with them.

Kent looked at his holo again and realized what day it was.

"Happy Birthday, Luna. I am sure tomorrow will be better."

Luna smiled softly, said thank you, and curled under the heap of blankets on the air mattress. She usually stayed over more often this time of year, maybe once a weekend, so he hadn't taken the air mattress down.

As Kent lay back, he could feel his ability pulling at his mind again, but he tried to ignore it like he would a sore knee. Soon, he drifted to sleep.

4

LUNA

LUNA ONLY GOT A few hours of restless sleep. Somehow, Kent was still up before her and was in the kitchen making coffee with a "birthday breakfast," whatever *that* was. Luna had to admit she was mildly concerned.

Thankfully, it was the weekend, so Luna didn't have to give tours at the art museum. Kent didn't usually work weekends either, but was scheduled for an overtime LEO shift today. Luna loved working at the art museum; it was truly one of her favorite places. They displayed both Behtari and human art. Luna had no idea how some of the humans managed to make the pieces without being caught.

She was sitting on Kent's bed when she turned the projection on in his room, letting the news play, though it served more as background noise. She tried to focus on the news beats to distract herself from everything. On the projection, they discussed the weather in Solles, a local robbery, and a spring festival scheduled for the end of this quarter. Luna continued to attempt to tame her copper curls as she watched. She would have to put her hair up in a braid; without any proper conditioner or curl cream, it was bound to go nuts. Although Kent had wavy hair, too, he was a typical single male, and the only items in his shower were a three-in-one body wash, shampoo, and conditioner, and a comb.

As she finished the braid on her hair, she shifted, catching a glimpse of herself in the mirror on his dresser. She looked like a ghost. She had dark circles under her eyes, making the freckles across her nose and cheeks stand out even more. Her face had a haunted look about it, reminding her of last night's events all over again. She really didn't want to deal with this right now, but she knew if she didn't, she would have to do it later. Frankly, that sounded even worse.

Luna leaned over the edge of the bed, grabbed the black bag from the night before, and placed it next to her on the bed. She pulled out two of the knick-knacks her mother had put in the bag to—

Knock, knock.

Kent poked his head into the room and asked, "Hey, can we talk?"

Luna nodded and scooted over, patting the spot next to her as an invitation to sit.

When Kent came into the room, she realized he looked just as haggard as she did.

Just before he sat, he handed her a plate heaped with scrambled eggs, toast with an obscene amount of butter, and an enormous mug of coffee, complete with cream and sugar.

As soon as the smell of the coffee hit her nose, she felt the ghost of a smile cross her lips. She took the mug almost greedily from Kent.

He smiled and said, "Happy Birthday, Luna."

She couldn't help but return the smile as she took the coffee and plate, which had her mouth watering with the butter from the toast and the eggs spiced with a bit of garlic. Luna took a long sip of the coffee, allowing the heat to wrap around her hands and warm her from the inside out. She began shoveling eggs and toast into her mouth; she hadn't realized how hungry she was.

She looked up to thank Kent, only to realize he was utterly still. His eyes were fixed on the projection. Time slowed. Luna moved her eyes from Kent to the projection. She stared at the image–unable to believe what she was seeing.

Her parents were the breaking news.

On the projection, Luna watched as their parents were shoved to their knees in front of the camera. The food in Luna's mouth felt as if it turned to ash; she swallowed it down, on reflex, but her mind was not there.

Her mother looked filthy. She still wore the clothes from the night before. Her father appeared to be in worse shape; his clothes were the same he had worn to work three days ago, and his right eye was so bruised it was swollen shut. The projection showed them in a room with floor-to-ceiling white tile; the only distinctive feature was a drain at the center of the floor.

There was only one thing for which the New Republic used this room on news broadcasts: public executions.

The news program's anchor explained that Daphne and Silas Bardin were traitors to the New Republic for assisting the Resistance. He was cut off when Senator Asher Dawson stepped into the frame of the projection.

The senator began reading the paper he held in front of him, his voice so firm it was almost robotic. "Daphne and Silas Bardin, you have been found guilty of the following charges: treason to your government, conspiracy to overthrow the New Republic from within, attempted murder on the First Citizen's Life…"

The senator continued, but Luna wasn't listening; she was staring at her parents' faces. Their arms were bound behind their backs, and they were forced to the ground in compliance. All Luna could do was watch.

Kent grasped her hand in his.

She could feel the sweat on his palm; she knew hers must have felt the same.

He gave her three squeezes. *I love you.*

She returned it with four squeezes back. *I love you, too.*

Luna knew, at that very moment, this would be the last time she saw her parents. On her birthday, in her brother's apartment, on the news projection.

Senator Asher Dawson concluded, "For these crimes against the New Republic, you are sentenced to death by firing squad." Without further warning, their mother and father, Daphne and Silas Bardin, were riddled with bullets.

Their bodies shook violently before their lifeless bodies slumped to the ground. Dark blood pooled around them like spilled ink, slowly pulled by gravity to the drain in the center of the room.

PART 2

The Siblings

10 YEARS LATER

5

LUNA

LUNA LOOKED OUT HER double-paned window to the endless rooftops covered in cardboard and metal as the rain continued its relentless onslaught. Most of the cardboard was already soaked through and sagging. The humans who weren't lucky enough to have metal roofs would have been soaked to the bone inside their small "buildings"—if they could even be called that. Their homes were stacked on top of each other, looking almost unsteady beneath the elevated street.

She shivered against the cold, her skin prickling as goosebumps blanketed her exposed skin. Taking the blanket from her bed, she covered herself, her eyes still fixed ahead on the rain steadily thrumming against the window. She twisted one of her copper curls around her finger as she checked her holo to see if Kent was on his way. Of course, he was. Which meant he would be early, so she needed to get moving. But this morning? This morning, it was always hard to do anything.

For the past ten years, Luna had moved from one shabby apartment to another. She didn't stay more than two years at any place. She couldn't believe she had moved five times in the last ten years since her parents' death. She never fully settled and grew antsy after a while, craving something new. There was always something missing, but she could never figure out what.

In all her moves, Luna had worked for Governor Seymour. He had always given her fair raises, but she barely took home any of it. The New Republic had a special deduction from her paycheck for her parents' treasonous activity. The fine lasted in perpetuity, or was removed by the First Citizen herself, which was unlikely. Kent got off easier; he hadn't been considered a co-conspirator.

Luna groaned, looking out her windows down onto the city.

She lived at the edge of Solles. Even though she was only on the sixth floor, her apartment was on a hill, giving her the best perspective to see the entire city—and its clear segregation.

The beauty of Solles came from its enormous white arches that flowed over the elevated streets. Each arch was at least forty stories high, cresting at the top and merging to create a garden space on the roof. The arches were the main support for the elevated streets and walkways that rose at least twenty stories above the ground, if not more. However, each arch contained offices, apartments, and shops, all located at street level, which was *not* ground level. Suspended between them was an infrastructure of woven walkways that resembled a beautiful cream ribbon, guiding pedestrians to different corners of Solles.

Directly below the elevated streets was the underrail—a train suspended beneath the underside of the streets by electromagnets. The train was a sleek silver bullet that could take you from one side of the city to another in a blink, or close to it.

At ground level was housing for the enslaved. Every time she looked out at their homes, she felt a familiar rage at what the self-appointed senators of the New Republic had done, enslaving the humans. That was the senators' solution to the war between the humans and Behtari: submission or death. The humans had no chance against the Behtari's abilities, and the Behtari knew it.

Luna then focused on the slight gray cloud that seemed to move around the slums—MAVs, each equipped with a camera. They buzzed in and out of homes, into the streets, ensuring there was no disruption, no unrest, and even no individuality. Privacy in the slums of Solles meant execution. The cloud of MAVs resembled a variety of tiny insects, crawling over everything or buzzing through the air, some of them climbing the slums. MAVs were initially designed as spies, intended to be used against the Resistance. The leader of the New Republic, First Citizen Kasandra Sanders, quickly decided it was a much easier way to control the humans. Constant surveillance, nearly undetectable, especially when the humans weren't paying attention.

She backed away from the window, turning to her closet to get dressed for work. She grabbed a pair of gray, form-fitting pants from her closet, along with a pale-yellow top and a cream-colored cardigan that fell to her mid-thigh. As she pulled the items out of the closet, she scratched her left arm against the latch on the closet door. Her closet was so shallow and narrow that getting anything in or out was almost impossible. She looked down at her left arm and realized the cut wasn't deep, but she was bleeding.

Luna inhaled, annoyed, but knew she needed to clean and bandage it, or it would make a mess of the yellow blouse and white cardigan. She closed the closet door and took the five steps from her closet to her bathroom, tossing her clothes on the bed as she went. Once she cleaned her scrape, she added antibiotic cream and wrapped it with gauze. Although the cut wasn't deep, it was long and awkward. Finally, she was satisfied with her wrap and gently pulled on her yellow blouse, making sure not to disturb the bandage.

Once she was finally dressed, it was time to tame her copper curls. At her third attempt to get her hair to cooperate, she huffed. One curled lock of hair bounced in front of her face, up and back down again, mocking her. She gave up and pulled her hair back, as she usually did. She finished securing the final pins and stared at her reflection for half a second.

The gold flecks in her green irises were brighter than usual. She loathed the gold. Luna was jealous of the beauty of human eyes; they were not marred by the unnatural glow from within.

Knock, knock.

"Shit," she said under her breath. Then, she yelled, "Coming!" Luna threw on an oversized teal scarf, black boots, and a black trench coat. When she left her bedroom, the knocking had grown more persistent, as well as obnoxiously loud.

Kent's voice was muffled from the other side of her front door. "Hey! I'm hungry!"

Luna grabbed her holo, keys, an umbrella, and a small bag with her wallet inside before finally opening the door. Her brother, Kent, was leaning against the far wall in his black LEO uniform, complete with a bulletproof vest and combat boots.

"Happy Birthday!" he said, his green eyes, flecked with gold, shining at her. Kent's hair wasn't the bright shade of copper Luna's was, his was brown with dark auburn hues. He handed her an extra-large iced coffee with cream and sugar, along with a sugared donut filled with custard and jam. "Do you really need interference up all the time? I don't like not being able to sense you when you are home."

Her eyes sprang to his, and her face contorted in disgust. "That's the last thing I want, you sensing everything I do in my apartment! Quit being such a snoop."

Kent ran a hand through his hair in frustration, but still smiled. "Never going to stop asking. One day you'll agree."

She knew Kent liked to use his Prophet ability to sense her, to make sure she was safe. She was grateful she had kept the knick-knacks from the bag their mother had packed ten years ago. Luna loved them for the nostalgia and memories of her childhood, but most importantly, they protected her.

No one would think the golden cat with a paw swinging up and down would be holding a one-inch cube her parents had created. Or that two other knick-knacks in her apartment shared identical cubes. One was a white crystal pyramid, and the other was a polished, pear-shaped river rock. When all three were placed in a triangle, they prevented a Behtari from successfully using their ability within that space. Sure, it didn't cover every inch of her apartment, but it covered a lot of it, and that worked for her.

Their mother originally described the cubes to Kent as a frequency that interfered with the Behtari's natural abilities. Kent explained it to Luna after their death.

When the contamination occurred, and a portion of Arelia's humans transitioned to Behtari, their genetics also changed. A human's gamma brain waves increased by the hundreds when they became a Behtari. Whatever their parents had done to these cubes prevented the gamma waves from forming when a Behtari wanted to use their ability. If they tried for too long, they could get a headache or even a bloody nose.

Luna eyed the coffee like a predator.

"You can't get the caffeine in you by staring at it."

She rolled her eyes as she shut and locked her apartment door.

He chuckled. "I never understood how you could ingest this much sugar; it's gross." She scoffed. "How would you know? All you do is eat protein and go to the gym."

Kent pulled her from the doorway by the elbow and said, "Come on, Moon Bug, the Governor needs you to take notes, or make meetings, or whatever you do, and I don't need to be late."

Luna sighed. She knew he was trying to be gentle, but he was right; if she were late again, it would be a problem. She already had two tardiness warnings this month. She was Governor Seymour's administrative assistant. If she wasn't there to take notes during a meeting, the meeting didn't happen on time.

She fell into step with Kent, briskly walking down the hall. The walls were a light, soft green, almost the color of spring grass, while the floor was white stone, and every time she walked down, she could hear the click of her boots. They rounded the corner to the elevator, and she pressed the button for the lobby. She lived on the sixth floor in her apartment building, so the stairs to the elevated street weren't unbearable, but she didn't feel like taking them today.

She looked at Kent with a tight smile, but he saw straight through her. She quickly faced the closing elevator doors—she would be fine today.

Everything would be fine.

After several blocks of silence in the cold rain, Kent glanced sideways at Luna. "What are you thinking about?"

Luna shrugged, adjusting her umbrella. "Lost in thought, I guess."

He bumped her shoulder. "Spit it out, Moon Bug."

She rolled her eyes. She couldn't remember the last time he called her Moon Bug, but that was the second time this morning. "I don't know..." she said. "This day always makes me feel...exasperated."

He arched an eyebrow. "Exasperated?" She looked up at him, scrunching her nose. Her curls caught in the wind and danced into her face.

He gave her a questioning look, silently saying, *"More information, please!"* as he looked at her from under his black umbrella.

She sometimes forgot how much taller he was than she, but it didn't stop her from punching him in the arm.

He put on a good show—dropping his jaw in shock, complete with a fake gasp. "You wound me."

She smiled a smile she desperately wanted to be real, but wasn't. The worst part was that her brother knew. Kent always knew. Her birthday was the same day their parents were publicly executed. Even though they didn't talk about their parents much, she still missed them fiercely, and it made her birthday that much harder.

"I guess I always feel disconnected this time of year. This day especially, I feel lost. So, when today is finally here, I'm not only disconnected and lost, but I am now *also* emotionally empty. The worst part is I'm *annoyed* about feeling disconnected, lost, and emotionally empty. Exasperated was the best word I could think of," Luna explained.

Kent bumped her shoulder again. "Always here if you need to talk, Moon Bug."

They continued in silence along the white stone pathway. Cars rushed by on their left, while on the right, they passed several large arches lined with shops and restaurants. That was all at the elevated street level. At ground level, there were LEOs stationed almost every twenty feet. She knew LEOs had increased in recent months because of Kent's role within the organization. He told her there were now two or more LEOs in front of every base entrance to the arches. The arches connected the ground level with the Behtari's elevated street level.

Their mother always said the city was two sides of the same coin. She looked out over the town of Solles. She could see the massive white arches not only supporting the streets but also providing walkways, spaces for shops and businesses, greenhouses for vegetation, and parks. It was stunning.

But beneath them, hidden below, was a completely different city. A city that was starving, beaten, broken, and most of all—angry.

6

LUNA

LUNA AND KENT APPROACHED the state building with haste. Luna quickly double-checked her watch, and the small, blue hologram appeared above it, projecting the time. She was five minutes early, and with that knowledge, she felt the tension ease between her shoulder blades. A genuine smile spread across her face for the first time in days, maybe weeks. Even though it was small, she let herself feel joy for a second, one brief second, trying to savor it.

Finally, they rounded the bend towards the Kellmont State building, the rain eased its onslaught enough that the siblings closed their umbrellas. Upon entering the courtyard, Luna caught sight of the increase in stationed LEOs in the surrounding area. She quickly scanned the courtyard, and she realized how many there were. She glanced up at Kent, who gave a slight shake of his head. Later, they would discuss this later.

The state building was not one of the structural arches holding up the elevated streets. However, the building was nestled between the base of one of them. It was set back enough to allow for a courtyard, where food vendors set up each day. On either side of the building, massive arches held beautiful luxury apartments on the lower levels and multiple greenhouses overflowing with fresh produce. Luna couldn't deny the beauty of the curated neighborhood. The state building was all white, like the rest of the street level of Solles, with fifteen steps leading up to the building's entry.

There were two security checkpoints to enter the building. The first was outside, before she ascended the stairs, with a LEO who scanned her right hand to ensure she had authorization and clearance to enter the building. The second was beyond the automatic revolving door.

The automatic revolving door was one of Luna's least favorite things. The door was enormous, with three sections, each designed to accommodate a maximum of twenty people. Today, Luna and Kent entered the revolving door with at least fifteen others.

Luna felt a pinch in her chest; she always hated this moment. She felt like she was trapped for a few seconds, but those few seconds were long enough to cause her heart to race and her breath to catch.

Kent gave her a sidelong look as his mouth pulled into a frown. He knew, he always knew. Sometimes she hated that he was a Prophet. Even if it was only two seconds before she knew, it was the most frustrating thing.

Kent never bothered to hide his Prophet ability from Luna; it never mattered between them. He never shared his ability publicly. He would have immediately been pulled from his position, moved to some unknown location, and Luna would never see him again.

Even then, seeing an adult Prophet was rare. Occasionally, the First Citizen Sanders would bring one into one of her public broadcasts, but even that was highly uncommon. Luna assumed the Prophets were taken for some abhorrent experimentation. When she tried to research where the Prophets were taken slyly, she was taken in for questioning within an hour.

Given her family's history with the New Republic, the LEOs questioning her ensured Kent did not know she was being questioned. In addition, they made sure she knew how lucky she and Kent were, having Solles's governor, Seymour, take pity on them, vouching for them after their parents' execution. They also ensured to inform her that if she ever looked into the subject, or anything related to it again, her and her brother's lives would meet the same fate. She never tried to look again.

Luna exhaled a sigh of relief as she exited the rotating door. Even though it was only a few seconds, it felt like an eternity to her.

Before they could reach the second checkpoint, they had to pass through the main foyer. The foyer was grand. It had a black, marble floor that was flecked with gold, and enormous, gold-dusted white columns drew Luna's eyes up to the glass ceiling, where she could see lush plants on the roof of the building. She always marveled at the entry's architecture—it was truly breathtaking.

She stepped into line for the second checkpoint. When it was her turn, she scanned her ID badge on what looked like a solid, flat black table, only about the size of her hand, as the device registered her presence. It slowly registered her ID card as a larger MAV that looked similar to a dragonfly, hovered a few inches from her face, and scanned the iris of her eye.

The MAV was fast, usually holding steady in the air even before her ID finished scanning. Luna stood still in front of the MAV. She looked at the tiny camera, which settled right where the dragonfly's head would be. Upon her eye scan, the MAV descended beneath the table to wait for the next check-in.

Metal doors clicked open in front of her, and she entered. As she turned, she nodded goodbye to Kent before the doors shut behind her with a hiss and *click*. Even though she didn't know their plans for this weekend, she was excited to go out tomorrow to celebrate her birthday properly.

Luna climbed the five steps following the final checkpoint to the elevators. She felt an unease settle in her gut again. She needed to get through this day.

Governor Seymour's office rose ten stories above the elevated street within the state building. Luna exited the elevator as it opened into the familiar waiting area, styled with four plush, green velvet chairs with large, flared backs. Between the four chairs was a small table made of black glass that held Luna's favorite flower, the delta lily.

The delta lily's name came to be because it was after the contamination, and after the Behtari. Most of the delta lilies grew right near the riverbanks and only opened at night. The rich colors of the flower were luminescent under the night sky, but Luna loved seeing it in the daytime, too. Like the Behtari's eyes, it was flecked with luminous gold within its blue hue. Delta lilies were extremely delicate, so this one was hand-dipped in resin to preserve it. Once cut, they would last only a few hours at most, making them very expensive.

Luna crossed the room to her desk, which faced the elevators. Her station was situated to the left of the two dark-wood doors that led to the Governor's office.

Luna sat at her desk, which was made of the same sleek, black glass as the table in the center of the room. She placed her right hand on the right side of the desk, and a holographic interface instantly appeared in front of her, allowing her to begin work for the day. Most interfaces had adjustable settings and the ability to form an opaque background, making it easier to work on and providing privacy. However, she only turned it on when she was expecting guests or various individuals for meetings. Most meetings were held in the Governor's office, where she would use a portable interface. The portable interface connected directly to the central hub at her desk, allowing her to transfer information easily.

She started typing on the keys projected onto her glass desk. Luna had to adjust her sleeve so it wouldn't pull on the bandage underneath. After she adjusted both the shirt and bandage not once, but twice, she opened her interface and began initiating her reports for the day.

Luna heard the elevator chime and looked up as Governor Seymour stepped out, his face grim. Luna felt her stomach plummet. He was never this early. Which meant he was here for some other reason. Then Luna remembered what Kent said—he had a meeting with the governor today about the cells, and Kent had planned to meet them in the cells upon their arrival. However, the plan must have changed without his knowledge, because right behind the governor were Senators Dawson and Yeo and First Citizen Kasandra Sanders.

Luna stood from her desk. She plastered the most genuine smile she could muster onto her face, but one look from Governor Seymour, and Luna knew she was not convincing.

Governor Seymour quickly recovered, his smile stretching across his warm, dark flawless skin, like the night sky without stars. She noticed the smile didn't quite reach his eyes. He had brown irises, and like all the Behtari, they were flecked with gold. "Good morning! Hope you aren't too surprised by our guests, Luna," Governor Seymour said with a hint of ice behind his tone.

"Not at all, Governor. It is wonderful to see you all again," she said with as much politeness as she could muster. All the while, her hands were clasped behind her back, nails digging into her skin. She would kill these people if given the chance. They took her parents from her and executed them publicly and without trial. Luna had to control her emotions. Instinctively, she ensured her shields were securely in place. Being a Shielder, Luna could create a protective shield around her mind, almost as if flexing a muscle.

Luna caught First Citizen Sanders's gaze. A smile bloomed across her lips that could only be described as sinister, before she looked away from Luna. First Citizen Kasandra Sanders was the leader of Arelia, Voice of the Republic—at least that was the title she signed every official edict with. She oversaw all five senators and the regions they governed. She was also one of the oldest Behtari. Behtari lived longer than humans, but they weren't immortal. It was not unheard of for an individual to reach the age of one hundred sixty years. First Citizen Sanders and Senator Asher Dawson were two of the founders of the New Republic, even though they both looked like they were in their mid-fifties. They were easily the oldest Behtari Luna knew of, and Luna didn't even know their exact ages.

The First Citizen was wearing a deep green blazer and matching pants, paired with a black blouse that fit so loosely around her frame that the clothes appeared baggy. Her dark hair was shorn close to her head, as if she couldn't be bothered with anything such as her appearance. Her face was haunting; her skin looked as thin and as white as paper, as if she never spent time outside. Her lips were covered in an almost black, blood-red lipstick. Luna couldn't place what felt different. She had only met the First Citizen twice before this moment, but something was not the same. The First Citizen's irises weren't just flecked with gold—they were entirely gold, and they were glowing.

Luna met the First Citizen once after her parents were executed and once eight and a half years ago. After their parents were executed, she and Kent were brought before her and the New Republic's senators, who would decide their fate. Luna and Kent were held in cells beneath the capital of Zuros, Hazleton, for almost a week. During that time, they endured beatings, sleep deprivation, starvation, and any other torture tactic the New Republic could come up with that wouldn't permanently scar them outwardly.

Luna and Kent were asked the same questions repeatedly during that week. She could still remember them by heart.

What did your parents tell you about their work?

When did your parents become sympathizers with the Resistance?

What did your mother take from the apartment?

The first two were easy to answer. Luna had little to no idea what they did for the government—only that they mainly worked in a lab and were highly valued by First Citizen Sanders. The second question was easy as well; she didn't know.

The third question, however...Luna lied. Over and over and over, she lied.

It took everything her mother taught her about shielding to protect the lie. She didn't even know what the items in the duffel were at that point, but she was not going to let the New Republic have them.

The second time, Luna, Kent, and their best friend Darin were walking back from dinner in downtown Solles when they passed the courtyard of the Kellmont State Building and heard someone begging and sobbing. The words were almost indistinguishable, but Luna still heard them.

Please, no. Please, they haven't done anything....

They froze. They were out of sight, but they could see enough. The trio watched the scene unfold as Kasandra and three other LEOs forced a family of four—two adults and two children, maybe around the age of thirteen—to their knees. Kasandra then took a gun from under her jacket and, as if it were a practiced dance, she and the three LEOs stood behind each person, placed the guns to the back of their heads, and all fired at once.

Luna blinked as she was jolted back to the present, feeling something painful against her shield. It had only been a moment, but it felt white hot, as if someone was trying to get through.

Still standing, Luna surveyed the group. They spoke quietly amongst themselves as they sat in the four chairs around the table. She scanned the governor and then two senators. Luna looked at First Citizen Sanders. She was looking back, almost as if she had been waiting for Luna to notice her.

As if the governor could sense the shift in tension in the room, he stood and walked in front of Luna, breaking eye contact between Luna and the First Citizen. Governor Seymour gave Luna a wink as he tapped her desk. "We won't keep you any longer, Luna. I know I keep you busy!"

Without another word, the governor led the way back to the elevator. The two senators followed swiftly behind him. But First Citizen Sanders walked up to Luna's desk and placed a small pink box with a deep green bow on it.

Before Kasandra walked back to the elevator, she said, "Happy Birthday, Luna. I hope you know I didn't forget. Hopefully, this will bring back some memories for you, as I no longer have use for it." The First Citizen turned toward the elevator, but paused and half-turned back to Luna. "Oh, right... It isn't *just* your birthday, is it?" With that, Kasandra Sanders, First Citizen of Arelia, walked onto the elevator as the doors shut behind her.

7

<u>KENT</u>

KENT WATCHED THE ELEVATOR doors close behind Luna. She used to be full of life, going out with friends and hosting art events at the museum, but it was as if she had dimmed over the last ten years, even more so recently. He could sense something changing within her, and he wasn't sure he was going to like what was coming. He wanted her to be happy. Even though he told himself he only wanted her to be happy, he knew it was a lie. Pathetically, selfishly, he wanted her not to need him. Somewhere deep in his being, he knew she always would, especially today.

It had been ten years since their parents were publicly executed. They had been killed for helping the humans, the thought made his gut churn. On top of all of that, the execution happened on Luna's birthday, and that made it so much worse. Kent was grateful he planned for her birthday this year; he had gotten tickets to an exclusive concert with Luna's favorite band, Infiniti's End. Their friend Darin pulled some strings and hooked him up.

Typically, celebrating with Luna would have been exciting, but the idea of going to a concert put Kent on edge. He had tried to use his ability and sense how the coming days would go, including the concert itself. Every time he tried to use his ability, things were gray, foggy, or there were too many emotions, with flashes of images that made it impossible to decipher anything useful. Even when he tried in earnest to focus—which he had—he couldn't glean any insight like normal. The reality was that he had been too preoccupied with work recently, which was clearly affecting his Prophet ability.

Being a Prophet meant he could sense certain aspects of what *could* be, but only to a point. Some things were fixed—a massive storm, a shooting star, or someone becoming ill due to genetics. However, a Prophet could never sense the future if it all depended on a significant decision yet to be made. Sometimes a Prophet could sense days in advance, but at other times, only minutes. Another setback was that Kent had to know someone personally to sense their unique frequency. To say the Prophet's ability was unpredictable was an understatement, but to the government, it was still valued above all other abilities.

Kent's parents knew that the New Republic, especially First Citizen Sanders, desired Prophets to work for it. Once discovered, the New Republic trained them as soon as their ability manifested because it gave the government additional control. The New Republic literally collected Prophets, keeping them in the capital city of Zuros, where they were rarely seen. Children who showed any signs of the Prophet ability were immediately reported by a LEO and collected by their local senator. Prophets were even more coveted, because Behtari parents tried to protect them at all costs. Unfortunately, most parents failed to find a solution.

The only way to escape the fate of a Prophet would be if a Behtari had two abilities, which seemed to be a trait only the Signalborn carried. However, even among the Signalborn, it was uncommon. Kent was lucky his Inflictor ability manifested first; no one questioned when he had been absent for months, learning to control his Prophet ability. Anytime he used his Prophet ability as a child, he became extremely fatigued. Sometimes, to the point of illness, or sleeping for days, which meant learning to control the ability took even longer.

Kent knew he was lingering too long. He was due to have a meeting today with Senator Dawson from Lembalt, Senator Yeo from Kellmont, where Solles resided, as well as the Governor of Solles, Governor Seymour. Kent knew they were meeting to discuss the state building's infrastructure regarding the cells, and Kent was to be their tour guide—whatever that meant.

He also had to deal with a human who had been arrested last night, painting Resistance graffiti on the walls of the support arches not far from the state building. It was Kent's job to obtain the confessions First Citizen Sanders wanted. It didn't matter if it was the truth; it only mattered that the accused admitted they were guilty, even if they weren't.

Kent walked to the back of the building and then descended a set of metal stairs to the sublevel of the state building, where the holding cells were located. There was only one floor beneath them, the interface data room. He thought the room was excessive. The Kellmont state building needed only three fan systems to run the servers, and he signed off on the ledgers every month. The interface data room was vented by four systems.

Once Kent noticed the discrepancy, he had to trace it back to the source. As suspected, only ninety percent of the servers were associated with the State building or held state information. The other ten percent was completely unaccounted for in the entire system, or at least within what he had access to. However, he was able to track where the information was being sent. There was a small, unnamed island off the coast of Zuros, Hazleton, where data was regularly sent. Kent tried to dive deeper and figure out what this island was holding, but he met firewall after firewall. He considered asking Darin to get involved, but he had already crossed enough lines. It was dangerous enough to search for this information, even under the guise of old files.

So, for the time being, Kent let it go. He knew he would come back to it eventually—he had all the information gathered, even the encrypted files. It was on a ghost drive secured under his desk, which he updated regularly, almost daily if he was being honest with himself. The ghost drive itself was tucked between two drawers under the lip of his desk, so no one would easily see it. He even had to remove both drawers from his desk to access the ghost drive itself.

Kent took the last turn to the cell where the human he was assigned to interrogate was being held. He almost ran straight into Senator Asher Dawson, Governor Seymour, Senator Yeo, and First Citizen Sanders. He knew they would come to speak with him, but he should have had another hour before their arrival. He had hoped to get to the interface data room to upload recently-encrypted files before the meeting, but now that would have to wait.

Kent immediately felt Senator Dawson staring at him; he loathed Senator Dawson. He could tolerate the other senators, but Senator Dawson's interrogation techniques were beyond torture. He savored the task, drawing it out longer than necessary, even after the prisoner confessed. "Captain Bardin," Senator Dawson said authoritatively, "are you here to interrogate SO-12536?" All prisoners were assigned two letters corresponding to the city where they were arrested, followed by a sequence of five numbers. The first three numbers comprised the quarter and day on which the prisoner arrived. The last two numbers indicated the number of individuals, both human and Behtari, brought to the cells that day. The system kept track of everyone who came through those cells. However, the reality was that those who entered these cells weren't leaving again.

"Yes, Senator."—Kent lied, hoping the group would not notice— "However, I would be more than happy to show you the improvements we have made, along with the enhancements in security and protocol to the state building. I can reschedule my interrogation."

Senator Dawson stiffened at Kent's suggestion. The senator looked to the First Citizen for the final decision.

First Citizen Sanders eyed Kent coolly as she said, "Proceed. Lead the way."

Kent's skin pricked as his Prophet ability tried to surface and flood his vision. He would not—*could not*—use his ability right now. That would land him a one-way ticket into one of these cells, and he would rather be dead. Nothing stopped the senators from getting their intel and confessions, which meant someone like Kent, an Inflictor, was vital to the New Republic. What made matters worse was that his role as a LEO also made him critical for the Resistance as an informant.

When Kent joined the Resistance, he knew the danger of collecting and sending information—information that would get him killed—and he willingly agreed. However, initially, when Kent and Milo Winton, the leader of the Resistance, discussed the details of Kent's endeavor, Milo decided that Kent should remain with the LEOs for an additional two to three years. After that, Kent could return to Hamdon, the capital of the Resistance. Kent never wanted to be pushing undercover information as a LEO for over six years.

He brought the group of four to the new cell block while explaining the specific improvements. This new block was built directly above the interface data room, unnaturally heating each of the six cells. They were also pitch-black; the only light source in the space came from the hallway when the cell door was opened.

The senators nodded in approval as he showed them the interior with a handheld light. The governor followed the senators in assessing the room's size and overall state. The First Citizen said nothing as she peered inside, her eyes taking in every detail.

Kent cleared his throat; certain he was becoming visibly nervous. "Are there any questions I can answer for you regarding the new improvements or budget?" He had memorized everything they might question before this meeting. He was not going to be caught without an answer.

When his gaze met First Citizen Sanders's, he realized there was something different about her eyes. He hadn't caught it earlier, but...her eyes were pure gold, not flecked. They glowed.

"No, I don't have any questions, but I want your four healthiest enslaved to be sent to my facility in Zuros for additional testing on their compliance—or lack thereof. We are working on a chip that will be installed into the base of their spine, forcing compliance, and we need some test subjects."

Kent felt the color drain from his face.

Then she said with malice, "Will that be a problem?"

"Not at all, First Citizen." Kent could feel his last thread of sanity pulled taut. He could not keep sending humans to their death—he had enough blood on his hands.

As if the First Citizen read his mind, she smiled at him and made her way into the cell with the others.

The tour lasted much longer than Kent had anticipated. He lost the majority of his morning over it. Finally, back at his office, he sat down in his desk chair, exhausted. His seat was far from comfortable, but it was the most comfortable thing in his office.

He had two simple black chairs in front of his desk, sturdy and made of metal and plastic. Behind the chairs were three four-drawer filing cabinets, crammed with documents and paperwork. He also had a four-drawer filing cabinet behind his desk on the right-hand side, positioned next to a large window.

He looked out his window on the third floor of the state building, noticing the rain had begun again, coming down in sheets against the arches. He was sure some of the greenhouses on the top floors would be overflowing the drains, which would funnel down to the humans on the ground level. He felt that normal frustration course through him as he closed his eyes. He leaned back in his chair when he heard a quiet *ping* that seemed to come from his interface.

His eyes immediately flew open, staring down at his desk. His desk was off, and his interface had not even been pulled up to start the day. Kent realized he hadn't yet come into his office today because of his meetings, so the interface hadn't been turned on.

Kent quickly scanned his desk, looking for anything out of place. When he found nothing, he activated the interface on the right-hand side of his desk with his handprint. The system hummed to life, and Kent froze.

Before he could log in, a message lit up the screen, making him freeze with fear.

They know.

8

KENT

KENT HAD BEEN PACING back and forth across the navy-blue carpet for over five minutes now. He always found movement helpful while using his Prophet ability. This time, it wasn't helping; every time he tried to sense into the next few hours, he felt slight emotion, but nothing more. He had been focusing solely on himself, but he still had too many decisions that hadn't been made yet. Which, if he was being honest with himself, made sense—they knew his cover was blown. That was the code that was previously agreed upon between him and Darin, his best friend and the Resistance's best hacker.

What am I going to do?

Initially, he planned multiple options to leave Solles when the time came. However, he had not gone over them in recent memory. Kent sank into his desk chair, weighed down by frustration. He had no idea what to do. He spent eight years undercover, gathering vital information and getting it back to the Resistance. The process was agonizingly slow; he would collect any information he found and put it onto a ghost drive. About once a month, he would have a meet-up and pass it along to the next person, who eventually passed it to Milo Winton, the Leader of the Resistance. It had been months since he had gotten more intel to the Resistance. The intel he had now—he knew it was dangerous, even with the encryption. Beyond that, he didn't even have the most up-to-date information now because the senators, First Citizen, and governor had been early.

Kent's mind spun. He was starting to feel queasy after overexerting himself. It wasn't abnormal for him to feel off after using his Prophet ability, but this was too much; he pushed too hard.

Kent rose from his desk, reaching for the top of the filing cabinet to pour himself a glass of water. He poured a large glass, but all it took was one sip before he retched into the trash can at his feet.

Kent rushed to the bathroom across the hall to clean himself. Not only did no one need to know he was sick, but they didn't need to know why.

He entered the bathroom, shut the door behind him, and locked it. He turned on the stone faucet that poured into a thick glass basin through which he could see the blue stone floor. He made the water as hot as it would possibly go; he needed to feel something beyond rage at this point. Running his hands through the water and cupping his hand, he brought the water to his face, washing the area around his mouth as best he could.

Kent looked at himself in the mirror. His hair was up in a half-bun today, but he looked haggard, exhausted; his green-flecked eyes were hollow, empty. He wasn't sure he recognized himself anymore.

A sudden burst of fury rushed through him. Fire ran through his veins as anger permeated every cell in his body. Without thinking, he yelled, "Godsdamn it!" and slammed his fists on the clear glass of the sink. When he pulled his hands away, they were trembling, with anger, fear, and pain; too many emotions to process. Even with all his rage, he hadn't even left a crack in the glass sink.

There was no way he could stay here. No fucking way. He knew he was letting his emotions get the better of him. He let his feelings spiral, let himself feel everything he hadn't felt these last ten years. Everything he shoved away to protect Luna.

Luna.

If they knew he was undercover, they would take Luna, too. She wouldn't be given another chance. He was truly fucked, zero of his escape plans included her.

Kent had no way to easily get out of the city without implicating Luna. Even then, Kent had to force himself to think logically. That message could be a trap—something the New Republic had set up to ensnare him. The problem was that he didn't know if it was a trap or a genuine warning.

After Kent returned to his office, he paced for another ten minutes. Then, he decided the best course of action was to remain calm and collected. He would act as if he were ignorant of the entire message. The New Republic never touched him before; maybe they were waiting for something, or for him to trip up. If he could act as if he had not been sent life-altering information, it would be fine.

Which will be super simple, he thought sarcastically.

Kent tried to use his prophet ability now that he'd made a decision, but there was still nothing to sense; a few emotions here and there, but he couldn't quite grasp them. He wanted to know what the feelings were, who was feeling them. Kent knew he was truly pushing himself to the limit, and still, he channeled deeper into his ability. Finally, he could sense something, a profound sadness, screaming. He felt ice prickling his skin, and his body seemed to plummet in temperature.

Kent's eyes snapped open. What was wrong with him? This was beyond anything he had experienced before, and he needed to know why. He sometimes felt unable to sense when there were complex decisions that would alter not only that person's life but also the lives of many around them. He knew those could take days to get past sometimes; what worried him most was the cold. He had never felt that sensation while using his ability before. He was trying not to worry, but there was no way to search for the information without it triggering the New Republic. The only other Prophet he knew was Milo, and there was no good or easy way to contact him.

The only person he could think of who might understand or have an idea, simply because she knew about it, was Luna. Even then, what would she do for him? Kent knew she already had so much going on, and he, of all people, didn't need to add to her chaos right now—especially today.

He hadn't wanted to think about today being the anniversary of their parents' death. His focus had been on planning Luna's birthday gift, but for the first time in a long time, he let himself think about his parents. He missed them so much, especially on days like this. He knew at a young age that their parents were involved with something big. As he got older, his father shared some of what they had done.

Kent knew he wanted to follow in their footsteps after their execution. Still, nothing truly pushed him over the edge until he, Darin, and Luna accidentally watched a family executed with no trial. He wasn't sure why that was the catalyst for him. Maybe he healed enough to move forward? Or perhaps he had been trying to rationalize the New Republic's actions. Whatever the reason, it threw him headfirst into the Resistance. And now, he would meet the same end as his parents if he were caught.

He couldn't bear to be in this building another minute. He stood and grabbed his holo and umbrella. He sent a quick message to Luna that he wasn't feeling well and would have to cancel plans later tonight, but he still planned to get together tomorrow for her gift. After pushing his ability beyond its normal limits, he needed a night to rest.

Kent left the office, backpack slung over his shoulder, leaving the ghost drive tucked between the two drawers under the lip of his desk.

9

LUNA

LUNA LOST HERSELF IN her work for the next several hours; she even skipped lunch without realizing it.

The governor approached her desk at the end of the day and asked, "Are you enjoying your birthday so far?"

Quickly looking up, she gave him a genuine smile. Governor Seymour had been so much like a father to Luna, she knew she relied on him too much. He put his life on the line for her and Kent to save their lives, even though it was evident that they were not part of the Resistance, as their parents had been accused of. Luna still didn't know what her parents were charged with beyond treason; the documentation had never been released, and she doubted it ever would.

She remembered when Governor Seymour stood before all the senators and explained that he would be responsible for Kent and Luna, ensuring that Kent would keep his job and that Luna would have one. He gave Luna a job that let him keep an eye on them both. The governor saved them, and Luna knew she would never be able to explain her gratitude in words.

Governor Seymour looked at the pink box with the green bow on Luna's desk—the one she had contemplated throwing away—from the First Citizen and cocked an eyebrow at her. "You aren't going to open it at least?"

Luna looked at the box and then back at the Governor, stating matter-of-factly, "I don't think I want whatever she is trying to give me."

The governor shrugged before saying, "Normally, I would agree with you, but I know what is in that box, and I can promise you, you want to open it."

Luna narrowed her eyes at him. He had never spoken to her this frankly. She tentatively took the box and opened it slowly, as if spiders would come crawling out onto her hands.

"The New Republic confiscated both of them," Governor Seymour continued. "Why, I don't know...but the New Republic, specifically the First Citizen, has had them these last ten years. The only reason I even knew they were being returned to you was because the First Citizen wanted to hand the box to you personally."

She looked up at him incredulously.

He threw his hands up as if in surrender. "Trust me, I know. When I resisted—and I did resist—the First Citizen finally showed her hand, explaining what it was. Upon getting that information, I knew you would want to have them."

Neatly laid within the pink box was her mother's gold necklace and her father's gold bracelet, which they each wore in place of wedding rings. Luna took both pieces out with trembling fingers; she hadn't seen either since the last time she saw her parents. Tears welled in Luna's eyes as she gently lowered them back into the pink box. Without thinking, she stood from her desk and threw her arms around Governor Seymour.

"Thank you," she whispered as she released him. Even though she knew he hadn't been the one to return her parents' jewelry to her, she still felt the urge to thank him. The governor had done his best to protect her and her brother, and deep down, she knew he had their best interest in mind.

"Even though I wish she hadn't been the one to give them to you, I am glad you have them," he said, still smiling at her as a father would a grieving daughter—not a happy smile, but not a sad one either, one full of empathy.

Luna and the governor continued to engage in small talk while they completed their tasks before leaving for the day. Before leaving, Luna put her mother's necklace on. The necklace was a simple, delicate gold chain that had almost a bluish cast to it in the right light. It was long, easily put on over her head, and tucked into her shirt. As soon as it set on her skin, she felt like something clicked into place, giving her a small sense of peace.

She made sure to leave the bracelet in the box for Kent later, knowing he would appreciate it.

Right before getting on the elevator with the governor, he stopped suddenly. "Oh, wait! I forgot something." Luna turned to see what Governor Seymour had forgotten, but he had already disappeared behind the doors of his office. He emerged from his office with a skinny box. The box was light brown, with only a piece of twine holding it together.

"It isn't much, but I know today is hard. After everything with the First Citizen, well, I hoped this might make you feel a little better." He spoke with sincerity as he handed Luna the box.

Luna opened the box slowly, as if she would jostle the contents and break whatever was inside. Once she removed the lid, she gasped in surprise. Governor Seymour had bought her a delta lily, dipped in resin, like the one on the black table.

Luna couldn't help the wide grin that stretched across her face. "Thank you," she said quietly.

He gave her arm a tight squeeze and, without saying another word, gestured to the elevator.

They rode the elevator in silence, leaving Luna's mind to wander. It was curious to her how this one flower sprang out of so much hate and violence. It was part of the reason it was her absolute favorite—it was not easy for her to find strength when everything around her always seemed to be in ruins, but then there was this flower, it became something new, something strong.

Upon exiting the elevator and moving to the front of the state building, Luna finally reached for her holo and responded to Kent. She told him she hoped he felt better and that she would see him the next day.

Her exit from the state building was not nearly as complicated as her entry. She scanned her eye and ID badge to check out and then made her way through the front doors into the brisk air. Solles was still one of the warmer cities of Arelia, but even at this time of year, it was cold at night. She decided to stop in two of her favorite shops in the courtyard of the state building. The first shop she could already smell as she walked toward it, and her mouth was salivating. It was a small bakeshop toward the center of the courtyard stores; the exterior was white brick, trimmed in navy blue and green, with a green awning. Smiling, she stepped through the bakery doors.

When she entered the store, she was immediately greeted by the comforting scent of baking bread. She breathed deeply, relishing the smell. The small interior matched the outside, with white tile flooring and navy blue and green accent tiles. She stepped up to place her order and could see huge ovens in the back, each holding at least six loaves of bread. She paid for a large loaf of white bread, hot from the oven with a light brown, floury crust, which smelled of garlic and rosemary.

She tucked the neatly wrapped bread into the extra canvas bag she usually carried. She was already planning what she was going to have for dinner—this bread with an enormous plate of pasta with a rich, white cream sauce heaped with extra garlic and cheese.

After the bakery, she went to the small bookstore two doors down. It was her birthday after all, so why shouldn't she treat herself? A tiny bell tinkled overhead at her entry. Luna stepped inside and inhaled deeply at the paper smell that could only come from new books. The two stores truly had some of her favorite smells, always brightening her spirits. Luna had come to know the shop owner, Magdila, personally over the last few years. Magdila constantly encouraged little ones to read, which was one of the reasons Luna cherished the store.

Luna had been waiting for the newest release from her favorite author. After she paid for her new book and gave her respects to Magdila, she stepped back into the brisk evening air.

She could smell the bakery, the new book, but most of all—she could smell the delta lilies from the flower shop across the way. The resin-dipped lily in her bag no longer held a scent, but that didn't stop her from relishing the freshly cut ones. The fragrance of the delta lily had always been almost intoxicating to Luna. She stood on the edge of the courtyard, closed her eyes, and let herself exist for a second. She listened to the murmur of foot traffic, the muffled conversations coming and going, the buzzing of an electric light nearby.

The bells on the shop doors gently chimed as they opened and closed.

Luna suddenly felt unsteady on her feet, and she stumbled to catch herself. Upon opening her eyes, she realized almost all foot traffic was gone.

How long were my eyes closed? It couldn't have been more than a few seconds. When as Luna looked around the courtyard, almost every single store was closed for the night.

Luna knew most stores closed shortly after dinner, after the evening rush faded. She looked around again in disbelief; it was as if it had been hours since then. The sun had long since set, and stars twinkled in the sky.

What the fuck happened? Why is it so dark?

Luna began to panic. She searched for her holo. Her palms began to sweat, and when she finally found her holo, she quickly lit up the screen to see the time.

The holo was wrong; it had to be wrong. Luna turned the screen off and looked at the time again; it was almost the middle of the night. Her pulse rate increased as panic started to set in. How long had she been standing here? Was she drugged? She knew the bookshop owner, Magdila, would never let her stand out here for that long. So the question became... Where did they take her? Beyond that, why did they bring her back?

Luna clutched the canvas bag tightly and took off toward her apartment as fast as she could. It was so late, and she had no idea what had happened.

Rechecking her holo, she swore. She lost hours of her life and had no idea how or why... She knew she would have to call Kent once she was in her apartment. Luna inwardly groaned. He was going to be pissed, but what else could she do? She knew if she didn't call him, he would be *extremely* pissed. If she did call him, he would be *mildly* less pissed.

The more she considered what had happened tonight, the more she worried. It made no sense. She was perfectly fine; she had no bruising, no bleeding—except her cut from this morning was painful, as if it were freshly cut again. She looked down at her left hand and watched the small drop of blood fall from her middle finger to the white walkway.

Luna knew she had not been bleeding like that earlier. She started walking again, picking up the pace. As much as she wanted to inspect her wound, she was not dying and wanted to get to her apartment, where she would have frequent interference and no Behtari could spy on her.

Her mind was turning over itself with all the possible options, each less realistic than the last. She then wondered if Kent could pull video feeds from the courtyard. There must have been a MAV or two present during the evening commute. Luna felt more secure when she realized how helpful Kent would be in figuring this out. Her mind wandered back to the moment she walked out of the bookstore into the courtyard.

What the hell happened to her?

Picking up her pace even more, Luna rounded the last few turns to her apartment. She was getting the sinking feeling that something else had happened, but she didn't know what. At the opaque door to her apartment building, she scanned her retina. The device whirred and clicked, and the opaque glass door cleared to transparent. It slid into the left wall to let her into the building. She rushed through the small entry area, almost running down the hallway to the elevator, where she pressed the button for the sixth floor.

Off the elevator, Luna rushed to her door, fumbling for the keys in her pocket. She pushed through her apartment door, turning to lock the door immediately. She felt the familiar pulse of the cubes' frequency at her back. All she had to do was take one small step into the apartment, and she would be within the frequency interference produced by the three objects in her room. She let her shields fall away. If she continued to use her ability in that area, the frequency would become unbearable, leading to headaches or nosebleeds. If a Behtari refused to stop using their ability, they'd begin to bleed from their ears, eventually passing out.

Luna grabbed her holo and called Kent.

The holo rang twice before a low, groggy voice answered, "Hey, you okay?"

Luna knew she wasn't okay, but she wasn't sure what to say without spilling everything over the holo. Anyone could hear him talking right now, so she would have to be patient.

"Can you come over? It will be easier to explain in person," Luna said with a shaking voice. She knew she was doing a terrible job of staying calm.

"I'll be there in ten."

10

KENT

KENT STUFFED HIS HOLO into his pants pocket. He did not need to drop anything right now and make more noise. He almost dropped his keys as he crept out of his apartment, trying his best not to disturb Marcella and Wyatt, who were in town on Resistance business and staying at his place. The trio hadn't lived together in years but made time to see each other when they were able. It had been several months since their last visit.

Thankfully, Wyatt was passed out on the couch, snoring. There was a beer bottle falling from his hand, and what appeared to be a roll of splice on the table next to him. Kent could smell that it had been smoked recently. Wyatt always loved splice, but Kent never got the appeal. He always liked knowing exactly what he was thinking and how he would react. Splice slowed his reaction time, making him feel stupid. With everything going on, he could not feel ridiculous right now.

Marcella had taken the second bedroom in Kent's apartment. Kent glanced back to make sure he hadn't woken her with his fumbling. Mercifully, the door to the bedroom was closed. Kent looked at his holo and realized he would have been waking for work soon anyway. He groaned inwardly as he ran his hand over his face before he stepped out and locked the apartment door.

Kent wasted no time, jogging the white bridge between his apartment and one of the grand, white archways toward Luna's apartment. He hated not being able to live with her, but when Governor Seymour vouched for them, additional parameters were established. The two most significant things were their government job requirements and inability to live together. They had to either live alone or choose people whom the New Republic must vet. Kent was already living with Wyatt and Marcella, whom he had known for years, even though they moved in together only three weeks before the execution.

Luna had been a different story. She chose not to find a roommate after the execution and instead lived alone. Marcella had offered to move out of the apartment with Kent and Wyatt to get an apartment with her, but Luna declined—more than once.

Not only was Luna required to move from their family home, but she was forced to leave her job to become the Governor's administrative assistant. Luna had been working at an art museum that specialized in various forms of art, made by humans and Behtari alike. While it didn't pay well, she loved it. The museum was small but beautiful. It had large windows facing a local park filled with delta lilies. Luna's entire life was uprooted because of their parents' execution. He knew she was making her way, but it felt like a punch in the gut every time he saw her, even years after everything happened.

Kent finally arrived at her apartment and scanned his eye to be let in. He was the only person with retinal access to her apartment. He made his way to the sixth floor via the elevator and took a deep breath. He and Luna had agreed a long time ago that if they were called and asked to come over, they would without question. They both knew everything and anything was recorded and reviewed for "security purposes."

What a load of shit, Kent thought. Then, the sudden pang of reality set in.

He left his apartment in the middle of the night, knowing the New Republic knew about him. Maybe not all the senators, governors, or LEOs, but at least one knew—and he had been reckless. He ran his hands through his hair, creating more frizz than there already was from his less-than-satisfactory sleep. In no way would this look good on any tracking camera, given the information they already knew. He had to get out of Solles...today. He couldn't wait; every moment he stayed was a risk.

Kent had questioned Darin after work about the message. Kent had to be sure his friend, the Resistance hacker, didn't send it. Looking back, Kent knew their plan regarding that emergency message was not well thought out. Kent was only supposed to be undercover for a few years. Now that so much time had passed, Kent had to be sure it was sent from his friend Darin.

Only to find out - it hadn't been, which made Kent even more uneasy. Darin suggested Kent leave immediately, but Kent shook his head in disagreement. He had to stay one more day for Luna, just one more day to celebrate her birthday, then he could go. Darin eyed Kent warily but ultimately agreed to let him do what Kent felt was best; in addition, Darin had promised not to bring up the message to Luna. Kent knew, in hindsight, his plan was short-sighted.

As he knocked on the door, he had no idea how he would tell Luna or keep her safe. He knew it had only been seconds since he knocked, but the panic began to set in. He went to knock again, but he heard the door unlock and saw her face. He pushed into the frequency interference and locked the door behind him.

Kent paused briefly, listening. Then, he asked, "What, Luna? What is happening?"

Luna had her head between her hands; she was shaken.

Kent slowly moved toward her, as if he was trying not to spook a wild animal. "Hey," he said quietly. "What's going on?"

She turned to face him.

Kent saw her cheeks were crimson, and her eyes looked like she had three times the amount of caffeine someone should have, bloodshot but wide.

Luna looked right at him and said, "You are seriously going to think I have lost it." She shook her head, looking at the floor. "I feel like I've lost it."

It was Kent's turn to look flustered. *What is she talking about?* He gestured to her couch. "Let's sit, you look like you might need to."

She nodded and walked over to the couch, but started speaking before she sat down. "I went shopping in the courtyard after work. I bought a new book and a loaf of bread. I stepped outside and closed my eyes, I don't even know—breathing, I guess? Then I stumbled, and when I opened my eyes, it was dark and no one was around! So, I checked my holo and get this: It was *five hours* later. I have no idea what happened or what caused it." She looked up at Kent. "Can you pull courtyard footage? Maybe there was a MAV recording?"

Kent paused as he processed Luna's experience. Before he answered her, he had questions of his own. "Wait, you literally were standing in the same spot five hours later and have no recollection of those five hours?"

Luna shook her head. "Kent, I have no idea what happened. I don't know what to do. If I report this to anyone, they will lock me up for testing for weeks." She wasn't wrong, and he knew it. Luna didn't have a history of brain trauma.

Kent continued with his questions, "Do you have any injuries? Headache? Feel like you hit your head?

"No, but there is this." Luna held out her left arm, rolling up her sleeve to show Kent a fresh cut, no longer a small scratch as she had described earlier. This cut was deep—were it any deeper, she would need stitches. Luna continued as Kent's mind raced. "It is directly over where I cut myself this morning. I don't know how I tore it back open."

He looked at her as he sank onto the green couch. "Lu, I don't think *you* tore it back open at all; it is too perfect."

Luna looked back at her arm and then at Kent. "You think someone cut me?"

Kent nodded, rubbing his temples; he was getting a headache. "I'll look for some footage, but let's start there, okay? We can even ask Darin for help if we don't find anything and need him to pull encrypted files. I do *not* want to bring this to anyone else's attention before we can get some footage of you. We do not need the New Republic up our asses more than they already are."

Luna nodded in agreement. Kent sank back into the couch.

Suddenly, Luna perked up and said, "Well, I was going to give this to you tomorrow, but since you're here, I have something for you." She reached into the canvas bag at her feet and produced a pink box with a dark green bow.

"Luna, what is this?" Kent asked.

Luna gestured to the box. "It's Dad's bracelet."

Kent stilled. He took the box so gingerly and opened it. His throat closed as he slowly slipped the bracelet on his wrist.

Before Kent could ask, Luna explained, "The First Citizen gave it to me yesterday at work. She also gave me this." Luna pulled their mother's long necklace from under her shirt, and Kent recognized it immediately as the matching chain their mother wore. Luna continued while Kent studied the gold chain in his hand. "The First Citizen said she didn't have any use for them anymore," she continued. "What is she talking about?"

This time, Kent was honest. "Luna, I don't know." He opened his mouth to say more; to tell her he was part of the Resistance—had been for years—and he hadn't told her so he could protect her, but he stopped himself.

He watched as she stood and made her way to her bedroom. She turned back to Kent and said, "I'm going to try to rest. You can sleep on the couch. I think I have a couple of pairs of clean clothes for you in the bottom drawer of the coffee table. Love you. Thank you for coming."

He was already horizontal on the couch with one of his favorite blankets, a knit, light blue one that felt soft as butter but was so warm. Before he completely succumbed to sleep, he managed to say, "Love you too. Always, Moon Bug." He curled up as much of his body as he could on the couch and tried to sleep, but shame coated his thoughts. He would have to tell her the truth tomorrow, and that would be a dumpster fire.

11

<u>LUNA</u>

LUNA'S ALARM WENT OFF a few hours later. She tossed off the rumpled sheets angrily, as if they were the cause of her poor sleep. When she stood and looked out her window, she was greeted by the familiar sight of the slums beneath Solles. It was some strange morning ritual she started when she moved to this apartment. She wasn't sure why, but she felt like she had to see them—see that they were real.

Tearing her gaze from the window, she quickly dressed in flowing black pants that cinched at the ankle. She paired them with a sky-blue shirt with sleeves that fell just above her elbows and a small scoop neck. Luna carefully tucked the gold necklace into the scoop before rechecking her arm. She carefully bandaged the cut last night, after cleaning it thoroughly, especially because she didn't know what had reopened the cut again.

Luna tried again to grasp her missing memories from last night, but there was nothing. She felt like she was standing on a razor's edge, and a soft push of the wind could throw her over.

She finished dressing and threw her copper curls—which were even frizzier and wilder than usual—into a high bun. Luna opened the door to the living space and heard Kent snoring on the couch. His leg was dangling over the front of the couch, with one foot on the floor, and the other leg was bent, his foot resting on the couch cushion and his knee against the back.

Walking past the couch, she smacked his knee and said, "Get up, we need to go."

He groaned and rolled over, face down, into the couch.

Luna padded into the kitchen, hollering over her shoulder, "I will not make you coffee if you do not get up." She went over to the coffee machine, clicked a few buttons, and the machine started up. The smell wafted from the kitchen into the small living space, finally getting Kent moving. She quickly made herself a cup with some sweetened condensed milk, ice, and a splash of regular milk. She also poured Kent a cup with regular milk and placed it on the coffee table in front of him.

He thanked her as he rose and went to the bathroom through her bedroom.

Luna's eyes slowly drifted back to the coffee table in front of the faded green couch. Atop which stood a resin delta lily she had been gifted yesterday, in a slim glass vase which flared at the bottom. The lily was so perfect, frozen in time, unlike the table, which had seen better days, much like the rest of her place. She painted the table a warm yellow when she started working at the art museum. There was always extra paint lying around, and although she wasn't skilled, she loved putting on music or an audiobook and listening while her mind unwound, focusing on a task with her hands. She lovingly touched the edge of the coffee table, where the paint was chipping.

Kent came out of the bathroom, and Luna turned to face him. He'd changed into tan pants and a white button-down with his wet hair pulled into a low bun. Not his everyday LEO attire, but they both knew he had extra sets of the black uniform in his office.

They were silent the rest of the morning.

Luna suggested taking the underrail today, to which Kent quickly agreed. They were both exhausted from last night, and even though they didn't use the underrail much, it was a faster way to get around. The underrail ran underneath the streets of Solles, functioning with a magnetic system Luna didn't quite understand.

Entering the underrail was simple enough. They scanned their monthly passes before descending one level below the streets of Solles to board. The underrail looked as if it should be underground. However, it was still high above ground level. At their stop, they exited the underrail, ascended the stairs, and stepped into the courtyard of the Kellmont State Building.

Back in the sunlight, Luna noticed Kent's pinched features. She gave him three squeezes and said, "I'm excited to go out later. Thank you for always making time for me."

He smiled tightly at her.

Yeah, something is wrong.

"Wouldn't have it any other way, Moon Bug," he said, giving her four squeezes back. Before walking away, he looked at her and said, "Meet you back at your place at eight tonight?"

She grinned. "I can't wait! You still need to tell me what we are doing!"

Kent shrugged with a devious grin, but his smile fell before he turned away.

Luna could feel her brother's panic—white hot and angry, but for once, she knew his panic was not for her. She decided that tonight she would get Kent to tell her what was going on. She'd spent far too long feeling sorry for herself; she needed to step up and help her brother. Luna would do everything Kent had done for her and more. They would get through this together.

She ascended the stairs of the state building and felt a small bubble of hope form in her chest, something that had been absent for far too long.

Luna was almost giddy with anticipation as they exited from the underrail later that evening. She had no idea where they were going or what Kent planned. He only promised she would love it.

Luna tucked her arm into the crook of Kent's elbow, matching his pace as they walked, and asked, "Okay, where are we actually going?"

Kent looked down at her bright pink, three-inch pumps. "How do you even walk in those?"

Luna smacked Kent's arm.

He gave her a wink and said, "I got us an exclusive invite to an Infiniti's End concert." Luna stopped dead in her tracks. She felt heat rush to her cheeks and tears prick her eyes. "Are you serious? How did you get the tickets?" Infiniti's End was one of the most popular bands not only in Solles but all of Arelia. Getting tickets to their performances was almost impossible, not to mention extremely expensive.

"Serious as I ever am!" Kent said, pushing Luna along from behind. "We actually have to get the tickets first, and if we don't hurry, we will be late."

Luna was ecstatic. She and Kent had been through so much, endured so much; they deserved a night filled with joy. She felt good in her black leather pants, pink pumps, and simple white t-shirt with her mother's golden necklace tucked beneath. She hadn't wanted to take the necklace off since receiving it.

The city seemed almost charged with electricity. Luna let herself feel happy for the first time in a long time. She felt alive; she could feel everything around her, pulsing like its own heartbeat. It made her feel invincible.

"Come on, Luna," Kent singsonged. "You don't need to be beaming so brightly, you'll take out a MAV by sheer lumens." Kent had, of course, said this loud enough that Luna was sure everyone within a two-block radius could hear him.

She pinned him with an annoyed glare and flipped him off for good measure. "With everything going on, let me soak it in a little."

Kent truly was the best brother, even if he pushed her buttons regularly. He'd opted for dark brown, slim-fitting pants and a gray short-sleeved button-down, currently open, exposing the light gray shirt beneath. Kent placed their father's gold bracelet on his right wrist. If Luna was being honest, he looked good and almost happy. *Almost.*

Kent took them down a narrow side alley.

"Um, okay." Luna took in the dark alley, her mind whirring with where he was leading them. "Where are we actually going?"

Kent's eyes brightened as he said quietly, "To see the best hacker we know. So, let's move, because if we do not get there on time, he threatened not to give me the tickets. As much as I love him, he is also very fussy."

Luna snickered but kept walking. "Do you guys still play that game together?"

Kent cleared his throat as an incriminating pink blush crept up his neck. "Um, No."

Got him. Luna was absolutely loving this now. "You both still play *Dragon Fight*?!"

Kent's blush deepened to a searing red.

Luna knew he loved to escape in video games, but he rarely talked about it. Kent had been streaming the interactive game *Dragon Fight* with Darin ever since they were kids. Kent had been so captivated by dragons as a child. She truly had no idea he still played, much less played with Darin. She stared at him with a raised eyebrow.

His lips were pursed in a thin line, trying to give nothing away, even though he already had.

"So..." Luna crooned, not at all trying to diffuse the awkwardness, "where are we meeting the Dragon Master?" She was enjoying getting under his skin at the moment.

Kent scoffed. "First off: He is not a Dragon Master, I am. He is a High-Class Wizard."

"Ah, I see. Our friend is one of the best hackers in Solles, but he is also a High-Class Wizard in *Dragon Fight*, very impressive." Luna's tone was thick with sarcasm, and her grin widened. She couldn't remember the last time they teased each other like this.

Kent gave her a sidelong glance that made it very clear she was being a pest. "We're almost there, please promise not to bring up the *Dragon Fight* thing, okay?"

Luna's eyes were merciless, but she nodded.

A few minutes later, they turned down another small alley and reached a brick building in disrepair on their left. Its windows were either broken or boarded, the front door was missing a handle, and the roof had a large hole in it, seemingly caused by water damage.

"Well, this looks...awesome. Are you sure he lives here?" Luna asked, concern lacing her voice.

Kent nodded as he walked up the three dilapidated stairs and knocked on the door.

"State your Name and Rank!" A voice from the other side requested.

Kent sighed deeply and said so quietly that Luna almost didn't hear it, "It's Eladon, Dragon Master level twelve."

Luna almost couldn't stifle her snicker.

Darin threw the door open, beaming at his friends. He had a deep, caramel-colored skin tone with black, curly hair that hung in his honey-colored eyes, making the gold flecks in them even more poignant. Darin wore a pair of tan shorts, flip-flops, and a bright blue hoodie. He threw himself into Kent in a giant bear hug. "It has been too long, Dragon Master! When are you going to get online again?"

Luna was really struggling to control her laughter now.

"I can't believe you, man!" Darin continued. "I haven't seen you in months, and then you message out of the blue asking for tickets for Luna? Shameful! I feel you owe me at least two hours of *Dragon Fight*, but I'll make an exception because this is Luna's birthday gift." Darin looked at Luna and winked.

She had known Darin for years, and they had tried what it might be like to be together but agreed that they were happier as friends.

"I am so excited to see you guys finally! Luna, how long has it been? Oh, my bad, come on in." Darin waved his hand, motioning them forward as he turned and walked into the structure.

Kent looked over at Luna, shrugged, and whispered, "I forgot how much he likes to talk."

Luna broke out laughing, and Kent followed until they were both cackling.

Darin yelled from inside, "Hey, assholes, get in here. I have beer and some splice if you want it!"

The siblings obeyed.

As Luna crossed the threshold, she felt a familiar frequency—the same pulse she felt at her own apartment. Luna quickly checked to ensure her shields were still in place—they were—but as she turned to close the front door behind her, she saw the slightly blueish cast just beyond it.

Darin, an Illusionist, had not only obtained at least three of the cubes her parents had created but also reprogrammed them as a hologram for the exterior of the house. The interior was *stunning*.

Luna almost gaped as she looked around at the perfect decor. A black, metal spiral staircase to the left led to the second floor. Directly to her right was a beautiful archway, painted a very dark green. Beyond it was a large, black dining table with benches and chairs. The kitchen was located around the corner, from which she could smell several different herbs and spices in the air. She felt a sense of home that she hadn't felt in years.

Luna looked straight ahead to the room in front of her, where three large, deep navy couches faced a small fireplace and three projection screens. Slightly to the left, tucked into the corner, was a desk facing a window, with fifteen security camera monitors mounted in front of it. The window looked out into the alley, but it also allowed some of the sun's fading light to filter in. The security cameras were arranged in three rows of five, stacked on top of each other, each attached to three metal poles that secured to the desk itself. The cameras seemed to capture every angle of the house, inside and out. Suddenly, she didn't know if she should feel at home or if she should be paranoid.

Kent stared out the front windows in amazement. "I knew you reworked the cubes, but I hadn't realized that you didn't simply invert the way the frequency interference projected, but you added an illusion!"

Darin shrugged as he joined Kent. "It took some tinkering, but I got it to work. The biggest positive is that you can still utilize your ability both inside and outside the house. Just not in that tiny space as you pass the illusion. I haven't been able to recreate the cube, though. I'm not sure how they did it, but moving them is a delicate process. If I adjust them, even slightly, it messes with the Illusion and the frequency's concentration. I had a lot of bloody noses the first week. I literally had to glue one to the roof; it's under a shingle. Shit's stuck there now."

Darin went to his couch and grabbed a keyboard from the floor. He sat and placed the keyboard on the small table in front of them. "Come, have a seat, and I'll send these to you." With a wave of his hands over the table, the mechanism under the keyboard lifted to elevate the table, which now sat slightly above Darin's lap. He typed away as all three projection screens came to life, connecting to the interface.

One projection was filled with code—Luna assumed this was where most of Darin's programming happened. The second had multiple tabs open, and even though she only got a glance, Luna was pretty sure they were classified New Republic documents or secure websites for which Darin should not have access. The third contained the tickets for tonight's show.

With a few swift keyboard clicks by Darin, all three projection monitors went dark.

Ping!

It was Kent's holo in his pocket.

"All set, my man!" Darin said with a smile. "Those tickets will get you in with VIP access. But there's a catch!"

Kent's face deadpanned, but Darin's eyes twinkled, and his smile broadened.

"I'm coming with you!"

12

<u>LUNA</u>

LUNA, KENT, AND DARIN left the house and returned to the underrail. The concert was held in a smaller club space in the heart of the city, a truly exclusive event.

Four LEOs guarded the doors from outside. The first was checking tickets, the second ushered concertgoers through an archway with a slight shimmer. Luna knew her parents must have had something to do with the technology—disrupting the frequency so the LEO can ensure no one is shielding. The third and fourth LEOs sat at a security desk, checking bags.

While they stood in line, Luna watched a slender female in a backless black jumpsuit place her small, matching clutch on the table inside the outline of a black circle. The circle on the table opened, revealing a large hole where the clutch hovered for a moment before lowering into the table. Luna watched alerts and buttons appear on the table for the LEO's assessment. Some he clicked through immediately, others created additional screens as he processed. Eventually, the clutch reappeared, hovering slightly before the hole was covered, leaving the clutch in its original position.

The line inched toward the first LEO scanning tickets. Thanks to Darin, the tickets worked perfectly, and the trio moved through the security measures with minimal fuss.

Luna descended the stairs into the basement club space. She could already hear the thrumming bass from the opening band. She felt a swell of relief; they hadn't missed the main act. She wove through the crowd to get as close to the stage as possible, leaving Darin and Kent behind in her excitement.

She spotted an open high-top table with a few chairs and sat in one to hold the spot.

Darin and Kent were still making their way through the crowd as she waved her arm to bring them over. Kent stayed at the bar waiting for their drinks.

Darin came right over to sit.

Luna was so excited she could barely contain herself. "These tickets are amazing! I cannot believe you managed to get them."

Darin gave her a sly grin but said nothing as Kent approached with drinks.

Luna noticed several enslaved people moving about the small bar space, serving drinks to patrons. There were also a few cleaning tables and bringing drinks out. It was rare to see the enslaved amongst the Behtari. Many worked behind walls so as not to disturb the Behtari. Luna suspected it was so the Behtari did not have to acknowledge their cruelty.

They all wore a similar uniform, regardless of post. The uniform consisted of steel-gray pants and a steel-gray long-sleeve shirt with a hood that covered their hair. A steel-gray mask concealed their faces, generally made of rigid, thick plastic. The mask covered their nose and mouth, even going around their chin. It was secured at the back of the head and could only be opened when they were released from their shift and returned to the ground level. The mask was barbaric; it ensured the enslaved person could not speak or eat without permission. As the enslaved moved about the space, they seemed like ghosts, never looking at any of the Behtari—except one.

Luna felt eyes on her, but every time she looked, the human's gaze was cast down. She was setting drinks on the side of the bar where Kent had come from. Luna tried to ignore the nagging in her mind that the enslaved was watching her, but she continued speaking with Darin and Kent over the music. When the next song finished and the clapping faded, Luna finally gave in to temptation. She looked at the bar, and sure enough, the enslaved woman was staring at her.

Luna noticed immediately that her eyes were slightly upturned at the corners. They were beautiful, a rich mahogany color. A touch of her silver hair peeked out from the top of her hood. Luna immediately wondered if she got in trouble for that...but as quickly as Luna looked up, the human looked down. Luna inwardly chastised herself. Of course she didn't want to look at a Behtari—who knows what she thought might happen if she was caught looking at Luna?

Kent then grabbed her arm when the lights flashed and the stage lit up.

Luna was already on her feet, hollering. She always dreamed of seeing Infiniti's End, and now it was finally happening—in an intimate club setting with only one hundred guests. Darin must have pulled some strings to make this happen.

As soon as the band came onto the stage, Luna was on her feet, and Infiniti's End did not disappoint.

Luna's mind emptied while the drums pounded a heavy beat as the intense vocals soared over the accompanying guitar. The guitarist sang various harmonies with the lead vocalist, and Luna couldn't help but sing along with every word. They wove a spell of raw lyrics and passion, filling the room.

Luna loved every moment. Her face hurt from smiling so much. She honestly could not remember the last time she felt so much joy. When she caught Kent glancing at her, he looked pleased, too.

As their final song wrapped up, Luna had tears streaming down her cheeks. She whistled and hollered along with everyone else, asking them for an encore. The band quickly exchanged knowing glances with each other and stepped back up to the mic.

Suddenly, Luna was consumed with the sudden sensation that something was incredibly wrong. She couldn't explain what she was feeling apart from the electric buzz in the air. She looked at Kent and tilted her head toward the door to leave.

She didn't know what was happening and, quite frankly, didn't want to find out.

Kent nodded, and they stood to leave.

Suddenly, Darin had both of their arms held so tightly that it was almost painful.

"We want to leave, Darin," Luna said as politely as she could. "We will catch you later."

Darin's grip didn't waver; his eyes were glassy, but wide with panic. He looked straight ahead at the stage—unmoving, unblinking.

A Behtari is using their ability on Darin. Luna's mind raced. *Shit. Shit. Shit.* She looked around for someone using their ability or even looking at them, but as her eyes swept the room, it was eerily quiet.

She realized the only other person moving in the entire club was Kent. Darin was not the only one who was still as stone—the band hadn't begun their encore, no human moved from the bar area or the back room, and there was not a LEO in sight. Everyone in this club was frozen, which meant that everyone except Kent and Luna was being Manipulated.

Luna's panic surge in her chest.

How are we moving? How is this possible?

She could think of no reasonable explanation as to how she and Kent were somehow resistant to this Behtari's manipulation ability. She knew that the cubes at home created a frequency interference, but this was something else. If a system similar to the one in her apartment were here, it would have protected everyone, right? Luna was rattled back to reality when Kent grabbed her hand and mouthed.

We have to go. Now. Carry him.

Darin was gripping her arm so tightly that Luna knew it would bruise, but she nodded once at Kent. They would not leave their friend.

Clink.

From the back corner of the bar, the enslaved woman Luna saw earlier came out from around the back storage area. Her eyes went wide with surprise, taking in all the still figures and the absence of music. She started trembling and turned to leave. Luna couldn't blame her; the club was like something out of a horror movie. When the woman faced Luna and caught her eye, she looked down.

Luna instantly scoffed in annoyance and said, a little too forcefully, "Get over here!"

The enslaved's cheeks flushed red out of embarrassment or anger, Luna wasn't sure.

Luna didn't mean to be rude, but they needed help.

As the enslaved hurried over to them, Luna asked, "Can you help us get out through the back?" With that question, the enslaved's face looked up to meet her own. Luna stared into the woman's beautiful, deep mahogany eyes, but with a light brown rim around the edge.

She nodded only once, unable to speak due to the mask.

"Good," Luna said at the same time Kent said, "Fuck this, let's go."

Luna and Kent wedged Darin between them and walked as quickly as possible behind the enslaved.

Darin was like a dead weight between them. His body was stiff, but not completely unmovable.

Luna felt it then: a high-pitched whirr. Time slowed. She was aware of everything all at once. In less than one second, she decided Kent had Darin, and she had to protect this enslaved woman. Her body was stronger than a human's—the human had no protection. She also had a strange sensation that, at this exact moment, something had shifted. She couldn't understand what she was feeling, but she knew, sensing it from the depths of her being, that this decision, to save this enslaved, changed the trajectory of her future.

That was the last thing Luna thought when she felt the shockwave through the air, followed by the blast of heat from the explosion. Her back was so hot, and Luna was thrown to the floor with the enslaved tucked to the side of her body.

Luna's ears rang—she could barely think straight. When Luna came back to her senses, the human was gone, and all she could hear was screaming before everything went dark.

13

<u>NAOMI</u>

NAOMI COULDN'T BREATHE; SHE couldn't think. She couldn't get out of that club fast enough. After being tackled by that Behtari, Naomi was sure she would be killed if someone found out the Behtari protected her.

This is not possible. This could not be possible. There was absolutely no reason that a Behtari—*this* Behtari—would have protected her unless she knew.

That worried Naomi more than anything else. Suppose the Behtari found out... *No.* That didn't make sense. If the Behtari knew, she would not have saved Naomi. So what did the Behtari have to gain?

Naomi couldn't help but feel conflicted. She would have been dead if the Behtari hadn't saved her, but if that Behtari found out who she was—what she had done—Naomi was as good as dead.

When the First Citizen gave Naomi this assignment over a week ago, her instructions at the club had been clear: Keep an eye on Luna until Infiniti's End starts the encore; once the first song starts, leave. The problem was, they never played the encore. In fact, everything had happened *before* the encore.

Those moments played on a loop in Naomi's head.

At the bar, stacking clean glasses.

Catching the copper-haired Behtari's eye.

Realizing who that Behtari was.

Knowing the Behtari was supposed to perish in the blast.

As soon as Naomi realized the timing was wrong, she panicked. She tried saving her own hide and, in turn, saved the Behtari. Naomi felt sick at the thought that the New Republic had been trying to get rid of her. But why? She had been nothing but obedient—not that she had a choice. She had never even been late apart from this morning.

Each day, it was every human's duty to ensure they were at their post on time. If a human was late for their post, they were punished. Naomi had been whipped once for being late to her dishwashing post on the north side of Solles. It was her first job at the age of thirteen, when all humans were assigned posts. She was eleven minutes late and received eleven lashes, one for each minute, after her shift concluded.

She barely made it home that day, her uniform soaked with her own blood. Her mother caught her as she crossed the threshold, sobbing into their small home. Her mother tended to her back while Naomi lay on the lone table in the house. She remembered watching her own tears and blood drip onto the table and then the floor, mixing with the dirt and cement floor of their home.

That was the first time she had felt genuine fear—thinking the LEO who whipped her was going to end her life. The only other time she had felt that fear was tonight. Had they adjusted their plans because she was late to her post with the First Citizen this morning?

Naomi had assumed she was too valuable to be removed. Clearly, that was not the case. Did they now see her as a liability? She knew many secrets, including the people they had contracted Naomi to remove discreetly—never by her own hands, though. A human caught controlling a MAV with enough poison to drop ten grown Behtari would be enough justification for a public execution.

Naomi had arrived only two minutes late to her post at the state building, where the First Citizen was reviewing cell improvements with Governor Seymour. Naomi had rushed through the back entrance of the building, weaving through the hidden walls the humans used to get from post to post. The First Citizen usually worked in a conference room while in Solles. It was by far the easiest location to navigate multiple meetings back-to-back.

Naomi clicked her mask into place and opened the door, which looked like a section of the wall in the meeting room's interior. The room was only half-lit, illuminating the First Citizen where she sat at the end of a long table on Naomi's right, in front of the large, floor-to-ceiling windows. The floor was a deep, rich cherry wood, and the walls had an almost sky-blue hue. Other than that, the room was sparsely decorated. The long table could easily seat twenty-five. Naomi could see the greenhouses on some of the buildings stretching up into the sky.

All this beauty covering what lay beneath, she'd thought.

The First Citizen did not look up from her holo as she tapped the surface with her too-slender fingers. "Sit."

Naomi's skin went ice cold. She had never been asked to sit by the First Citizen before and didn't need to be told twice. Naomi pulled out the chair directly in front of her and sat, waiting for the First Citizen to continue.

The First Citizen, still looking at her holo, pursed her blood-red lips and said, without looking up, "You are late."

Naomi said nothing; she knew the First Citizen would ask her to speak if a response was required. Naomi kept her eyes trained on the table in front of her, tracking the First Citizen's movements in her peripheral vision. She willed herself not to show fear.

The First Citizen allowed the silence to stretch on before putting her holo face-up on the table. She took a small key from her pocket and slid it to Naomi. She intertwined her fingers on both hands to rest her chin atop them. She tilted her head, her golden eyes flicking up to Naomi's face as she asked, "Why?"

Naomi closed her eyes, bracing herself for what would happen after she spoke. She could be whipped, she could be forced to a different post, a different city, Ethan and Ella could be taken from her. *No*, she just needed to focus and be honest. She reached for the key and unclasped her mask so she could speak.

"I had to wait for a second lift."

It was the truth. Naomi had left at the same time as she did any other day. She wove through the ground-level streets to a lift inside a structural arch, which brought her up to the elevated streets. There were lifts for humans in each of the large arches along the central part of Solles, allowing them to reach the elevated streets without climbing twenty flights of stairs. However, when she arrived at the lift, it had already departed. She went a block in the other direction, hoping to grab the lift on the other side of the arch. It had also departed, so she waited there and took the next one.

The First Citizen eyed her warily. "You are aware of your requirements tonight?" Naomi nodded, still looking at the table while keeping her peripheral vision on the First Citizen.

As if the First Citizen knew what Naomi was doing, she pursed her lips again and said, "Look at me, human. Spying is rude."

Naomi obeyed and made eye contact with the First Citizen. She was dressed in a deep burgundy, oversized pant suit, creating a startling contrast with her porcelain-white skin and golden eyes, which Naomi could have sworn were glowing.

The First Citizen placed her long fingers on the table and drummed slowly, taking in Naomi. "If you are aware of your duties, and you arrived late this morning, you are clearly in need of rest to ensure you perform tonight. Your post has been covered for the day. My LEO—" The First Citizen snapped her fingers, and a broad female LEO stepped out of the shadows. "—will escort you back to the ground level."

Before Naomi could stop herself, she asked, "I am not being punished?"

The First Citizen looked Naomi up and down as if she were an insect, a pest to be removed. "Do you need to be reminded to be on time?"

Naomi shook her head firmly.

"Good. See that you are not late this evening."

With that, Naomi returned to her home on the ground level.

Now, as Naomi sprinted to the lift, she wondered if she was just a pawn on the New Republic's giant chessboard. Useful but expendable. Sweat dripped down her back and into her eyes. Finally, Naomi stopped to catch her breath. She was almost to the lift; she didn't need to draw attention to herself. She turned and looked back at the way she had come, under the giant white arches. No one followed her.

Naomi was supposed to be the only one in that club who could resist Manipulation, but those two Behtari resisted. *How was that possible?*

She had left as soon as she felt like she could get her weight under her. She hadn't been able to see much through the debris, smoke, and gore. When Naomi stumbled into the alley behind the club, LEOs were already closing in. They pushed past her; she was unimportant, human. So, she ran as fast as she could to the nearest lift. Each could hold about fifty people, but only two others were waiting to go down. Neither gave her a second glance; one had clearly been working in the sewers beneath the elevated streets, covered in grime and smelling of waste. It took all of Naomi's effort not to vomit. Combined with her adrenaline from the explosion, it was almost too much.

The lift ride was short—five minutes at most—but Naomi couldn't help but feel jittery on the lift. As soon as the doors opened at ground level, Naomi pushed her feet out from under her, wasting no time before running again. She could not get away from the elevated streets fast enough.

She finally felt like she could breathe back on the ground level, which was so ironic she almost laughed aloud. The smell on the ground level was putrid on good days, suffocating on bad. The Behtari didn't care what ended up down here, as long as they didn't have to deal with it.

Naomi arrived at the building that she, her brother, Ethan, and her sister, Ella, shared. They were eight years old and eleven years old, to Naomi's twenty-seven. As she entered the structure, she saw both were asleep on the twin cot in the corner, a small fire burning in the makeshift stone hearth she made for them. They couldn't ever have a roaring fire, but they managed to keep a few coals going on cold nights.

Naomi kissed both of her siblings on the forehead and settled into the cot on the other side of the room. She knew Ethan was going to have to take this one soon; he was already almost too big to share with Ella, but Naomi wasn't ready to give up a bed yet.

As Naomi drifted off to sleep, all she could hear was screaming.

14

DARIN

DARIN'S FIRST CONSCIOUS THOUGHT was that he was on his back. His ears were ringing from the explosion, but muffled screams pierced the sound. As he took a breath, he could taste the dust and blood in the air. He blinked a few times as he tried to reorient himself. Sitting up slowly, he surveyed the scene, brushing off the small bits of rubble and dust that had fallen on him.

This was wrong. He could see blood on the walls, on the floor, as well as pieces of people. He couldn't fathom the carnage he was staring at.

Darin panicked as he looked himself over to ensure he didn't have any life-threatening wounds. He was certain that even if he did, he wouldn't have felt them with the adrenaline coursing through his veins.

After scanning himself, he realized he was mostly fine. He had a nice-sized gash on his back across the bottom of his left ribs. He could feel the pain slowly increasing as his adrenaline waned, but he could also feel the blood soaking through his shirt, sticky and felt like it was gluing to his skin.

He shook his head. What had he been doing leading up to the explosion? He had been holding onto Kent and Luna because he couldn't let go... Someone had taken over his body to force Kent and Luna to stay, but Darin was utterly powerless. He let his guard down, and it had endangered his friends.

Darin looked around, frantic. *Where are Luna and Kent?* As he continued to scan through the smoke, he could feel the dust and ash coating his mouth and lungs. After what seemed like an eternity, even though it was only mere seconds, he spotted an arm resting on the ground behind a flipped table with a small truss of curly, copper hair peeking out above the arm.

He gripped the tabletop edges and righted it to get to Luna beneath. Her eyes were shut, and she lay unmoving on the ground. Darin knelt, placing his hand gently on her neck to feel for a pulse. Simultaneously, he watched her chest to be sure she was breathing; thankfully, she was. He could feel her pulse hammering against his fingertips. Even though she was passed out, her body was still on high alert. She was bleeding from her temple, not severely, but she would need stitches.

Darin gently tapped her face.

Luna's eyes flicked open. Her frightened gasp made Darin jump, even though he had been expecting her to wake.

As she and Darin looked at each other, he gave her a moment before he said, "I'm okay. Are you okay?"

She nodded and tried to stand, but she wavered, her hand flying to her temple. "Shit," Luna exhaled a whisper amidst all the commotion, screaming, and sirens.

"Well, not okay. Apparently, I got slammed in the head." She brought her fingers to her forehead and winced as she touched the gash. Before Darin could speak, she asked, "Are you hurt?"

Darin helped her up amongst the rubble and broken glass. "Cut on my back, it'll need stitches, same as your forehead, but I don't think it's serious."

Luna nodded as she stood. She looked around at what was left of the club, and Darin watched her take in the severity of the damage. As Darin took in their surroundings, the most damage came from the stage – or what was left of it. The band had very clearly not survived the explosion. The lead singer's eyes were open but unfocused, her body bent at odd angles, and blood dripped from her mouth. Luna paled.

Darin sometimes forgot that not everyone had seen dead bodies in person. He rested his hand on her shoulder, knowing her pallor was not only due to the bodies, but the absence of Kent. "He's fine. We will find him."

As if the universe was listening, he heard Kent call Luna's name weakly from about five feet behind them. Darin felt his chest immediately relax. He and Luna followed Kent's voice, carefully navigating the chaos and rubble. They had to climb over a large piece of concrete amid the rubble that seemed to have fallen from the wall during the explosion. It was obscuring their view of Kent just enough that they could see the top portion of his face just above the nose, but nothing else.

Darin let Luna go first. The large piece of cement wasn't enormous, but it was tall enough that he had to use his hands to swing his legs up over it. As he did, he felt the pain from the gash in his ribs radiate red-hot. His adrenaline was masking most of the pain, but he knew he needed to be more careful or he would make the wound worse.

Yep, definitely going to need stitches. He grunted.

Kent's face was too pale. He wore a small smile, relieved to see his sister, Darin assumed. Kent was under some debris, which Luna and Darin would have to move to get him out. Then Darin saw the weakness of Kent's smile; sometimes he wished he didn't see so much.

Luna fell to her knees and tried to wrap her arms around her brother, but Kent's face winced in pain. The rest of his body remained still. That's when they noticed the two-inch-thick metal rebar sticking straight through Kent's chest on his left side.

Darin knew instantly, between the size of the wound, the fact that Kent already had blood coming from his mouth... Kent's wound was fatal. He watched in horror as Luna's hands trembled, reaching for her brother's too pale face.

This cannot be happening, not again. She can't lose someone else. Kent was the only person she had left. What had she done to deserve this?

What could she have possible done to deserve this? He knew the answer already. Nothing. She had done nothing to deserve this, and Darin could do nothing but watch.

Silent tears left trails down Luna's dirt and blood streaked face. Luna framed Kent's face with her hands, gently so as not to move him.

Kent attempted to move his right hand, but it was too painful. He gasped, which turned into a cough, spilling more blood from his mouth.

Luna carefully took Kent's hand, holding it away from his injury.

Her tears were falling faster now.

Darin wasn't sure what unspoken words were being shared between them, but he watched as they slowly eroded Luna's strength.

Luna nodded and then slowly unclasped the golden bracelet around Kent's left wrist.

Kent's eyes slowly found Darin. Darin had stood back to give the siblings privacy for this moment. When Kent's gaze found his, he knew his friend needed him one last time.

Darin then knelt beside Kent on the floor. He kissed Kent on the forehead, then pressed their foreheads together. He loved Kent deeply, even if they had never said it aloud. As Darin pulled away, he watched panic flicker in Kent's eyes.

He tried to tighten his grip on Darin's hand.

"Please," Kent whispered.

Darin knew what Kent was asking. Kent was one of the only other people Darin knew with a second ability, like himself. Not only was Darin an Illusionist, but he was also a Mind Reader. He honored Kent's request, gently probing through anything at the surface of his mind.

Three things came away very clearly. First: a message on Kent's screen at the state building, *They know*. Darin felt a pang of regret in his chest that he didn't encourage his friend to leave when he should have.

Second was an image of a ghost drive tucked between two drawers under the lip of his desk.

The third and final thing Darin felt was an overwhelming sense of sadness, and his heart broke. Darin couldn't have that. He pushed every happy memory of Kent he could back to his friend—memories of playing as children at the farmhouse. Years spent playing games together online. Flashes of Kent, Luna, and Darin being together and laughing. Every happy memory Darin could muster in those brief seconds flooded through him and into Kent's mind.

A whisper of a smile crossed Kent's face, and a tear fell down his cheek.

As Darin backed away, he nodded to Luna.

Luna gently took Darin's hand, placing Kent's bracelet in his palm before she knelt beside her brother again, one last time.

They didn't have long now. Kent's breaths were becoming shallow, each a labored effort.

Darin placed his hand on Luna's back, trying to give her his strength. Luna kissed Kent on the cheek. Then, so softly that Darin almost missed it, she whispered, "I love you more than all the stars."

Kent closed his eyes and released his last breath.

It took too much time to get out of the club. Darin guided Luna as best he could, but she was like a ghost next to him.

He could feel the emptiness in the air from their loss. The pain was almost unbearable; he could not imagine how Luna felt.

Outside, the pair was taken to an ambulance for stitches and evaluation at a nearby hospital.

In the back of the ambulance, Darin closed his eyes, resting his head against the dividing wall.

Luna placed her head on his shoulder and wept.

The quiet ride was short, but the chaos at the hospital was a nightmare. There were so many people, and everything took hours. Finally, once Darin and Luna were both stitched up and evaluated, they were moved to a small room to await a LEO for their witness statements.

While they waited in the cramped room, Darin could not shake the nagging feeling in his brain that he wasn't entirely innocent in the night's events. He felt he should have come across a document or piece of information within the New Republic that would have tipped him off to this targeted attack. He clearly missed something.

Darin was a hacker, plain and simple. At first, it wasn't anything significant—tickets to a game, a concert—but the requests grew. He couldn't say no to the money. His family had a rough time financially, even though his mother never seemed to stop working. Because his mom was with the Resistance, she always seemed to need his unique skillset. As much as his mother loved him, she loved The Resistance more, which meant every extra penny she earned went to their efforts.

Even though he was still not legally able to vote, she often had him hacking into New Republic databases. Sure, he agreed with what the Resistance was doing—they never had to force Darin—but a mother willing to sacrifice her son's safety made him bitter. Despite his resentment, he was now a ranking officer in the Resistance, which came with its own problems.

"Hey... You want to talk?" Luna asked gently, likely sensing his frustration.

Darin sighed deeply. "No, I'm trying to figure out what to do next. If I'm being honest, I'm overwhelmed."

"Me too." Luna pulled one leg to her chest as if using her limb as a physical shield. She'd discarded her pink pumps and had even asked the hospital for extra clothes. The only thing she still had on from the club was a gold necklace. Darin could see it; Luna was shutting down, becoming a shell of herself.

He could not let her walk this path again.

"I'm sorry you have to go through all this, Luna. At the same time, I'd be lying if I said I wasn't also glad I'm not alone right now." Darin slowly reached for her hand and gave it a tight squeeze.

"Same," she said softly.

Darin blew out a breath. "Lu, you know he and I were working together, right?" Darin was excellent at many things, but uncomfortable conversations were not his forte. He hoped Luna would catch his drift. Between the LEOs, cameras, and staff, he didn't want to ask her directly if she knew Kent had been working with the Resistance.

Luna sighed, her voice breaking as she said, "I do now. I always suspected, but we never talked about it," and then she said more to herself than Darin, "I wish we had talked more."

Darin didn't know what to say; he put his head against the wall and tried to stay awake, but it was impossible. He felt exhaustion deep in his bones; the adrenaline had clearly worn off. He turned slightly, closed his eyes, and let sleep take him.

15

<u>DARIN</u>

IT HAD BEEN OVER one week since the explosion at the concert, and Darin still had no explanation for it. Once he and Luna were discharged from the hospital, they went to Kent's apartment. Marcella and Wyatt agreed to watch over Luna and take care of her for the next week or so while she finalized Kent's affairs.

Darin only stayed in Solles for a few days, helping Luna through everything. He had to piece this together—something wasn't adding up. He waited to leave until after the funeral was held for all who perished at the club's bombing. There were only thirty-four Behtari survivors out of the one hundred guests; none of the band survived.

There was no mention of how many enslaved survived or died. Darin shouldn't have been surprised—the New Republic never included human casualties in public documentation. That was one of the first things Darin intended to find out: how many enslaved were at the club and who they were.

Darin spent a disgusting amount of time in other people's business as a hacker. He knew it was not mathematically possible that the explosion, the discovery of Kent's participation in the Resistance, and Luna losing hours of her life on her birthday were mere coincidences. No, he believed in numbers, science, and data.

Once Luna was safe, he took the underrail to the coast, where he chartered a private boat to Hamdon, headquarters for the Resistance. It cost Darin way too much coin to charter the small boat. Typically, when he came to Hamond, a ship would be sent for him. This time, Darin didn't tell anyone he was coming, apart from the Resistance leader, Milo. Not that it would have mattered anyway—Milo could use his Prophet ability to sense others' intentions.

Darin had always admired that Milo was transparent about his Prophet ability. It was unheard of for a Prophet to tell people about their ability. It made Darin trust him more, even when he knew he couldn't trust anyone. The message sent to Kent's interface had all but confirmed that.

Going to Hamdon was dangerous, but Darin needed the Resistance to open a proper investigation into the explosion. If he were a betting man, he'd bet this wasn't just an explosion, but an attempt to target Behtari associated with the Resistance.

Darin had gone over in his head how he would properly explain this to Milo. He knew there was more behind this explosion; even with little to no evidence, there was no reason to kill all the other Behtari, enslaved, as well as the band. Every conversation he had with himself, attempting to explain the situation, didn't end well. Darin was so clinical that sometimes he drove himself mad.

Any loopholes he found? Start again.

Hit a dead end? Start again.

He was the same with hacking and coding, which is why he was so damn good at it.

As the boat crested the next wave, he spotted land in the distance.

I'm going to kiss those rocks when we dock.

Hamdon was notorious for its rocky shores and rough waters, which meant the small boat would circle to the south side of Hamdon, toward a large bay. The Resistance's compound was not marked on any map. The only city listed on a Hamdon map was Arlo Bay, the easiest port to access, used only for diplomatic conversations when necessary. Arlo Bay was only minimally manned, but several tunnels connected the bay to other locations within Hamdon, doubling as easy escape routes when necessary.

Ping!

Darin reached for the holo, ensuring with medical precision that he didn't lose it in the waves. He also wrapped it in a waterproof bag and attached it to his wrist, in case. He didn't care if it was excessive; he lost a holo to these waves before, and he was not doing it again.

The notification was from one of Darin's contacts who worked with security cameras and MAVs in the New Republic. A while back, Darin had cleaned up a mess for him, and now Darin had called in the favor he was owed for footage of the night Luna lost hours of her life.

After three passwords and an eye scan, Darin finally pulled up the video. First, he saw a courtyard with no Luna, but then she appeared, exiting a shop. Darin watched Luna stand there, joy evident on her face. A moment later, her face went blank, and she stood unnaturally still. A tiny shadow crossed the left side of the frame.

Darin opened a sequencing program on his holo to slow and enhance the video as much as possible. While the boat rocked, Darin struggled to stay still as he edited the footage. Finally, after a few extremely irritating minutes, he got it. The small shadow moving away from Luna was a Stinger MAV. She was drugged.

Darin was so focused on the shadow; he forgot to watch the rest of the video. He brought the footage back up and pressed play. Almost as soon as the MAV left the area, an enslaved person approached Luna, looking around to ensure no one was watching. The camera captured her whole face. Darin recognized the enslaved woman almost immediately.

He exhaled through his nose in frustration and said, "Well, shit..." as he stared at the face of the enslaved woman who helped them the night Kent died.

Once Darin arrived, he made his way through the regular checkpoints until he reached the main base within the compound of the Resistance. He went to the security officer on duty and requested an audience with Milo, which was granted almost immediately.

The meeting with Milo was brief, lasting only about ten minutes. Milo agreed to call an emergency meeting with all the other ranking officers in the Resistance compound.

It took an hour or so to gather everyone, but once they were assembled in the old auditorium, there were over two hundred officers in attendance. Darin wasn't sure what it was used for before the war, but he had always loved the gilded designs on the wall, which were now faded and chipped. His focus was brought back to the meeting when Milo approached the podium.

A hush fell over the crowd. Milo had a charismatic presence; he didn't command respect, he earned it. Milo was in his early fifties with silver hair and deep-set wrinkles on his forehead. His skin was deep amber, but his eyes were striking—a bright honey color flecked with luminous gold.

Milo explained the purpose of the emergency meeting. News of the explosion in the club spread quickly in the media. Everyone in the compound was already aware of the attack in Solles and Kent's death—that they'd lost one of their own.

What they didn't know—and Darin had asked Milo not to share—was that a MAV had injected Luna and that she'd lost those five hours.

Darin had also asked Milo not to mention the message sent to Kent's interface. Milo agreed reluctantly. They needed to determine the source of the message before acting. If a Resistance member had sent the message, they needed to know who as soon as possible. The sender had covered their tracks well. In Darin's opinion, it reeked with the workings of the New Republic.

Darin was brought back to the meeting when Milo said his name. Milo explained that not only had Darin been there, but he'd also seen the propaganda the New Republic spun about the explosion. They told the Behtari it had been a Resistance explosive device, and they had done it to kill Behtari out of spite. Hearing Milo talk about it so matter-of-factly made Darin feel even more hollow than he already did. Milo wrapped up his introduction and handed the podium over to Darin.

Darin went over the evening in as much detail as possible. When he finished, he stepped down from the podium to an eerie silence.

Milo sensed the shift in the room and stood.

"I am not only appalled by this, but also worried." Firmness coated his voice. "We are being framed for something we did not do, nor would we ever do. Unfortunately, I cannot say I am surprised. Over the last twenty years, we have quadrupled the number of Resistance members. We also know that the First Citizen has been keeping track of our numbers by any means she can. While we know she does not have accurate figures, thanks to an undercover agent higher in the government. We also know that she is scared, which will do one of two things for us. The first: It could work to our advantage. It could cause both panic and curiosity. Or the second: It could make her more unpredictable than she already is, which is terrifying."

Milo paused and scanned the room. "I respect each of you. I would not have put you in this position if I did not trust you with my own life, let alone the success of our mission. We will investigate this situation. I suspect this was orchestrated by the First Citizen and the New Republic, but we do not yet have proof. I have assigned each of you specific research points to review. There are intentional duplicate assignments to catch misinformation. However, in the meantime, please return to your daily tasks. We will have another meeting in seventy-two hours. Thank you all. Dismissed." Milo turned away from the podium and approached Darin.

"You handled that well," Darin said with a grim smile.

Milo gave him a sidelong look. "Thank you for bringing that to us so quickly. I'm worried that if we don't act quickly enough, we are going to have more incidents."

Darin nodded.

As the old auditorium emptied, Darin heaved a sigh of relief. He never liked public speaking; it was always worse when it was bad news.

Once everyone left, Milo turned to him. "Alright, well, let's get on the encrypted interface and see what we can figure out." Milo turned on his heel and left with Darin following closely behind.

Darin spent the next few days poring over data and leads and hacking into the club's cameras but found nothing. Darin couldn't understand it; there was no footage of anyone putting an explosive device within the club. That meant there was nothing to tie the attack to the New Republic. He was grasping at straws at this point. He even looked into the deceased band, who, of course, was not involved. Darin, for the first time in recent memory, could not find anything to go on.

After looking over everything again, he felt like his head was going to explode, so he returned to his temporary room in the compound. It was small, but well-kept. He had a small bathroom with a shower, toilet, and sink. The bedroom itself was large enough for a dresser, a twin-size mattress, and a small desk. Papers, notes, and photos were taped to the walls and strewn on the floor and dresser. As he stared at the ceiling from the desk chair, he noticed the open vent blowing warm air from the furnace into his room, warming his skin. His eyes suddenly widened, and

16

LUNA

LUNA LET OUT A shaking breath to calm down. Typically, any excuse to go out in Solles was something she'd look forward to, but it had only been three weeks since the explosion in the club—three weeks since her brother was murdered. She couldn't say he died, because she knew better. Someone targeted them.

Her last moments with Kent played on an endless loop in her mind. She could feel the sadness and rage she felt that night as if she were living it again. She refused to give in to the rage as Kent slipped away—she wouldn't let anger ruin her last moments with her brother.

She remembered the feeling of his hand in hers, how cold it was. What truly caused her heart to break over and over again were his three faint squeezes. *"I love you."* Luna had kissed the back of his hand and squeezed his hand back four times. *"I love you, too."* That was the first time since the day of their parents' execution that Kent had initiated their silent communication. It had always been Luna, up until the night Kent died.

For ten years, she kept that tradition of love alive, and for what? To be the sole surviving member of her family? The medical staff told her she had been lucky. She scoffed he quickly picked up his holo from where it was charging on the desk and opened it to Milo's projected image.

"Milo," Darin said, looking at the projection of him on the holo. He was breathless with excitement. "How quickly can you get me video footage from every source in a one-block radius from the club and blueprints for the club and surrounding buildings within a two-block radius?"

"Probably a few hours, why?" Milo asked.

"That will be perfect. I've got an idea. Let me know when you have them," Darin said, not missing a beat.

Darin saw a smile spread across Milo's face as he said, "I will," before he ended the call.

He felt a surge of adrenaline and used his holo to review the footage of Luna again. If he was going to have to wait to hear from Milo, he might as well do something else productive.

As Darin watched the footage for the millionth time, his excitement evaporated. He was missing something; he was sure of it. It was only a question of what. Suddenly, it felt like he had been smacked by a sack of bricks.

The human was the only other person in that club who could move—the only other person besides Luna and Kent. He was going to find out everything about that enslaved woman. Darin was certain: She was the key to everything.

at the memory. If there were such a thing as luck, she never had any; everyone she loved died.

The armored vehicle's driver easily maneuvered the evening traffic of the elevated streets, carting her to Governor Seymour's annual fundraiser. In past years, Luna enjoyed this event, but she was filled with dread. Not only was the fundraiser at a museum around the corner from the club, but the First Citizen was attending this year.

Luna knew the First Citizen attended various political fundraisers throughout Arelia, but Luna detested having to see her again so soon. Beyond her own dislike of the First Citizen, she had a nagging feeling in the back of her brain like a thin thread that leads to something larger. As if everything that happened was woven together, but even though the thin thread was within her grasp, she couldn't quite reach it.

The stress overwhelming her entire being was unbearable. Luna knew the vehicle would arrive soon, but nothing was happening quickly enough. She wiped her sweaty palms on her navy-blue pants, hoping no one else in the vehicle noticed. The only others in the private vehicle were the driver, herself, the Governor, the Governor's wife, Margaret, and one LEO.

Luna shifted uneasily in her seat, trying to calm her nerves. She bounced her leg mindlessly and played with the gold chain around her neck—she'd do anything to take her brain off where she was going.

This is ridiculous, she thought to herself. She tried to focus on something else, but her mind kept returning to the Resistance, Kent, her parents, and her own complete failure as their daughter and his sister.

Luna was unable to save them; she blamed herself. She had never done anything to help her family, herself, or others. Luna wanted no part of the Resistance after her parents died. She'd blamed them for her parents' death for so long, even though she knew it wasn't true. It had only been after Kent's murder did Luna realize it didn't matter who was responsible. She didn't care anymore. She just wanted her brother back.

After what seemed like an eternity, they arrived at the fundraiser. Thankfully, Luna kept her panic under control—at least for the most part. She waited, her leg still bouncing as the vehicle came to a stop in front of the museum entrance. When the vehicle's wheels finally stopped, Luna quickly rose, grabbed the briefcase of documents she had for the Governor, and exited the vehicle as fast as she could. She didn't need to be in enclosed places tonight. Or ever, frankly.

As she exited the vehicle, a hand touched her elbow, causing Luna to jump and almost drop everything. She looked in the direction the hand had come from, realizing it was only the driver. She felt her cheeks heat with embarrassment. The driver got out of the vehicle before anyone else to assist them all out, nothing more.

Once everyone disembarked, Governor Seymour came up to Luna, eyeing her with concern. "Hey, you okay?"

What could I possibly say to him that he'd understand? "Yeah, I'm still dealing with a lot right now. But I'm fine," she replied, her tone as calm as she could make it, as if she wasn't a complete ball of nerves.

Governor Seymour smiled sadly and nodded. Then, he turned to offer his arm to his wife, and together, they headed into the museum.

All the while, Luna felt like she should be screaming.

Two sweeping staircases with black iron railings and wooden cherry stairs flanked the museum's foyer. Luna would have thought the juxtaposition of the black railing and warm-colored wood would not work, but it gave the stairs a soft, almost whimsical feel, as if they grew from the floor itself. The rest of the flooring throughout the entry space continued in the beautiful, warm cherry color. Luna's favorite part, of course, was the art.

Paintings in all styles lined the walls so densely that there was almost no wall space. Statues, pottery, glass, and other artifacts were placed throughout the space on small tables or in glass cases. The sheer volume of art and artifacts took her breath away.

After the Governor reviewed the evening's timeline, he suggested that everyone enjoy the exhibit before the fundraiser began in twenty minutes.

Luna excused herself so she could try to get her head on straight before all of this started. She felt like her skin was almost buzzing as if she would catch on fire. She wore a cream-colored blouse with four buttons at the top, but the movement of the fabric rubbing against her skin was too much. The gold chain that swayed against her skin with every step irritated her. She was feeling everything too much.

They were only four blocks away from that club. Four damn blocks.

She walked under the sweeping staircase into the next room, where the floor was a deep green slate. Luna was sure she had gone in the direction of the restrooms, but she got lost along the way. She rounded the corner and saw a sign reading, *Employees Only*, directly on the left. She figured that was as good as anything; she didn't need a restroom, she needed privacy.

Luna barged into the employees' only room. Mercifully, not only was the room empty, but it was a storage closet with a mop, sink, and a mirror.

Luna locked the door behind her and braced herself on the metal sink basin so hard her knuckles turned white. She unclasped the gold necklace and stuffed it in her pocket—anything to reduce the sensation on her skin.

She could do this.

She could calm down.

She would force herself to calm down.

She would calm down.

Her mouth felt so dry and hot, she was afraid she was going to vomit. She started inhaling too quickly, and her heart rate was too fast.

Panic rose like a wave inside her. Luna couldn't do this. She had to get out of here.

She closed her eyes so tightly it hurt. Her breathing was even faster now; she felt it coming out in short gasps that were painful with each exhale.

Hot tears streamed down her face, which she was powerless to stop.

Her whole body was trembling now. She felt dizzy and defeated and like she was suffocating. There was not enough air in her lungs; there was not enough air in this room. At the same time, she felt everything, and everything was too much.

Calm down, she thought.

CALM DOWN. Her mind only made the increasing wave of anxiety rise.

The tears were now a hot flood down Luna's face. Her body was trying to sob, but her breaths were coming so fast she worried she might pass out.

Luna squeezed her eyes even tighter, gripping the sink harder. She wanted to scream.

"Shh..." a soft voice came from behind. A cold, wet cloth was gently pressed to Luna's forehead. Luna felt a jagged breath leave her body as she tried and failed to regain control. "Shh..." the soft voice came again. "Breathe slowly. Take deep breaths. It's okay."

Luna's body still trembled, almost violently, when the stranger placed their hand on her back and began moving it in small circles. The circles were small at first, almost tentative, but grew firmer as Luna's trembling stilled.

Luna had to make an active effort to calm her body. First, she relaxed her grip on the metal bowl of the sink.

Next, Luna focused on her breaths as the stranger said.

As if the stranger next to her could sense what she needed, they said to her, "In, one, two, three. Out, one, two, three. Again. In one, two, three. Out, one, two, three." The stranger continued counting for four more complete breaths.

Luna felt the stranger's calming presence. She took another deep breath through her nose, and the scent of lavender wafted toward her. The smell was so comforting. When Luna realized it was coming from the stranger, it brought Luna back to reality.

Luna opened her eyes and looked into the mirror. The stranger soothing her was the human from the club the night of Kent's murder. Luna hadn't realized how beautiful she was, but the thought faded quickly. The human's face drained of color, recognition flaring in her mahogany eyes. She knew who Luna was.

Luna slowly rotated to face her. Luna knew her anxiety attack was over, but her heart was racing once she was face-to-face with the human. The space was so small that Luna could feel the human's breath against her hair.

The woman's face was exposed—she didn't have her mask on, and her hood was down. Even though she still wore her uniform, her beauty couldn't possibly be dimmed. She had long, silver hair that reached her chest. Her skin was a smooth ivory, contrasting the mahogany color of her upturned eyes, which stood out even more on her heart-shaped face. Full, dark pink lips complemented her features perfectly. Her beauty was only enhanced by her irritated stare.

The stranger pursed her lips slightly, and her eyes crinkled at the edges.

Luna didn't register that the stare was pinned on her.

The more Luna looked at her, the more she felt a loss of words. With nothing to say, Luna reached out and brushed her fingers against the human's. A warm spark flooded through her.

The human flinched and backed away. She lowered her eyes, as was customary for a human to show respect to a Behtari.

Luna felt a frustration ripple through herself—not at the human, but at the reason the human wouldn't look her in the eyes. It didn't matter that Luna wasn't supposed to be in this closet; the human would always be the one to suffer the consequences. In this case, the consequences for initiating an interaction with a Behtari, even to comfort.

Instead, Luna said softly, "Thank you."

The human was still looking at the floor, but Luna watched her cheeks flare a bright pink. She wasn't sure if it was embarrassment or anger, but she forced herself to continue. "I—I'm..." She couldn't help but use her thumbs to fidget with her nailbeds; she just wanted to thank the human, and she couldn't even do that properly.

Luna could feel her heart rate rising again—not from nerves, but that hot, creeping anxiousness threatened to flood her. She closed her eyes and took slow, deep breaths, just as the human had instructed before.

In, one, two, three. Out, one, two, three. Again. In, one, two, three. Out, one, two, three.

When Luna opened her eyes again, the human was gone.

Luna knew she had been a fool to close her eyes; she wasn't sure why she was surprised. She looked around the small room, but she didn't see any other door besides the one she was directly in front of. Luna wondered how the human had left without her realizing. In the small room, there was a yellow plastic mop bucket, a rack of hooks for cleaning tools, and another rack of hooks holding four coats.

A surge of curiosity went through her as she reached for the coats. She must have been dreaming—no way could there be a door behind there. She pulled back the coats, but of course, there was no door. Luna sighed, feeling her spirits drop, but when she looked down, she saw a return air duct, uncovered and hidden behind the coats.

She stared at the uncovered air duct for a moment before replacing the cover as it should have been. She hadn't wanted to hurt or yell at the human. She wanted to know if she knew anything about the club. Or maybe she could help Luna.

Luna turned back to the sink. Splashing water on her face, she tried to rid her mind of this human. She knew the water would ruin her makeup, but she didn't care. She needed to get it together for the fundraiser.

She glanced up at the mirror, which was broken in three places and so worn around the edges that it was hard to see her face properly. She quickly wiped her running makeup away with her fingers, wondering why she even bothered. She knew tonight was going to be hard, and she'd done nothing to prepare herself, to distance herself. Her mind was in a different place entirely.

She stepped out of the supply closet, briefly checking her holo and exhaling in relief that it had only been ten minutes; she wouldn't have been missed at all yet.

As she retraced her steps to join the governor on the other side of the entryway, she saw that human again. She was being roughly escorted by two LEOs—who seemed to each have an iron grip on her arms—as if she wasn't supposed to be there in the first place. Before Luna caught the human's eye, Luna turned away, pretending to be an obedient citizen of the New Republic.

Luna couldn't help herself. She glanced over her shoulder to see that they already had her in a vehicle in front of the building. She could do nothing.

At that very moment, something in Luna snapped. She was no longer going to be a lap dog. She was not going to let the New Republic decide what she could do or who she could be. She was not going to allow them to keep spewing hatred and enforce the inequality they bred into the cities. She might only be one person, but it only takes one grain of sand in the right place to destroy a machine—and she was ready to finish what her family gave their lives for.

Luna knew then and there that she would either give her life to help the Resistance and the humans wrongly enslaved, or she would live to see Arelia be the democracy it was meant to be.

She then pulled out her holo and messaged the only person she knew could help: Darin.

17

DARIN

THE AIR WAS COOLING as the afternoon passed into evening. Darin stood across the street from the museum, waiting for Naomi to exit the building. Naomi—he finally learned her name.

The enslaved weren't documented in the New Republic's system by name, but rather with an identification sequence of numbers and letters. Initially, the sequence was tattooed along the enslaved's upper left forearm, but now the government relies on fingerprints, retinal scans by MAVs, and DNA swabs.

A human's common name was documented in the New Republic files, but most enslaved people were referred to by their identification sequence. The sequence was similar to prisoner classification—two letters, followed by a sequence of twelve numbers.

The two letters were for the city where the enslaved person was born. The twelve numbers comprised the date and time the enslaved person was born: six numbers for the day, month, and year, and the following four for the time of day. The final two numbers indicated where the enslaved individuals fell on the daily birth count for that specific city. Naomi's ID was SO-413128-2034-56. Darin knew that some of the enslaved still used last names from before the New Republic, but that was never part of the records the New Republic kept.

Darin hadn't had any trouble locating Naomi's file; he had to bypass a few firewalls and encryptions, but it was nothing he couldn't handle. He pored over the information, hoping to find any scrap of information that might help him. Suspiciously, most of the information was redacted or absent altogether.

So, Darin did what he did best: followed her. When he returned to Solles earlier that day, his primary goal was to find Luna, but by a happy accident, he found Naomi first, so he trailed her. Darin followed her all the way to the museum and hid in an alley across the street, watching her duck into a ventilation system at the back of the building.

It was at this point that he realized there were no LEOs with her. It was rare for any enslaved to walk alone. Most were not even allowed on the streets of Solles. They all existed below, performing posts no one else would.

As selfish as it was, Darin hated going to the ground level. He knew he shouldn't hate it; the humans didn't choose their circumstances—they were victims. They didn't ask to be on the ground level with shacks for homes beneath enormous white arches.

Finally, Darin watched as Naomi exited the building, though not in the way he hoped. Two LEOs were forcibly escorting Naomi out. Darin didn't dare intervene—he already had a plan in place in case things went sideways, but he didn't anticipate they would. Darin couldn't risk giving himself away. The New Republic had long wanted him, but they only knew him as a hacker. They had no idea who their most-hated hacker was.

Naomi was thrown into a black vehicle with tinted windows. Then both LEOs, as if spooked, quickly got into the vehicle and drove away. Darin promptly entered the vehicle's features into his holo, and with a few clicks on his program, it was tracking. Darin hacked the camera system of Solles years ago to ensure he could track a vehicle if necessary, and this program proved invaluable more than once. There were usually six to eight cameras in any given block of Solles—all with wide lenses that captured as much as possible. Most of which were nearly impossible to spot. Although Darin despised them, there were times like these where they were beneficial.

Darin then sent a quick message to Marcella with the tracker information. When he pressed send, a message from Luna flashed on the screen.

Can we get together in person sometime? Nothing bad, promise.

Darin forced himself to shut the holo. Not only because he itched to see where the vehicle was going, but he also wanted to reply to Luna's message. Darin knew getting Luna out of here was more important, and he was going to see her in a few minutes. When Darin looked up from his holo, he saw Luna through the glass windows of the museum. Relief flooded him; she was who he had returned to Solles for. He needed to get Luna to a safe house. The way things were going, Solles was no longer safe for either of them.

Darin moved to the front of the building, and his mind wandered. He knew the explosion in the club was meant to kill both Luna and Kent. Luna missed the central part of the blast because she leapt to cover Naomi. Naomi was the puzzling element—the New Republic was either trying to protect her or couldn't risk her getting away because she knew too much. So why not kill her if she was a liability? Darin couldn't figure it out.

Naomi's parents were taken to the city of Zuros four years ago. The same as the Prophets, when humans went there, they didn't come back. When Naomi's parents were taken, she'd been old enough to care for her younger brother and sister. Darin was pretty sure Naomi's siblings were being used as a bargaining chip against her. He could think of no other reason she would do anything for the New Republic.

Darin opened the museum doors. Luna, the First Citizen, and the Governor were already in the ballroom. Darin was going to have to get Luna alone, and the sooner the better.

As the pieces clicked into place—Naomi being forcibly taken meant she was not supposed to be here, meant she was doing something she shouldn't have been. Or she was trying to atone for past mistakes.

Darin ran.

Darin ran through the foyer, not caring who he bumped into. He could hear the introductions, already beginning the fundraising festivities, or whatever they were called—frankly, he was numb to all of it. He wanted his friend out of there.

He made his way into the opening of the ballroom where the event was taking place, and spotted Luna to the left of the stage, by the Governor. Even from this distance, he could see her fidgeting; she was a nervous wreck. Luna did not want to be here, and there was no easy way for Darin to reach her. Darin held back the urge to charge up to the stage; he would have to get to her discreetly and quickly. Before Darin could come up with a plan, the Governor approached the microphone.

"Citizens of Solles, my friends," he said, "welcome. I know we can all appreciate how far we've come in recent years with structural improvements to our city. However, I believe that unity is our best step forward."

Darin knew Governor Seymour was sympathetic to the Resistance's cause; however, the Governor was a mainstay of the New Republic's government. So much so that the Governor was able to persuade the Senators and First Citizen that he would keep Kent and Luna safe and under control after their parents' execution. As much as the Resistance was Darin's found family, Kent and Luna had become his family even more in the last few months. Especially Luna.

"I know we are always looking toward the next horizon and how we can improve ourselves in our abilities and strive to be the best we can be."

Get Luna out of this building. The New Republic knows I am sympathetic to The Resistance, Governor Seymour said directly to Darin's mind while his speech went on.

Darin's eyes went wide as he looked around and saw everyone else laughing.

The Governor chuckled with them but quickly brought the microphone back up with a grin across his face. "Without further ado, I give you the First Citizen." A soft, polite applause followed as the Governor turned, waiting for the First Citizen.

Click.

Darin turned to find the ballroom doors closed. When he tested them, he found they were also locked. At that exact moment, white gas slowly infiltrated from the ventilation units into the room.

All hell broke loose.

18

<u>Naomi</u>

Naomi knew she had fucked up. Not only did she fail to stop the gas compound release at the fundraiser, but now—with two LEOs having caught her— there was no question she was going to be executed.

This morning, Naomi had attempted to hurry Ethan and Ella along, knowing what she needed to do would take her all day and into the evening. Naomi had even asked Zoey—their neighbor with a child the same age—to watch Ethan and Ella after school.

It was an enormous risk. If the LEOs even suspected what Naomi was doing, they would take Ethan and Ella from her. She had to be careful, and she had to be fast.

Schooling for the enslaved children was mandatory. The school was intended to prepare the children so that once they were given a position of their own, they would be more compliant and more willing to obey. There were no exceptions; once they turned five, they were expected to attend every day. The only time school was missed was if a child was ill. Even then, it had to be proven to the LEOs who ran the schools. At thirteen, they were assigned their post within the New Republic and forced into society like another cog in the giant machine.

The New Republic required LEOs to run the enslaved schools, fearing that if the enslaved had been tasked with teaching their own, it would be kindling for an uprising. They were probably right.

Between the ages of one and five, children were either brought to their post with their parents or given to a neighbor to care for during the day. Some enslaved were lucky to have partners or friends who had posts on an opposite schedule, and the children were passed back and forth. A few older enslaved people were tasked with looking after the little ones between the ages of one and five, but there were too many children. When you have twenty infants and one elderly human, it creates a time bomb; something must give eventually. Naomi was glad she didn't have to worry about that with her siblings.

Ethan and Ella were taught the basics of reading and math, as well as the Behtari's version of how the New Republic came to be. Then they were taught how to clean, how to work on various mechanical parts, and, most of all, how to obey.

The LEOs loved to punish the enslaved children. Ethan and Ella had come home with bruises, split lips, and various other injuries from their school days. They never went so far as to cause permanent damage, but the violence was enough to keep the children in line.

After dropping Ethan and Ella at school, Naomi made her way to the illegal entrance to the elevated streets. She'd used the passages through the homes of the slums humans had formed in response to the MAVs, almost like an interior street. Getting past the MAVs on the regular paths was practically impossible. Some days, they resembled a true swarm of insects.

Naomi didn't waste time when she made her way through the back corridors of homes, closets, and up different stairways that eventually led into one of the structural arches. Once she reached the exterior of the structural arch, she removed one of the long-forgotten vents and climbed inside, entered the HVAC system and ascended the arch. Naomi knew she was close to street level when she could hear the hum of the underrail. Navigating the ventilation system was challenging and required significant physical strength. Naomi was not the only human who used it for smuggling; most vents had makeshift rungs installed, turning them into ladder systems.

Naomi knew the city well—ground level and street level—so when she peered out of the vent onto a loading platform for the underrail, she could see she was only a few blocks from the museum.

Since her last screw up, she had been lucky enough that her punishment was only additional testing. Naomi was thankful they didn't take away her brother and sister. Everything she did was for Ethan and Ella—everything she endured from the New Republic, every test she underwent, every deed they demanded of her—it was all to protect them from the New Republic. Naomi knew she wouldn't be able to protect them forever, but she would as long as she was able.

Naomi went one block in the wrong direction. This would put her directly inside one of the busier restaurants in Solles. There was a room where a human washed dishes under supervision by a LEO. Any LEO put in this position was either an idiot or on probation, making Naomi's next part even easier.

She waited back a few feet deeper into the shadows so the Behtari wouldn't see her eyes peeking out from the vent, but the human could. The human would still help her get in—unplanned smuggling was not uncommon, especially in emergencies or when someone needed medicine.

After a moment, the human, who was chained to the sink, looked at the vent. They gave Naomi the tiniest nod.

Now all Naomi had to do was wait.

The human turned to the LEO, looking downcast, and tapped the mask on their face—a simple enough gesture, which the LEO wholly ignored. The human then tapped the mask again, louder this time, their finger creating an abrasive sound each time it struck the mask.

This time, the LEO looked up and laughed in disbelief. "No, I am not taking that off. You tried to bite me last time."

However, the human was tenacious and tapped the mask again.

The LEO grumbled under his breath but came over with the key and removed the mask from the back, stepping away as fast as possible. Then, in the meekest voice Naomi ever heard, the human said, "Bathroom."

The LEO gruffly asked, "You really can't wait another ten minutes?"

This human was very good at playing the part of pure obedience, looking down at their feet and shaking their head very softly back and forth.

The LEO relented. He placed his nightstick between their shoulder blades as he quickly unfastened the chain that prevented them from leaving. The LEO stayed behind the human as they walked out of the room.

Naomi slipped out of the vent and waited by the entrance to the room, making herself as small as possible against the wall. When Naomi was sure it was quiet enough, she slipped out of the sink room and to the back door.

Naomi made quick work of getting out the door, attaching her mask that didn't actually close, and walking several blocks toward the museum, keeping to the alleys. Once Naomi arrived, she slipped in through the vent in the back of the building and climbed to the small maintenance room.

She quickly realized that a Behtari occupied the maintenance room, which was odd, but she quietly moved back to take a different route. That's when she realized the person in the room was shaking violently. Naomi didn't know what came over her, but she slowly eased herself out of the vent to comfort the Behtari through the anxiety attack. Naomi was all too familiar with anxiety attacks—after her parents were taken, she suffered from them regularly.

Once the Behtari calmed down, Naomi realized that, despite her best intentions, this had been an enormous mistake. This was the Behtari who saved her at the club, the one Naomi took from the courtyard by order of the First Citizen. Not that Naomi wanted to, but the New Republic had her by the throat, threatening the lives of Ethan and Ella.

Naomi needed to get out of there. At the first opportunity, Naomi forced herself back through the ventilation system as quickly as possible; she didn't even bother to replace the cover on the vent.

In Naomi's panic, she exited a different vent into the museum, one she wasn't familiar with—that was her mistake. LEOs spotted her immediately and tried to suppress her using their abilities, but couldn't. They lunged for her and dragged her out of the building and into a black vehicle before she could have been of any help to anyone. Before she could sabotage the device that was due to release the compound gas in the ballroom.

After being gagged, blindfolded, and thrown in the back of the LEO's vehicle, they took off down the streets of Solles. Naomi didn't know where they were taking her. She had no sense of time, but knew the vehicle turned four times before coming to a slow stop.

Naomi expected the LEOs to get out of the vehicle, but instead she heard a high-pitched whistle for the briefest moment. Between the blindfold and the gag, Naomi had no idea what was going on. Then came a second whistle, which was followed by a third. Finally, there was a loud *thud* as the vehicle's horn honked persistently. The crunch of glass breaking under someone's boot was accompanied by swearing that seemed to run together into one long, unbroken swear word.

"Son-of-a-mother-fucking-bitch, you couldn't hit him the first time, could you, Wyatt? You had to miss. I told you, you needed to move two steps to the right," said a female voice.

Then, a male spoke. "You know what? It's not like you were Johnny-on-the-spot either! Come help me move this behemoth so the horn stops?"

There was more crunching of glass and swearing before the honking finally stopped. The two voices continued bickering while Naomi's mind spun.

What in the actual hell was going on? These people either knew precisely who she was and didn't care that she was listening to them or had no idea she was in the back of the vehicle.

"For tits' sake, get her out! You already fucked up once by missing, let's not take too long and fuck up again."

Well, that answered her question.

The back door opened, and she felt large, cool hands as they took the bag off her head and untied the gag from around her mouth. Naomi had tucked her mask into the hem of her gray pants before leaving the ground level, and if they found it, they'd find contraband. All humans were required to have their masks removed by LEOs before entering the lifts. Naomi stole this one and broke the back so she could take it on and off as she pleased.

Naomi blinked at the light. Even though it was already dark outside, the vehicle's interior lights remained on because of the open doors. Once her eyes refocused, she realized she was face-to-face with another Behtari. This one had blue eyes flecked with gold, jet-black hair, tanned skin, and wore what appeared to be combat gear. His attire was all black, consisting of a long-sleeve shirt, cargo pants tucked into combat boots, and a tactical belt holding two knives and a handgun.

The Behtari held his hands up as if in surrender. "We are not here to hurt you. We have questions for you that we cannot ask you here. I do not have the luxury of time to explain everything to you. You have two choices: You can come with us willingly, or I can tranquilize you like your buddies up there. What's it going to be?"

Naomi looked at the two Behtari slumped in the front of the vehicle and shrugged. "I don't have much of a choice."

The blue-eyed Behtari held out his hand and helped her out of the vehicle. "If you need to look at it that way."

Meanwhile, the female Behtari was frantically typing on her holo. She wore the same attire as the male Behtari: all-black combat gear. Although she was significantly shorter than the male, she was far more intimidating. Her raven hair was set atop her head, with a few loose ringlets framing her face, contrasting her warm golden skin. What Naomi noticed most were the two prominent scars that ran across her mouth. The female Behtari looked at the male again, the luminous gold flecks in her hazel eyes prominent even from this distance. With a simple glance at each other, they seemed to exchange information. Then the male Behtari came striding for her.

"I am of the mind to tell you exactly who we are. I think it will help. My friend back there thinks I am an idiot. I am going to go with my gut here. My name is Wyatt. We know you are Naomi, so don't even try." He said, waving a finger at her as if scolding.

If Naomi didn't know he couldn't use his ability on her, she would be questioning if he was. She sized up the two of them but ultimately decided she wouldn't stand a chance, even if she had proper training.

"Yeah. We know quite a bit about you. Sorry about that." However, he didn't seem sorry at all. Wyatt looked back at the female.

She groaned. "Fine! I'm Marcella. Now that we are all introduced, can we leave?"

Within thirty seconds, they were in another vehicle that had been stashed beneath a loose tarp. As they sped through the streets and onto the main highway out of the city, Naomi's mind kept wandering back to how she didn't help. She didn't stop anything. She wasn't able to save the copper-haired Behtari from the white gas suppressant. Naomi didn't even know her name, her thoughts now roiling in anger. That was all she ever felt recently—anger. She didn't want to hurt someone else, but she felt like she was hurting, as if she were internally bleeding.

It was pitch black when Marcella and Wyatt removed Naomi's eye covering. Now the black was fading to blue as the sun slowly crept onto the horizon.

When they pulled off the main road and onto a dirt road, Wyatt popped out of the vehicle and came around back. He opened the back door and gestured for Naomi to get out. When she didn't move a muscle, he said, "Here, you can hold this knife, if that will make you feel better." He handed Naomi the smallest pocketknife she had ever seen. Reluctantly, she did get out of the vehicle; this Behtari could force her with brute strength if he wanted, but he didn't want to.

"Okay, same thing as before. I am going to give you two options. Option number one, you wear this." As he pulled out a thick black cloth about the size of a small scarf. "Option number two, I put you in the trunk. Either is fine with me. I am assuming that you would prefer the blindfold over the trunk, but I have been surprised before."

Naomi looked at him, her mouth agape. He could not be serious. *The trunk?*

Wyatt sighed. "You have about three seconds, and then I am going to choose for you. You are not going to see this last bit. Even if we know you are not willing to work for them, that doesn't mean you won't spill—willingly or unwillingly—what you know if they capture you."

Naomi's features turned to stone as she took two steps toward Wyatt and grabbed the black cloth from his hand.

"Great!" said Wyatt, "You put that on, and I will tie it. Then you can get back in the vehicle, and we will be on our merry way."

Once Wyatt was satisfied Naomi couldn't see, he assisted her back into the vehicle, and they were "on their merry way," as he claimed. After about ten minutes, she could tell the road was rougher, and the vehicle came to a complete stop several more times.

Naomi tried counting the seconds and then the minutes, but had no real gauge of how accurate she was. She guessed the first stop must have been about two to three minutes. The second was the longest, about ten minutes. She felt her shoulders slump, as the vehicle slowed to another stop. She wasn't sure why she was disappointed; she had no idea where they were going or what they planned to do to her. She knew they treated her as kindly as they could, given the circumstances, and that they gave her choices no other Behtari had.

After a moment or two, the back door to the vehicle opened, and smaller, rough hands gripped Naomi's. "We're here. Come on. You can take that blindfold off once you're out." Marcella helped Naomi out of the vehicle.

As Naomi took off her blindfold, she blinked rapidly, her eyes adjusting to the sunlight. The sun was over the horizon now. She breathed in the balmy air.

Before her was a two-story white house with a wrap-around porch, complete with rocking chairs. The front door was slightly ajar, but the screen door in front of it was closed. Naomi was already sweating in her uniform—it was warmer here than in Solles. Naomi paused for a moment. She closed her eyes and listened closely; she could hear the ocean.

She had never heard it in person, only recordings. The push and pull of the waves, which only a natural tide could provide. It was loud and soft all at once, yet it had a melody, a give and take. The sound was more beautiful than she ever anticipated.

Wyatt strode toward the house, calling out, "Acadia?"

Naomi heard a clatter within the house, followed by the pitter-patter of fast footsteps and the excited cry of a child.

A female with a lean, athletic build and skin the color of amaretto ran out of the house. The screen door flew open, hitting the exterior of the house so hard that some of the windows rattled. The female, barefoot, in leggings, a hoodie, and an apron, rushed onto the dirt drive, calling Wyatt's name—a sound laced with both sadness and desire.

Desire was something Naomi had never felt before, something she hoped to feel for someone one day. Even hoped someone might feel that way for her, too.

The female leapt into Wyatt's arms, weeping and laughing at the same time.

Wyatt had caught her with ease, burying his face in her neck

She wrapped her legs around him, hugging him as tightly as possible. Her dark-black, corkscrew curls, which carried a streak of silver, bounced with her movements.

Naomi had never seen such devotion. So much of Naomi's life was performed out of necessity. She couldn't help but envy what they had; it was a reminder of what freedom she didn't have.

As the female and Wyatt continued to hold each other closely and speak softly, Naomi caught a glimpse of two small children running down the porch and joining the hug; they couldn't be older than four. Naomi looked at each child through their tears. A single difference was apparent—only one child had gold flecks in their eyes. Both were caramel-colored in skin tone. The girl on the left, wearing pink shorts and a yellow t-shirt, had the same bouncy black curls as her mother. She had blue eyes flecked with gold. The other child, a small boy on the right, wore green shorts and a military green shirt. He had short black hair and piercing, clear blue eyes. Only one child was Behtari. The other was human.

When the female finally stepped away from Wyatt, Naomi realized she had plain blue eyes. Wyatt's spouse was human.

19

LUNA

LUNA WAS WAITING ON stage for the First Citizen during the Governor's fundraiser when she felt an electric prickling across her skin. Almost painful, like an electric current. Then, Luna felt her mind push elsewhere. It was an active effort to resist disassociation from what was happening here and now. She struggled to maintain her focus as a flash of heat coursed through her body.

Time slowed. Luna realized it a moment before it happened—white gas would be released from the vents. She looked up, and sure enough, a white gas was seeping into the room from an air vent.

Luna rushed to leave the stage, almost stumbling when she felt the current again. When she looked up, her eyes found Darin. He was already sprinting for her.

She forced her legs to move faster, ignoring her discomfort, both physical and mental, and nearly collided with Darin. He pulled her in the direction he had come. No words were spoken between them as they rushed for the closed ballroom doors. Six Behtari on each side of a statue, charged full speed ahead, straight for the locked door.

It didn't fully give way, but it did fracture enough for a person to fit through. One of the female Behtari slipped through the door on the other side, unlocking it. That's when Luna realized there was white gas out there, too. The entire museum was being filled with it.

Luna and Darin sprinted through the main foyer. The gas was thick, almost cloud-like. Luna felt her nose tingle, and blood slowly dripped down her face. She looked at Darin, whose face was contorted in pain as blood trickled out of his left eye.

What is this?

Luna then experienced one of the most painful things she had ever felt. Her shields were forcefully ripped from her. She felt stripped to her bones as her ability was violently suppressed.

Darin was also fighting the suppression, fighting to keep his ability from whatever was in this white gas. There was an odd paleness that colored his usually soft-brown cheeks. He now looked almost as dark as ash. He must have used his ability before now—and having it taken from him by force was creating serious repercussions.

As the clouds of gas around them grew, Luna could barely see her hand in front of her face. All she could taste was the sharp tang of iron on her tongue while the blood continued to roll down her face. She was going to pass out. She must've stumbled a little bit because Darin grabbed her arm.

Then Darin threw something.

Bang!

Luna thought the sound that followed sounded like rain hitting glass.

Darin pulled them through the museum's broken glass window.

Taking in the outside air was exquisite. Luna still felt like a piece of her being was ripped from her, but she could at least breathe. Darin was gasping for breath, and Luna realized how awful he looked.

As if Darin read her mind, he gave her a weak smile.

Sirens wailed in the distance, and LEOs were arriving in black combat gear, complete with tasers and fully loaded automatic guns. The pair did not waste any time, taking advantage of the mayhem.

Luna ran, pulling Darin along. Two blocks later, Luna turned into an alleyway she was familiar with. They waited for a minute, watching LEOs run back and forth as people ran from the museum.

Darin was bent over with his hands on his knees, still trying to catch his breath.

Luna could feel the smallest of her abilities coming back. She used what she could of her limited ability, bringing a small sound barrier around them, only enough that they wouldn't draw any attention to themselves.

Luna slumped against a brick wall and let herself fall to the alley floor to sit. She wiped the blood from her face with the hem of her shirt. She couldn't see much because of the dim light in the alley at nighttime, but she thought she got most of it off her nose. She let her head rest against the brick alleyway and took her time as she looked up at the moon, peeking through the clouds as they whispered by.

Darin slowly regained his breath.

Luna turned her head to look at him. He was gaining color back in his face, giving Luna a slight relief. He was the only family she had left, and even though they weren't siblings by blood, they could always count on each other when it mattered.

"What are we gonna do now?" she asked.

Darin laughed, throwing himself into another coughing fit; thankfully, he was easily able to stifle it.

Darin opened his mouth to speak, when both their holos made the same blaring sound, causing both to flinch. Luna and Darin looked at their screens.

"Well, apparently, we are the breaking news." Darin read the alert aloud. "*'Wanted, by any means necessary. Darin Kiesel and Luna Bardin for releasing a gas suppressant at Governor Seymour's annual fundraiser in Solles. No additional information is available at this time.'* Huh, I always wondered when I would officially become a fugitive." Darin looked at Luna. "Didn't expect you to be, though."

"Safe house?" Luna asked.

The excitement of a child twinkled in Darin's eyes. "The best safe house," he replied.

Even though everything had gone to shit, and Luna didn't know what was going to happen, she felt calm. For the first time in a long time, she felt a sense of calm. Luna didn't know whether it was because they were going to the safe house or because she finally felt she was being true to herself. The latter filled her with a small sense of joy.

"So, when do we leave?" she asked.

Darin's smile faltered. "We need to figure out transportation. We can't take the underrail. We need to destroy these first, though." He shook his holo in his hand. "We don't need anyone tracking us." Luna nodded, rising to her feet.

Darin slowly followed.

She used what remaining strength to fortify their sound barrier. It was all she could muster.

Darin was efficient; he took a loose brick and smashed his holo to pieces.

Luna attempted to snap hers in half but relented and let Darin smash her holo as well.

Once both holos were nothing but tiny pieces of glass, Luna pointed to the street in front of them. "Vehicle?" she asked.

Darin's face contorted into a grimace as he shook his head and pointed below. "Sewer," Darin then used what little remained of his Illusion ability strength to create a brick wall to anyone passing by.

Luna could see through it, but only just. Luna watched the illusion slowly fade as she followed Darin into the sewer.

They climbed down a small metal ladder onto a walkway next to the water inside the sewer. Luna was relieved that she didn't land in the sewer water and grateful she had picked flats to wear to the fundraiser instead of heels.

It was so dark that looking around was difficult. Darin pulled a flashlight from his belt, leading the way.

Luna wasn't sure if she was thankful for the light or not—its beam illuminated all kinds of rats, spiders, and roaches. The smell was, well, like a sewer. It was as bad as Luna would have imagined.

As they made their way through the pipes underneath the main streets of Solles, they didn't see or hear anyone else. After what felt like an eternity with the putrid smell around her, they finally came across a locked door.

Luna slumped against the stone wall; she felt defeated. She wasn't going to go out without a fight, but she had no way to protect herself or Darin from the New Republic.

Darin walked toward her and snatched the pearl pin out of her hair.

"Ouch!" she exclaimed. "You scratched me!"

Darin shrugged. "Sorry, I've got to pick the lock somehow, and I don't have anything."

She watched while Darin fiddled with the lock for what seemed like ten minutes. Finally, they heard a soft *click*.

Darin swung the door open. Inside was a small room with three more doors. The door on the left led to an unlocked maintenance supply closet for the humans who had posts in the sewers.

Luna found a few human uniforms, complete with the gray hood and mask. She'd never been more thankful that the humans operated behind the scenes. She quickly changed, but not before putting her necklace back on. Once dressed, she threw on a pair of excessively worn and tired boots that were tucked in the corner. With her copper curly hair, she stuck out like a sore thumb in most places, but the hood made hiding easier. If she could pretend to be human and keep her eyes downcast, she might actually be able to sneak out of the city.

While she'd been in the closet, Darin found that both the other doors were locked. In a huff, Darin sat and began picking the lock on the middle door.

Luna couldn't find a proper uniform that would fit Darin. They would all be comically large or comically small. She grabbed one of the larger sets, a pair of boots, and a hood, tossing items to him one at a time.

He caught all of it and placed each beside himself, but Darin didn't try to catch the mask. He watched as it thumped to the ground. Darin looked up at her incredulously and said, "You think this is how we're getting out of here?"

Luna shrugged. "Got any better ideas?"

Darin looked back down at the mask, and after thinking for a moment, he said, "Actually. No, I don't." He returned to picking the lock.

Once Darin had both doors unlocked, there were minimal differences between the pathways. Both were dusty and lit with flickering lights. The problem was that neither Luna nor Darin knew where they would go.

While Darin changed, Luna looked around the small supply closet for anything else they could use. She noticed two sling bags tucked in the back corner. She grabbed both, putting their clothes and shoes from the night before inside the bags. Luna then turned from the supply closet toward the middle door and immediately felt the tingling sensation she had experienced at the fundraiser.

Something pulled her toward the door. Luna tried to ignore it, but her mind wandered back to it over and over. She sensed different aspects of the route. She finally shook her head, and she placed her fingers on her temples.

Darin looked at her with concern. "Are you okay?"

Luna sighed. "Yeah. But also, no. I have been having issues with my ability recently. I don't know what they are, but they're hard to ignore. It's almost like I'm developing another ability...but that's impossible. No Behtari has ever developed another ability as an adult outside of the original contamination."

Darin looked at her, his eyes betraying a concern he didn't want to voice. Instead, he said, "Luna, whatever it is, we'll figure it out, but at this point, I wouldn't rule anything out. If you think it is an ability, lean into it and see where it goes. See if it can help us."

Luna didn't like the idea, but she nodded. She closed her eyes and allowed the prickling, tugging feeling to spread. In an instant, she sensed different paths. Some things were gray. Everything was layered on top of one another—decisions leading to love, or loss, decisions leading to death, screaming, crying, the taste of ash in her mouth. There was so much noise that Luna felt her hands slamming over her ears.

Luna tried to make it stop, but she couldn't, she *couldn't*. She was going to seize up if she couldn't control this. She could *sense* it. As a sharp slap stung Luna's face and her eyes flew open.

Darin's face was full of worry as he said, "I didn't know what else to do. You were freaking out. Maybe you can try again once we're at the safe house."

"Yeah," Luna said with a sigh. "Let's do that." Luna did her best to explain to Darin what she felt—or sensed. She assumed it was the Prophet ability but didn't know how that was possible.

Darin shrugged. "Certainly sounds like the Prophet ability, but manifesting a power this late could be dangerous. Your brain is made to continue to grow and adjust to the new frequencies when you're young. It isn't built for that now. I'll reach out to Milo once we arrive. He helped train Kent; he might have some ideas."

Even though Luna was hesitant to trust anyone else with this information, she needed to understand how to control it, or it was going to kill her, or worse—drive her mad.

When they were ready, Darin agreed that going with Luna's gut was the best idea. He followed Luna through the middle doorway. The hallway walls were stone, but the floor was made of metal plates, and a metal railing lined each side. The metal walkway was covered in a thick layer of dust; it seemed no one had been here for quite some time.

It was only wide enough for one person at a time, so they continued in single file.

It struck Luna as odd that they didn't come across a single MAV or camera. She didn't know if she was relieved or worried, or if they were so well hidden that she and Darin missed them.

They walked in silence, catching the occasional horn from a vehicle or revving of a bike from the street above. They were still beneath Solles. After what felt like a few hours, the vehicles and street noises became sporadic, leaving only the sound of their footsteps.

Finally, Luna could see an end to the tunnel. At the dead end, a metal ladder, with eight rungs, led to what appeared to be a utility hole cover. Luna climbed the rungs, bracing herself on the ladder as she turned the utility cover to release the hatch. She looked back at Darin, knowing that they had no clue what was on the other side.

Darin gave her a reassuring smile. "Trust yourself. You led us here for a reason; we're about to find out."

Finally, the small wheel stopped. Luna gave a hard shove with her shoulder and pushed the utility hatch open.

20

DARIN

As Darin followed Luna up, exiting the utility hatch, his eyes adjusted to sunlight. The hatch opened eastward. After he had his bearings, he looked around, trying to gauge their location. Before he got a grasp on the situation, Luna, who was looking off in the distance, said with a heavy sigh, "Well, this is not what I expected."

Darin could not have agreed more - not at all what he expected. In front of them was a field that stretched into the distance, the long brown grass swayed in the soft morning breeze. The field seemed to go on forever until Darin looked up slightly past the horizon, where he saw the white arches of the city of Solles. About twenty feet behind them, there was a grove of trees. Their trunks were covered in moss, and if Darin was being honest, it was creepy.

Luna closed the utility hatch behind them, promptly sitting on the grass in her human uniform with her boots that were too big. She then looked at Darin and patted the spot next to her, an invitation to sit and exist for a moment.

Darin sat and put his head on her shoulder.

She gently leaned hers atop his. "I love you. You know that, right?" Luna said.

Darin didn't respond. He reached for her hand and gave three squeezes. *I love you.*

Luna picked up her head; Darin did the same. When he caught her eyes, they were full of tears.

Darin shrugged. "I pay attention."

Luna laughed as tears rolled down her face.

Darin knew it was all too much, and she needed familiarity, comfort, and love right now. The only people with whom she had ever done that were her mother, father, and brother—all three dead at the hands of the New Republic.

To Darin, it always seemed Luna was left out of her family's dealings with the Resistance as well as the New Republic. Kent tried to include her more once, but it seemed to be out of necessity—even Kent kept her at arm's length to protect her. Darin understood. It was Kent's own twisted way of showing his love for his sister. Luna had never outwardly chosen the Resistance. He knew she would never agree with the New Republic, but there was a difference between disagreeing and joining the coup d'état. Kent wanted to keep her out of it to protect her until she outwardly chose the life Darin and Kent lived.

Now there was nothing to protect. Luna was a fugitive, and so was Darin. Although Darin had been wanted for some time, the government didn't know his identity until now.

Luna sighed. "Well, before all this happened, when I asked if we could talk in person, I wanted to ask if you would help me join the Resistance." She brought her knees to her chest as she watched the horizon. "I will not be a lap dog watching the New Republic destroy more families. I have to do something."

Darin felt lighter than he had in days, not because he wanted Luna to join the Resistance, but because *she* wanted to join, and that made all the difference.

He smirked. "Well, as a Captain for the Resistance, I think we can find somewhere amongst our ranks for you."

She smiled, but it didn't meet her eyes.

Darin gave her a nudge with his elbow. "I actually have information for you, too." Darin explained what he found on the footage from the night of her birthday when she lost five hours. He told her she had been drugged with a MAV, and not only that, but the human from the club was there, guiding her away.

Luna was quiet as he spoke, taking everything in.

Darin went on to tell her that the only other footage was Naomi exiting the club hours later, without Luna. Even though he didn't have any proof, he suspected the New Republic coerced Naomi to plant the device in the first place. He wasn't sure about that, which was why Marcella and Wyatt took her to the safehouse as well.

At that, Luna looked at him, eyebrows raised in question and concern. "You really think that is a good idea? What if she is still working for the New Republic?" Luna asked, worry coating her tone.

Darin shook his head. "I really don't think so. She was doing everything she could to resist the LEOs who took her from the museum. I was surprised she didn't bite them."

At that, Luna chuckled softly.

Darin felt a smile stretch across his face.

"Thank you for coming to get me," Luna said after a few beats.

Darin gave her a shoulder bump, saying, "I'm always going to come for my sister."

Luna smiled as she wiped the tears from her eyes.

Darin's heart ached even though he was smiling. He knew Luna had been so hollow after Kent's murder. She hadn't reached out to anyone, especially once she returned to her apartment. The only time she left was to go to work, which included the fundraiser. Perhaps the Resistance wasn't the right way to get excitement back into her life, but for the first time in weeks, she did seem excited.

They sat on the grass for a few moments longer before Darin patted her leg. "All right, baby Prophet, what's next?"

Luna looked at him with a furrowed brow. "Baby Prophet? Seriously, Darin?"

"Well, what would you call it?"

Luna gestured to his entire body. "You're the mastermind!"

While Darin would never admit it, he was indeed at least two steps ahead in his head. In addition, he had three backup plans in place, in case more than one thing went wrong, except for the whole sewer tunnel situation.

When he didn't reply, Luna put her hands on her hips, staring at him with annoyance. "Seriously? You have no backup plan?"

Darin scoffed. "No, I always have a backup plan!" He lifted his pant leg, exposing what looked to be a simple bandage on his calf. He peeled back the bandage to reveal a tracking device, which sent a signal directly to Marcella. The tracking device emitted a very slight blue light.

"Wyatt and Marcella know what's going on. They should already be at the safe house with the human.

If I have programmed this correctly—which I typically do—they will know our exact location and come and get us.

Luna seemed to be impressed with Darin's thought process, but Darin didn't want to linger any more than they had. "Luna, we do need to get going. We have no idea if anybody followed us, and while I have a general idea how far we are from the safe house, it isn't nearly close enough."

Luna nodded as they both stood. They quickly determined West and stepped into the trees.

After several hours of walking, Darin's feet hurt. He was exhausted, hungry, and pretty sure that he could wring sweat from the human uniform. Thankfully, no one followed them. There were no MAVs this far from Solles. They did not have the battery capacity to fly this far, record data, and return; however, there was always the off chance they could run into a vehicle. Anyone working for the New Republic would shoot first and ask questions later.

The trees were denser the further they went, but Darin saw a road about five hundred feet ahead of them. That's when he heard the slow drone of a vehicle approaching. Darin stopped and held a finger to his lips. He motioned for Luna to stop as well. Darin knew it could be their chariot or their doom, so he decided caution was best.

The vehicle gently came to a stop, and Darin could hear voices. It was music to his ears because it sounded like arguing. As the vehicle door swung open, Darin listened to the most beautiful bickering he had ever heard, because it was his friends.

"You know why I didn't want to leave the human at home!" Wyatt said with irritation. He threw his head back, groaning into the sky.

Marcella came out of the driver's side, throwing her arms open. "I don't know what you want me to do. I couldn't bring her; if somebody found her, they'd kill her. We need her." Marcella looked at Wyatt and said, "She's human, too. Why wouldn't I leave them together?"

At this distance, Darin could tell Wyatt's features were pinched with worry. Darin was about to open his mouth to grab their attention, but something made him pause. Darin was sure they couldn't be talking about Naomi. Even if Naomi were left with Acadia, Wyatt's wife, Acadia wouldn't have done it out of charity; she would have wanted to spend time with Naomi.

Over the years, Acadia had easily become one of the most cherished people in Darin's life, even though he didn't see her as often as he liked. Not only was she a complete saint to her friends and family, blood and found, but to anyone else? Acadia was a badass who would rip out her enemies' eyes with her bare hands. Darin had seen her do it; he inwardly cringed at the memory.

"Wyatt! She *wanted* to be alone with her, regardless of what *you* wanted. That is what she wanted. I get you don't like the human. She makes you uneasy. She makes me feel that way, too. There is something she isn't telling us. Acadia might be able to get it out of her. Acadia was in her shoes; she has been there, Wyatt. Let her try, for tits' sake. We promised her three hours, and that is what we will give her."

Wyatt almost looked like a puppy being told it was bad. He brought his hands up, running them through his hair, and rested his palms on the back of his head as if he were resting on a pillow in the air. With a large sigh, he said, "Can you wait at least five minutes before telling her I went totally off the rails when we get home?"

Marcella narrowed her eyes at him. "Two."

"Fine."

Darin and Luna approached the edge of the forest by the road while Wyatt and Marcella bickered.

"We have problems," Wyatt said when he spotted them. "We have to get off the road. Acadia is a good hacker, but we have about thirty minutes before the cameras are operational again. Being on the road at all isn't worth the risk right now."

Luna nodded and headed to the vehicle. She hugged Marcella and Wyatt before getting in.

Darin pulled Wyatt into a bear hug before moving to the other side of the vehicle. Wyatt may seem like a stoned teddy bear, but the teddy bear was more like a wild grizzly bear, and he would ruin someone's day if they got in his way. On top of that, he was smarter than anyone Darin knew.

Wyatt was constantly thinking tactically. He knew who would be best suited for what and where at any given moment, or what kinds of threats they could potentially encounter beyond cameras. Darin also knew that even though he could see zero weapons on Wyatt that he would have at least three knives and one pistol, if not two, which meant the other would be semiautomatic.

Darin also gave Marcella a bear hug, and he could feel her weapons. He knew Marcella preferred concealable handguns so she could put them in her own pockets. Marcella modified most of her handguns over the years to retain the power of the larger ones. Darin had been there when her first trial broke her finger from the kickback. She was a little taller than Luna, but still shorter than him.

As Darin gave her one last squeeze, he tried to lift one of her handguns from her back pocket.

Marcella pushed Darin off. "Get off of me, douche canoe."

"Love you too, Marcella," Darin chided.

Marcella rolled her eyes and got into the driver's seat.

Once the four were in the vehicle. Marcella threw on her purple sunglasses and pushed the pedal to the floor.

21

<u>NAOMI</u>

NAOMI SAT ON THE front porch as Acadia came out with a large bowl of ice cream.

Acadia's black curls were tied up into a bun on top of her head, making the streak of silver even more pronounced. She wore a pair of cropped, loose-fitting jeans, an oversized, deep green long-sleeve shirt, and an apron. "Hold this," Acadia said as she turned, going back inside.

Naomi stared at the bowl. She didn't know how to feel about everything. She was so conflicted and confused. She knew this couldn't be the end—this house, this town. It was too good, too easy. Guilt coursed through her like a hot iron. Naomi knew that the New Republic had undoubtedly taken Ethan and Ella at this point. Not only did she go entirely against her vows to them, but she had also actively tried to prevent the release of the white gas at the fundraiser. Her fingertips went white from how tightly she gripped the bowl. She almost enjoyed the numb feeling—at least she was feeling something.

Acadia returned with a tray balanced on her right hip and a bottle of wine in her left hand. She didn't ask for help as she pulled the cork out of the bottle with her teeth and let it fall to the floor.

Naomi stared wide-eyed. She never interacted with someone so casually before, so freely. Acadia placed the wine down first and then the tray. As she finally sat, Acadia took a long pull from the wine bottle and looked straight at Naomi as she offered it to her.

Out of habit, Naomi looked at the floor. Cursing under her breath, Naomi brought her gaze back up, looking Acadia in the eye. Naomi would not apologize for finally letting herself feel like an equal. That was when it finally sank in: This place was a haven for humans...

Acadia was undoubtedly human. Her eyes were blue, not a speck of gold to be found. Acadia gave her a soft smile, and as Naomi took the bottle of wine, Acadia gently took the bowl of ice cream from her. She placed the bowl of ice cream on the front porch where they were sitting.

Naomi could see a small tattoo peeking out from under her shirt on her left arm. Acadia caught Naomi looking and said, shrugging, "Not my favorite piece of art." Pulling her sleeve back over her arm, Acadia continued, "Okay, so now that you know we are on the same playing field. We are having ice cream for lunch. And yes, it is necessary, given everything that has happened. What do you like on your ice cream?"

The question took Naomi aback. "Um... I don't know. I've never actually been able to have a choice before."

Living on the ground level, they would occasionally host small parties and celebrations, but they were few and far between. When they did happen, desserts were so rare and coveted that they were shared whenever possible. Even when she did get to enjoy the occasional sweet or dessert, there weren't options to choose from. As Naomi thought back, she could only remember two times when she ate ice cream.

The days her two siblings were born. They were both born early in the first quarter, only a few years apart; her eyes welled with tears as she thought of them.

Acadia let Naomi work through everything, waiting patiently for an answer.

When Naomi looked back at the bowl, she asked, "What is your favorite?" Acadia looked at the tray. There were two bowls filled with grilled pineapple, sticky rice, and thinly sliced pork. Next to the tray was an assortment of toppings. "Chocolate chips and sprinkles for vanilla ice cream. Wyatt says sprinkles have no flavor; I say they are for fun." Acadia took the chips and rainbow sprinkles and generously showered them over the ice cream. She then handed Naomi a spoon and gave her a nod.

Naomi didn't need to be told twice. The ice cream was like nothing they had on the ground level. This was so cold, and so sweet, it almost made Naomi's teeth tingle. The chocolate chips were the perfect addition, enhancing the texture and flavor. Although Naomi was loathe to admit it, Wyatt was right, the rainbow sprinkles had no flavor. There was something about them that brought her joy while she ate.

They sat in silence for the first few bites, leaving the bowl of ice cream and wine on the floor as they shared.

Then, Acadia asked, "How did they trap you?"

Naomi almost choked on her spoonful of ice cream as Acadia continued.

"My mother was 'sacrificed' for the greater good within the New Republic. I became a 'ward of the state.' I was lucky Senator Yeo presided over the territory. I would not be here today without her."

Naomi felt her eyes widen. She never heard anyone speak kindly about the First Citizen or the senators. Acadia nodded. "Senator Yeo hides it well, I know. The New Republic has your family, correct?"

Naomi nodded and said, almost in a whisper, "I assume they have my brother and sister. My parents are gone."

Acadia reached over to grab Naomi's hand and squeezed it gently before she continued.

"If you are not ready to talk about this, that is okay. I want you to know that you are safe here. The things you have done, or haven't done, are not your fault. You have been given an impossible choice—one that should never have been asked of you. It is okay not to want to talk about it or think about it. It is okay to sit here and eat ice cream if that is what you want."

Naomi looked up at Acadia. She still couldn't believe she was sitting with a human in a place where Behtari and humans lived together. She couldn't wrap her head around it. How did she not know this place existed? How had she been completely unaware?

As if Acadia read Naomi's mind, she leaned over and grabbed her next scoop of ice cream. "Obviously, a place like this cannot exist without Government knowledge," she said, seemingly unaware how Naomi was hanging on her every word. "However, they believe that this small town was overrun long ago by the Resistance and is now looted and empty."

Naomi took another scoop of ice cream, listening intently.

"What the New Republic does not know is that abilities do not work here. At least to a degree."

At that, Naomi stopped moving. *Abilities do not work here? How?* The wheels in her mind were turning with the multitude of possibilities as to how this place worked. As Acadia continued, her eyes were shining with such sadness that Naomi felt her heart break a little.

Acadia sniffed and wiped her eyes with the back of her hand. "Sorry, lots of memories over the years."

Naomi nodded but remained silent; she knew all too well about the memories that could haunt, linger, and sometimes threaten to tear her apart if she let them.

"There are two ways someone can be protected from a Behtari—one you already know—is to be naturally resistant. As with anything, life will constantly adjust and adapt. Over time, we have found a few naturally resistant humans. Some are only resistant to one type of Behtari's abilities. Others are resistant to all of them, like yourself. That is what the lab is—"

Acadia pointed to the white building that looked to be an old school about a mile away, down the hill from the house. "—trying to replicate. With any Behtari ability, the key workings of the ability itself are the brain waves within the mind. Specifically, the gamma rays that the brain can produce."

Never had Naomi been trusted so openly like this before, unless it was information she had to have to complete whatever *task* the New Republic made her do. It made Naomi's skin crawl in terror—knowing what they would probably do to her now.

Her facial expression must have changed, because without warning, Acadia placed her hand on Naomi's knee. "Are you alright to keep going? I know it is a lot to take in. We can take a break if you need a minute to sit with everything."

It was almost unsettling to Naomi to know how someone could speak and act so freely without fear of consequences. If she was being honest with herself, she was jealous—jealous she hadn't lived here or been able to bring Ethan and Ella here—but that wasn't Acadia's fault. Naomi cleared her throat. "Sorry, I'm good. You're right, it is just— It's a lot, and I don't know if I realized how different things could be." Acadia smiled.

"I felt the same way when I got my first taste of freedom. It was heart-stopping and blissful at the same time." Acadia shrugged, squeezing Naomi's leg before she let go.

Naomi sighed. She might be jealous, worried, sad, happy, and peaceful all at the same time, but she was going to try to soak in everything she could while she was here. That included all the information she could get.

Acadia didn't start speaking until Naomi gave her a slight nod. "So, the Behtari who were created by the water contamination went through the genetic shift, causing their gamma brain waves to increase significantly. We refer to this as high-frequency oscillations, or HFO for short. However, the Signalborn are born with the ability to have and maintain the HFO. The higher the frequency, the stronger the ability.

"When a Behtari uses their ability to adjust the frequency around a person's brain or being, it is not simply a change of that individual's brain wave frequency, but the person they are using it on as well. The only Behtari who causes a larger change is the Prophet. When they use their ability, it causes a frequency change not only within themselves but their surrounding area. We have tracked Prophets' gamma waves as high as 800Hz before, whereas a human can only reach 100Hz.

"The interesting thing with Prophets is that they can adjust the waves around them as well. We are still not entirely sure how the Prophet ability works beyond their internal gamma waves. Their ability seems to operate completely differently from all other abilities—" Acadia cut herself off, "Sorry." She leaned back on her hands.

"I know you know only some of this, about the gamma waves at least, but not the specifics. To truly understand how this—" Acadia gestured around to the valley below. "—and how all of it works together, I am going to need two things."

Naomi felt her spirit drop. *This is it.* They needed something, and she was the key. Again. Someone always needed something from her.

"Number one: I need you to understand that you are your own person. If you do not want to do something here, no one will force you. Period. Number two: If you choose to be an active part of this fight, I need you to study, learn how to protect yourself, and learn how to protect others. Regardless of your choice, getting your siblings back will be one of my top priorities, which means it will also be Wyatt's," Acadia said with a wink and a smile. "You've suffered enough. No one will judge you if you choose to remain here, or if you decide to move to Hamdon."

Naomi was stunned. This was her choice; she was *choosing* what she wanted to do. Naomi brought her knees to her chest, her silver hair falling around her. She'd borrowed some of Acadia's clothes—black sweatpants, and a plain, loose white shirt. As the wind blew the ocean breeze toward them, Naomi let the scent fill her lungs. "If I don't agree to join the Resistance, you aren't going to tell me any more information, right?"

Acadia looked at her with such fierceness that Naomi knew in her core she would not lie.

"Naomi, I will never keep information from you. This is information that should be public knowledge, not a closely-guarded government secret. The New Republic has kept that information so close that very few Behtari even know how it works. Anyone found looking into it has been executed or recruited for the New Republic's own needs."

Naomi was speaking before she realized she had even opened her mouth. "Why would they shut down anyone looking into it... what would be so dangerous about the information?"

Acadia smiled softly. "Ah, therein lies the New Republic's worry. It is surprisingly easy to disable a Behtari. You have to know the right frequency to project, which will interfere with their own, drastically reducing their ability, if not rendering it useless. Anyone who is extremely strong in their ability and well-trained will eventually overcome the frequency, so for now, that is the information we hope to distribute."

Naomi was familiar with gamma waves, but she had no idea how intricate the underlying mechanisms were. Naomi knew she was naturally resistant, and she was now suspecting Acadia was, too. Naomi's mind raced to keep up.

"There is a set of three antennas on each of the highest points that create a triangle of this area," Acadia continued. "That means this area is completely useless to anyone with an ability."

Naomi looked around at the three points Acadia was pointing out. One on the roof of the house, where they were sitting on the porch. One to the left that seemed to be on another small hill within a line of trees. The third, she could barely make out past the school on the right. It seemed to be a three-story house, but a large weathervane atop the structure made it the tallest of the other buildings. Naomi looked on in wonder.

Acadia offered her the bowl of mostly melted ice cream, which Naomi happily took another sloppy spoonful of.

"What do you call this place?" Naomi asked, awe enveloping her voice.

Acadia sighed. "Home. Salvation. Equality. But others refer to it as Omphalos."

22

<u>LUNA</u>

AS THEY BUMBLED ALONG the dirt road, Luna felt like her mind was somewhere else. All she could think about was the flashes she got when trying to access this new thing inside of her. Feelings, smells, some foggy images—all of them seeming like memories, but she knew they weren't. Luna never heard of a Behtari developing an ability this late, and she was worried. These images and emotions would not leave.

Luna looked down, holding someone's hand, warmth flooding her chest.

Luna was tossing a small child, features blurred up and down as the child squealed with joy.

She reached for someone and let out a scream full of sadness and heartache that was so loud she felt her vocal cords sting with pain even though she wasn't using them.

She was back in the tunnels again, but they weren't quite the same.

She was in a black room with a slight drip, drip, drip in the background, but her shoulder was in so much pain.

Luna rotated her shoulder in the vehicle to make sure her visions weren't real. She knew these moments hadn't already happened, but were they going to? How could she navigate this? The pieces were jumbled, and she couldn't make sense of them. At that moment, Luna missed Kent so much that her heart hurt inside her chest. She needed her brother.

Luna closed her eyes and took a breath, thinking of the human who helped in her panic attack the night before—the soft circles on her back, the subtle scent of lavender.

In, one, two, three. Out, one, two, three. In one, two, three. Out, one, two, three.

She did this four more times. When she opened her eyes, she realized the vehicle was coming to a halt.

Wyatt jumped out of the vehicle, walking through a wall of forest to...*nothing?* He disappeared.

She looked over at Darin, whose eyes were brightly sparkling.

"Same system as my house!" he said with a cheeky grin. "I designed this one myself. It isn't as good as your parents', but I did add an extra frequency!!" Darin was grinning broadly now, "If the frequency isn't disengaged and someone crosses it, they lose control of their bowels."

Luna whipped her head to Marcella in concern.

Marcella rolled her eyes and looked in the rearview mirror, saying, "Don't be so fucking dramatic." She turned to Luna and said, "Wyatt and I turned that frequency *off* before we left. Figured that was unnecessary."

Luna suppressed a giggle that somehow came out as a snort. "So, just a frequency?" Luna asked, unsure if she wanted to know about any other frequency Darin had put in place.

Darin nodded, letting his head fall back against the headrest, closing his eyes. "Just a frequency. More like a hologram frequency, but...six of a dozen, half of a chicken."

Luna laughed. "Darin, please don't use the phrase if you can't say it right. It's six of one, half a dozen of another."

He elbowed her in the ribs, his eyes still closed. "I needed to make you relax somehow. Don't need you to lose control of your bowels without the frequency." Marcella again rolled her eyes, and Luna chuckled under her breath.

Wyatt came running out of the hologram with his right hand in the air, making a circle with his index finger, as if to signal, *wrap it up, let's go*.

As Wyatt climbed into the vehicle, he said, "We have about fifteen seconds to get through there, or we are all going to shit ourselves."

Luna burst out laughing.

Marcella, already passing through the hologram, laughed, too.

"I told you how to disable it!" Darin lost his composure, falling into a laughing fit.

Wyatt shot Darin an irritated glance. "Well, I enabled it. Let's go before I need new pants!"

That only caused the three of them to laugh harder.

After another thirty minutes down the dirt road, Luna spotted at least five elevated lookout positions in the trees. Wyatt explained earlier that over the years, the safe house had grown into a small town and had become more of a haven. It was hard to find, harder to get in, and even harder to hear about. The city was named Omphalos, meaning "center."

Luna could finally see through the trees to a clearing ahead where the safe house came into view. It was a two-story white house with a wrap-around porch and four rocking chairs. Luna realized she had been to the safehouse a handful of times as a child with her parents and Kent. At the time, Luna didn't know the white farmhouse was a safehouse for her parents, or for those they sheltered there. Luna knew they came, played at the beach, and always met new friends in the area.

On the porch were two individuals with their eyes fixed on the two small children playing in the grass to the right of the house.

Wyatt leapt from the vehicle and ran up the porch stairs, giving the female on the left a kiss before joining the two small children playing in the grass.

Luna's jaw dropped. She knew Wyatt didn't date, but she assumed it was because he liked to date, well, everyone.

Marcella gave her a hard poke on her back. "Your mouth is open...and you're staring," Marcella said with a devilish grin on her face.

Luna turned to look at Marcella and then back at Wyatt and his family. "I...I didn't know."

Marcella shrugged. "No one did. It was Acadia and Wyatt's choice, as they are both a part of the Resistance. Some things they had to give up for a time." Marcella's face softened. "They both knew the risks of their relationship, but they love each other and look what it has given them." Marcella nodded to the children.

Their game sounded like Wyatt was supposed to be an enormous monster coming to attack the city of sticks that the two children built. Luna had never seen Wyatt like this. Wyatt was always happy and friendly, but she was truly seeing him in his element for the first time. Wyatt was so loved here and clearly loved the world he had created. The feeling was almost infectious.

Luna took a deep breath, savoring the balmy breeze and the salty scent of the ocean.

Marcella gave her a quick tap on the shoulder and then, nodding to the porch, said, "Um... Looks like you have some unfinished business."

Luna looked to the porch where the human girl with beautiful silver hair waited. She was here in Omphalos, safe.

She was staring right at Luna.

23

<u>DARIN</u>

DARIN EXITED THE VEHICLE quickly, stretching his legs, and watched Wyatt go to Acadia, kissing her quickly, then heading over to his two children.

Darin had known Acadia for years but hadn't seen her recently. The last time he saw her was for Wyatt and Acadia's wedding, when the two agreed to take on this chaotic life together. That was almost six years ago. He'd never met the twins, Cora and Owen, which bothered him deeply, but Darin couldn't risk their safety by coming here. Even Wyatt's visits every four to six months were a risk.

Omphalos made Darin's emotions feel raw, as if they were too much to bear. He didn't know if that was his exhaustion or if he was truly this emotional about the reunion he was about to have.

Acadia helped Darin when no one else would, after the government took his mother. Darin was seventeen when the New Republic took her. They came in the middle of the night and snuck into their home in Solles. Darin hadn't even heard the door open—he woke to his mother's screams as she fought back. They overpowered her quickly.

Darin hid like a coward under his bed, praying to a deity he didn't believe in, that whoever had taken her wouldn't know he was there. He stayed under his bed for at least two hours before he felt safe to move, immediately leaving for the Bardins'.

The Bardins wasted no time. Darin was immediately brought to Omphalos—to Acadia—so she could protect him and keep him off grid until things calmed down. Darin stayed with Acadia for just over five years. He moved back into his mother's home in Solles after that.

During those five years, Acadia taught him how to shoot correctly, as she claims. She also taught him how to disarm; she even had a few hacking tips up her sleeve. In turn, Darin constructed the three antennas that surrounded Omphalos. It was one of the happiest seasons of his life, and although Acadia was like a big sister to him, he still felt like she was the mother he had always wanted. Darin would forever be grateful for her. There was no way to repay her for her kindness and help, he knew that, but he would never stop trying.

He passed Marcella and Luna as they spoke in low voices near the vehicle.

Darin sighed. He knew she would have found her way to the Resistance one way or another. The best thing he could do was stand by her and teach her everything he knew. He would always try to protect her, but he wouldn't stand in the way of her battles. She was strong, and he knew that. He started up the porch steps.

He took the steps slowly, feeling the adrenaline wane from his body. By the time he reached the top step, he watched the human, Naomi, stand and stare him down, as if she were going to flay him alive. She was terrifying. Even though he stood above her by almost a foot, he knew that if she wanted to, she would end him. Thankfully, he helped get her here, even if she didn't know that yet.

Acadia opened her arms with tears in her eyes.

Darin brought her into one of the tightest hugs he could remember in a long time. When he let her go, tears fell down her cheeks.

"It is so good to see you, Darin," Acadia said, holding his face in her hands.

Darin nodded. "Thank you for helping us. I know it is a risk—" She cut him off abruptly.

"If you are about to be formal with me, you can leave. I have zero patience for that these days. I am glad you are here. You are family as you always have been."

Darin knew better than to argue. He kissed her on the head and said, "Thank you." Then he turned and jogged down the porch steps to play with Wyatt and his twins.

Cora and Owen had moved on from Wyatt being the monster who attacked the city of sticks and created a new town from wooden blocks. As Wyatt and Darin sat in the grass, helping Cora and Owen, the two Resistance Captains discussed next steps and how to push forward. They hadn't been speaking for five minutes before a stick came whizzing past Wyatt's head so fast it whistled.

"Hey! What was that for?" Wyatt looked past Darin to Marcella on the front porch.

Acadia had already turned around to go back inside and was shutting the screen door behind her.

Marcella looked at Darin with large eyes as if she was trying to convey something to him.

Darin was lost. "In case you forgot, I did not go to mime school for communication. *Words*, Marcella!"

Marcella rolled her eyes in annoyance, "I know you two wouldn't plan our next strategy without everyone present. Because number one: we don't all have the same information. Number two: some of us are *not ready to talk.*" Marcella gently tilted her head to the other side of the wrap-around porch.

Naomi and Luna sat on opposite sides of the stairs, but clearly, they needed to clear some things up. Darin couldn't blame Luna—Naomi was the direct cause of her brother's death, even if she had unwillingly done it.

Wyatt must have still looked confused because Marcella stomped down the porch stairs. "Get your slow butts in here and let's give them some privacy. Please? They need a minute."

Wyatt finally took the hint. "Come on, kiddos! Let's play inside!"

Owen and Cora groaned in protest.

"I bet your mother is working on some dinner."

That had both on their feet in an instant, racing for the door.

Wyatt smiled as he shook his head. Wyatt glanced at Naomi and Luna, then at Darin with a silent question.

Darin shrugged. "Can you blame Luna? She has got to figure this out on her own."

Wyatt stuffed his hands in his pockets. "I know, but something about the human—" His features pinched. "Naomi. Sorry. It always takes me a minute to shake the habit." Wyatt gently pulled Darin's shoulder and spoke softly. "Darin, she is resistant."

"What are you talking about, Wyatt?"

"Exactly what I said," Wyatt answered in a whisper. "She. Is. Resistant. I cannot use my ability on her outside of this place." Wyatt's eyes were wide.

Darin couldn't remember the last time he saw Wyatt afraid.

"Darin, are you listening to me?" Wyatt asked in an aggressive whisper. "I had to question her about the video footage you found of Luna. She answered everything, but she is lying."

Darin raised an eyebrow. "You're sure?"

Wyatt ran his hand through his black hair in frustration. "Would I lie to you about this? I have tactically trained for years to sniff out deception, and she is dishing it out on a silver platter. I don't know what she is hiding, and I don't know why, but there is something about that night with Luna that Naomi isn't sharing. Beyond that, she doesn't have a shield or anything I can feel with my ability. So, I will need to do a brain scan on her and see where her brain waves are tracking."

Darin looked at his friend in surprise. He had never seen Wyatt this wound up. "You can't force her, Wyatt."

Wyatt pinned his friend with a lethal stare, "Don't you think I know that? But she is here, around my *family*, my *children*, my *wife*, and I have no idea if she is safe. If I am being honest, I think she is more like Acadia than I realized."

Darin considered this. "Possibly. That isn't a bad thing, though. We could use someone else who is naturally resistant."

"Could we?" Wyatt asked Darin with steel in his gaze.

Darin realized Wyatt was not just afraid, he was worried, but about what? "Darin, do you really think that if she is naturally resistant that the New Republic isn't just a little interested in her? But in fact, she is one of their prized pets?" Wyatt took a deep breath. "What if she is naturally resistant and willingly working for the New Republic? I know we speculated that one of Kent and Luna's parents' devices protected her on the night of the club bombing, but it wasn't. She is resistant, just like Acadia."

Wyatt started pacing. "Naomi's parents were taken against their will, and we must assume her brother and sister have been taken as well. Darin, she is not a pawn; they are moving around, she is a key player—whether she knows it or not. The New Republic knows what she is, and she is important to them. Except there is *no mention of* this resistant ability in her file, which means it is in the classified files in Zuros, which we have zero access to."

His worry was infectious. Darin felt fear and panic take root in his gut.

"We took Naomi based on a hunch and some video camera footage. We had no idea what she was, and we absolutely did not have the full scope of who she is. Darin, we have painted a massive target on our backs."

With that, Wyatt retreated into the house without another word, leaving Darin to realize how badly he had screwed up.

24

<u>NAOMI</u>

NAOMI KNEW SHE NEEDED to clear the air with Luna—Acadia had told Naomi the copper-haired female's name—not only for her own conscience but because they were going to be living together in the farmhouse until a plan was set in motion. She needed to start somewhere.

Naomi asked Acadia for her opinion about talking to Luna. Acadia had, of course, encouraged Naomi to try. Now, as they waited for the vehicle to arrive, Naomi couldn't help but second-guess herself.

At the faint rumble of an engine, Acadia stood, as if her standing would will them here faster, even though it was only moments now.

When the vehicle came around the bend, Naomi also felt herself standing, some strange anticipation that felt almost infectious between her and Acadia. She inhaled deeply, relishing these last few moments of peace, savoring the balmy breeze and the salty smell of the ocean. Naomi had been here for only hours but was already in love with the place.

When Naomi opened her eyes, she caught Luna looking at her. Time stopped. All Naomi could do was stare.

The Behtari was just as Naomi remembered her.

She had pale skin, curly copper hair, a dusting of freckles on her nose, and the most piercing green eyes she had ever seen. The gold flecks ruined their beauty; she hated those flecks. Those flecks meant Naomi was less than, that she was not enough simply because she was human. The fluttering in her stomach grew, from fear, loathing, or something else which she was going to actively ignore. As if her own body heard her thoughts, her heart raced in anticipation when Luna stood and walked towards her.

Luna stopped at the bottom of the four stairs.

Naomi felt her mouth go dry as she looked at her feet before she corrected herself and met Luna's eyes. "Luna, I am Naomi. I know we have met before, but I wanted to properly introduce myself."

Holy gods, what is coming out of my mouth? Just shut up and move on!

Luna shrugged. "I figured that wasn't necessary, but sure. Naomi, I am Luna. I am glad to have met you." She then walked up the two stairs and extended her hand to shake Naomi's.

Naomi looked at Luna's hand and then back at her eyes before shaking. When their hands touched, she felt that same warm, crackling energy pulse up her arm.

Luna flinched, and Naomi realized she felt it, too.

She didn't want to get sidetracked, though, so she said, a bit too quickly, "Could-we-please-talk?"

Luna, without missing a bit, smiled. "Sure."

Naomi was dumbfounded; she had hoped Luna would say yes, but she hadn't considered what she would say if Luna agreed to speak. They had made their way to the far side of the porch, and now Naomi and Luna sat in an awkward silence on opposite sides of the porch steps. Naomi didn't know what to say. What could she say?

Sorry, I ruined your life? Sorry, I helped kill your brother, but I was trying to save my brother and sister? Sorry that I keep popping up in your life, because I know I am another problem to deal with? Naomi blew out a breath, causing her silver hair to blow around her face.

Luna stood. "I'm going to go see if they need any help—"

Before Naomi realized what she was doing, she reached out and grabbed Luna's wrist. "No. Please. Stay." There was that familiar crackling in her veins— this time, she embraced it.

To Naomi's surprise, Luna did stay, but she didn't sit back down.

Naomi had one chance to fix this, and she was blowing it. She released Luna's hand.

"I—I'm... I'm really sorry. I didn't know... They told me if I didn't—my brother and sister." Naomi's voice was starting to break. She looked up at Luna, her copper curls framed by the sun, seeming to glow. Naomi quickly caught herself before her mind wandered further.

"I'm sorry. I know I have no right to ask for your forgiveness or for your help, but I am so fucking sorry. I wish I could go back and change it, change everything..."

As Naomi quietly trailed off, Luna sat on the stairs again. She looked out over Omphalos, processing what Naomi had said.

"I know," was all Luna said for a moment. Her face was scrunched in concentration as if Luna was trying to gather her thoughts.

Before Naomi knew what she was doing, she was speaking again. "I get it, because you shouldn't need to forgive me—"

Luna cut Naomi off, saying coldly, "I know you are sorry. I wouldn't expect you to want to change it, because that would mean losing your brother and sister. As much as I want Kent back, I know that wasn't your choice. You were forced to be a part of something against your will. I cannot blame you for that."

Naomi sat there, stunned at Luna's declaration. Before she could think, she blurted, "Just like that?"

Luna blinked hard and turned to face Naomi. *Holy hell*, she was even pretty when she was pissed.

"Just like...what?" Luna asked with ire. "I haven't forgiven you. I have not said those words. I said I didn't blame you for the decision. That does not mean I forgive you for drugging me—"

Naomi's eyes must have gone wide because Luna's mouth grew into a beautiful smile that held no warmth.

"Oh, you didn't think they would tell me? No, they told me. We trust each other. That is what a family does for each other!" Luna looked up at the porch roof, and before Naomi could speak again, Luna was already cutting Naomi with her words.

"Am I *not* supposed to forgive you? Am I supposed to be miserable and *hate* you forever? Because that is not what I want. I don't want to live my life every damn day waking up with hate in my heart because some New Republic tyrant has it out for my family for reasons unknown to me. I do not want a life where I am so incredibly consumed by my hate and misery that all I can give back is hate and despair. Do I forgive you? No. Will I? I don't know. Do I blame you? Absolutely not.

"But don't you dare act like you need more from me. Because. You. Don't. You don't deserve more from me. Regardless of whether you wanted to, you still put that explosive there. You took my brother from me. My last blood relative is gone. Because. Of. You."

With those final words, Luna turned and stalked into the house, slamming both doors behind her. Leaving Naomi on the porch, alone.

When Naomi was sure she was gone, she put her knees to her chest and let the tears fall. Then, she buried her head to cover her mouth with the fabric of her shirt and screamed.

Naomi couldn't tell Luna now—she could never tell her. Luna could never learn this information from anyone. Because Naomi didn't put the explosive device in the club, Luna did. Only she didn't remember.

25

<u>LUNA</u>

LUNA SLAMMED THE SCREEN door and the regular door for good measure as she entered the farmhouse heated.

Just inside, there was a dining table with benches for chairs. To her right were two chairs and a large sofa with a projection on the wall. The large room had a wooden floor and one light-green accent wall. Past that were the stairs which led to the second floor. To the left of the stairs was a too-small kitchen, overcrowded by the living space, where everyone was staring at her. After a beat, they returned to their tasks.

Luna had been loud enough for everyone to hear, but Luna couldn't find the strength to care. She was so exhausted; she needed food and sleep. When she entered the kitchen, Darin handed her a plate of pasta with white sauce, spinach, and chicken.

Her mouth watered at the smell.

Darin then grabbed his plate and a bottle of wine, which he handed to Luna. Then, with that hand free, he grabbed two glasses and said, "Come on. You listen and eat, I'll talk and eat, and then you can sleep. We will go over everything else tomorrow."

Luna followed him up the stairs to the bedroom she assumed they were sharing. There were several extra rooms in the house. Most were equipped with at least two twin beds, if not bunk beds, to accommodate as many people as possible.

Their room was on the far end of the house, complete with two twin beds, a small bedside table between them, one dresser on the far wall, and a desk on the other.

Once she and Darin showered and changed into extra sets of clothes kept at the farmhouse for guests, they settled onto their beds. Their food was barely warm at this point, but Luna didn't care; it still smelled divine.

Darin placed the two wine glasses and the bottle on the small table between their beds and poured each of them a glass. As promised, Darin talked, and Luna ate.

Darin filled her in on their exact location.

She had been to the farmhouse but didn't realize that Omphalos and the farmhouse were the same place—another thing her family failed to mention. To Luna, Omphalos existed, but only in an imaginative way, the way a child thinks about unicorns or monsters. They could be real, but they most likely weren't. Except Omphalos was very, very real. Luna stayed here more than once as a child, not realizing where she was.

Darin explained how they rendered most Behtari abilities useless.

She knew these frequency emitters existed, but didn't realize how complex they were. Nor did she know that her parents used their knick-knacks at home as prototypes for the real thing here. Luna finished her plate and now toyed with her mother's gold necklace as she sipped the wine, running the gold chain through her fingers.

Luna now knew about the five hours she had lost and Naomi's role in it. Darin had explained his Mind Reading ability to her in the tunnels, along with what he saw from Kent. Then they moved on to talk about Naomi.

Luna filled in some gaps for Darin that she knew, including that Naomi seemed like a genuinely good person, or so Luna thought. Luna knew it was speculative—she didn't know Naomi at all, which had been evident from their earlier interaction—so how could she say Naomi was a good person? She couldn't. She only hoped her gut was right.

They were silent for a moment before Luna took another sip of wine when she had an idea.

"Darin..." Luna started cautiously.

"Oh no...I don't like that look," Darin said, clearly suspicious.

"Did you ever check Kent's desk after he was murdered?" Luna asked, already knowing the answer.

"Son of a bitch," was Darin's reply before he downed the rest of his wine glass in one gulp. "We're going to need more of this. You're going to have to come back downstairs so we can tell the others."

Luna's eyes felt so heavy, but she wanted to be helpful. She grinned as she realized she was part of the Resistance—this thing her family had always been a part of, she had been an outsider to. *Not anymore*. She was one of them.

Luna tossed on a gray sweatshirt and followed Darin back downstairs.

Once everyone assembled around the table, Naomi included, Luna shared what she knew.

After what felt like an enormous monologue, they all agreed that Kent would have kept the ghost drive for the Resistance at the state building to ensure he had plausible deniability. If Kent ever brought the ghost drive home, he would have implicated not only himself but everyone around him.

Darin told everyone Kent mentioned the ghost drive on their way to the club the night of Kent's death, but he and Luna both knew that was a lie. Darin wasn't comfortable sharing his second ability with the group, especially with Naomi present.

As much as Luna wanted to trust Naomi, she agreed with Darin. The implicit trust between them was the kind of trust best friends or siblings share. Luna knew she could trust Darin with anything, that there would be no judgment or fear, only love. She was thankful to have Darin; there was no question, but she was not going to let herself rely on anyone too much. She did that with Kent, and for ten years, she lived half a life.

She felt ashamed of it now, but while she was living it, Luna couldn't even see what had happened to her. She had stopped reading and stopped painting; her coffee table had needed repainting for years, but she never did it. She had the supplies, brushes, and more than enough paint to repaint it yellow or do something completely different. But she never did it. She closed herself off to the entire world, a shadow of her former self. Sitting around the table with everyone in the farmhouse, Luna felt like she had fire in her veins again. She felt like she had purpose.

Darin pulled up the blueprints for the Kellmont State Building in the heart of Solles. The place Luna worked for Governor Seymour, and where Kent spent the last eight years undercover gathering intel. Darin projected the floor plans above the dining room table, using Marcella's holo at the base.

Luna and Marcella sat next to each other on the bench. Darin and Wyatt stood. Naomi sat across from Marcella, staring at the blueprint with wonder. Luna realized she had probably never seen an interactive projection like this—one where you can touch it, zoom in, and adjust different settings. Luna's suspicions were confirmed when Darin caught her looking at the projected blueprint and bent to ask Naomi if she would like to guide the map to see how it works.

She nodded with excitement and stood.

Darin showed Naomi the controls, and she took to them quickly. Darin then moved to sit at the far side of the table, next to Luna.

"Wyatt, can you turn off the lights?" Marcella asked, halting the verbal jousting between the three of them.

Darin gave her a wink.

Luna watched as Marcella rolled her eyes and said, "Hey! Asshole! Can you turn off the fucking lights? It is getting dark outside, and to see these blueprints accurately, we need as little light as possible."

Luna sat forward, staring intently at the projection blueprint before her as Naomi shifted from level to level. "Darin, how did you get this?" Luna asked.

Darin scoffed. "Seriously?" When he looked at her, he registered her genuine concern. "Oh, sorry... I asked Milo to pull them for me the last time I was in Hamdon. He has access to the New Republic's security system and uses it to get in and out of their territories—at least until they find out he has access. I don't have every city and capital building, but I do have Solles."

Naomi zoomed out so they were looking at the entire building again and gave it a gentle spin. She glanced at Luna. "Where do we start?"

Luna couldn't hold a grudge against her, even if a small part of her wanted to. None of this was Naomi's fault, and Luna knew that. She couldn't stop her smile as she pointed to the back entrance of the Kellmont State Building. "Right here."

The sun had long since set, but Cora and Owen were still running around, unaware that the gravity had changed in the room.

They were doing this—they were going to break into the Kellmont State Building in Solles and find the ghost drive. The one they hoped Kent had left; the one they hoped the New Republic wouldn't have found yet.

The group had gone back and forth. Marcella argued they could go during the day, undercover as enslaved.

Naomi went into great detail about the security checkpoints, the mask that would prevent them from communicating, and the violence-prone LEOs who wouldn't hesitate to shoot.

Marcella didn't shrink from Naomi's disagreement. She thanked Naomi for her insight about the complexity the plan would require.

There were further discussions about which cameras to remove and which building to use to access the government Wi-Fi and hack into their network. Once they had agreed upon that, they opted for Luna's suggestion to use a nearby cafe full of old filing systems.

Darin hadn't realized he could go into the cafe and access the Wi-Fi. He had wanted to break in, as he had apparently done before.

Luna felt relief as they continued. Increasingly, the group took her suggestions and asked for her opinion. She realized she was more knowledgeable than she thought. She was familiar with the inner workings of the LEOs' schedules, having worked in the government building constantly for so many years. She knew the access passwords to several mainframes because even though she wasn't supposed to have them, Governor Seymour had asked her to remember them for him, in case he forgot.

Luna realized now the Governor had been planning for and preparing her, even though she hadn't realized it. The Governor had been spoon-feeding her intricate details of the inner workings of the New Republic—things she should not know—feigning his forgetfulness. Even though Luna never saw it, she always did as he asked, keeping detailed files and records for him.

She hoped that the Governor was still alive; she wanted to hug him and tell him she was sorry she hadn't seen everything earlier. Hot tears pricked the back of her eyes, but she furiously blinked them away.

Wyatt and Acadia took turns caring for the children and getting them to bed as the discussion continued. Once Cora and Owen were finally asleep, the six adults sat around the table looking at the blueprints, their notes, and a second holo projection from Wyatt's phone of an electrical map of Solles.

"Okay," Luna said, "cutting the system here—" She placed her finger on the map at a coffee shop a few blocks from the state building. "—will give us a ten-minute window without cameras and no power within the state building. *But* that means I must enter on this side of the building." As Naomi rotated the map, Luna pointed to the entrance closest to Kent's office. Although Luna had no tactical training, she knew the security within the building best and would be the most knowledgeable about how to get around, so the group agreed she'd participate.

It was also agreed that Acadia and Wyatt's relationship wasn't yet known to the New Republic, and they wanted to keep it that way so the pair would stay behind. Marcella, Darin, Naomi, and Luna would be the ones to go. Luna and Naomi were responsible for acquiring the drive within the government building. Marcella would stand lookout, and Darin would be stationed in the cafe for the first half, then leave to regroup at the sewer grate.

Luna reviewed the details again, covering where she and Naomi enter, how long each step should take, and how quickly they should be out. She also made sure to mention more than once that it had been weeks since Kent's murder. Kent's office was probably cleaned out at this point, but if so, their next move was to head to Senator Yeo's office to see if anything had been confiscated from Kent's office and brought there.

"What if we split up?" Naomi suggested. "What if I go to Senator Yeo's office? She is a Resistance sympathizer, right? So, it is plausible that if she were to see me, she might try to help me, but at the very least, wouldn't blow my cover." Naomi explained she had met each senator more than once—they were all very familiar with her and her family, but that was where her explanation stopped. She didn't offer *why* Arelia's political leaders would know her or her family, causing a film of tension to envelop the room.

Naomi hadn't talked about her family outside of Ella and Ethan. It didn't sit well with Luna—Naomi was intentionally leaving details out, and Luna needed to figure out why. On top of that, Luna could tell that Wyatt was not pleased with being sidelined. He had stood a step or two back for the entire conversation with his arms crossed. Luna thought the only times he had moved were when he took care of the twins. He was always the one in charge of tactile missions, and being removed from an important one was clearly aggravating him.

When they wrapped up, Luna stepped outside to breathe in the night air. The stars shone brightly overhead, the moon full, and from the top of the hill, she could see the pale blue light reflecting on the ocean water. Luna hoped it was a good sign, even though she didn't usually believe in things like that.

They had three weeks before they were scheduled to leave for this mission. Three weeks to gather intel, train, and learn as much as possible before Luna put her life on the line for not only the people in the house, but for a mission she believed was right. For her family. For the humans who deserved better than this.

It had taken too long for Luna to know where she should be and what she should do. She knew now—she would fight for what was right. Luna would fight for those who could not fight for themselves. She would fight for the memory of her mother, father, and brother. Most of all, she would fight for herself. Luna would fight for the ability to have a future she would choose. With the newfound resolve, she looked up and locked eyes with Naomi.

Naomi slightly cocked her head, as if asking, *All good?*

Luna nodded once, smiling. She knew no matter what happened, she was glad she made this choice.

PART 3

THE GHOST DRIVE

26

LUNA

They had been in Omphalos for five days now. Today was the first day Luna had free time to go with Darin to the small general store in town to grab new burner holos. Darin had suggested that Naomi join them, but since she never had a holo to begin with, she didn't see the point in getting one, so she had stayed behind.

On the way over, Darin had brought up again how they should reach out to Milo to help with Luna, but she brushed him off. She wanted to do this on her own. She wasn't sure why, but she needed to prove to herself that she could do this.

Darin relented once they entered the store.

Luna wasn't sure if it was because they went in opposite directions, or because he was going to let it go. The more she thought about it, the more she realized it was that Milo would be her best help, and they both knew it.

Luna walked up and down each of the fifteen aisles within the store. All were brightly lit with fluorescent lights, with goods ranging from clothing at the left end of the store to produce and frozen items on the right. She stood at one of the stands near the front by a case of sunglasses. She tried a few while fidgeting with her gold necklace.

It was nice to have a small break.

The morning after their arrival, Wyatt joyously walked the halls of the farmhouse while banging a pot with a wooden spoon. Luna had begrudgingly wandered downstairs to find Naomi already at the table, dressed in sweats and a white t-shirt. Naomi's hair had been freshly washed and hung, still damp down her back, and she was looking at a book of human art, some of which had been on display at the art museum Luna had worked at.

Luna smiled to herself. She grabbed two mugs, filled both with coffee, but only one with sugar and extra cream. The other she left black and took to Naomi at the table, along with cream and sugar.

She placed the coffee, cream, and sugar down, and quickly retrieved her own cup, coming back to sit to the right of Naomi, who was at the head of the table.

Luna began to speak, but her groggy voice betrayed her, cracking. She cleared her throat and tried again. "Sorry. I brought you some coffee if you'd like?"

Naomi slowly looked up at Luna, from her fingers to her arms, to her chest, where Luna felt her heart pound. Naomi's eyes moved to her neck, her mouth, and finally met Luna's eyes.

Naomi's obvious exploration made Luna's skin feel as if it were on fire. Naomi always saw so much of her—so much more than anyone else. It was a terrifying vulnerability to know someone saw so much of you. Luna admired how perceptive Naomi was, and surprisingly, yearned for Naomi to know her even more deeply.

"I didn't have coffee much in Solles, what do you like in it?" Naomi asked, her nose crinkling up at the black liquid in front of the book.

Luna chastised herself. Of course, Naomi wouldn't have had coffee regularly. Luna probably came off a bit pretentious, assuming Naomi would even want coffee.

As if Naomi could sense her unease, she reached her hand out, as if she were going to touch Luna, but thought better of it, returning her hand to her lap.

Luna tried to diffuse the tension by explaining she liked her coffee extra sweet, with cream and sugar.

Naomi nodded toward Luna's still-steaming cup. "Could you make it for me, like yours?" Then adding, almost as an afterthought, "Please."

Luna couldn't stop the grin that flourished over her face. She nodded with fervor and made Naomi's coffee the same way as for herself.

Once the coffee was made and the milk and cream were back in the kitchen for others to use, Luna and Naomi engaged in small talk—nothing meaningful, but everything felt meaningful, all at once. Luna learned that Naomi loved to draw and paint, but because she was on the ground level, she never had the opportunity. Luna had moved her chair closer to Naomi's—close enough she could feel the heat radiating off her body—to show her some of her favorite art pieces. Naomi hadn't heard of some of them, but Luna was impressed with her overall knowledge.

Naomi pointed out one piece of art to Luna while skimming the pages. Luna had skipped over it, the painting brought back too many memories. Naomi lingered on the page, her hands, calloused from years of enslavement, gently brushing the colors as if she could paint it herself.

Naomi said, "This one is my favorite."

The image spanned the entire page. The colors were not as perfect as Luna knew them to be in person, but the art itself was still stunning. It was a field of delta lilies at night. The night sky was a deep navy, with swirls of stars through it. The field's perspective was almost as if the viewer were sitting amongst the lilies themselves. Each softly glowed against the dark background. Each flower had been painstakingly detailed, none trying to outdo the others, apart from one. There was one lily that had drooped, a golden chain hanging around the neck of the flower, as if it were slowly crushing it. Yet the lily—despite the weight from the golden chain—still turned toward the viewer, casting its beautiful golden and blue hues more brightly than any of the other lilies. Its title was "Beauty found within the broken".

Luna chuckled. "I know it isn't funny, but it is my favorite, too. I worked at an art museum where the original was displayed, and it is even more breathtaking in person." Luna let the silence stretch between them before she continued. "I'd love to show you some day, if you would come with me?"

Naomi's fingers froze on the page. Her mahogany eyes searched Luna's before she asked, "Why? Why are you being so kind to me? I don't deserve it. I have broken everything around me."

Luna couldn't help herself and clasped both her hands around Naomi's, which had been resting on the page, and said in a fierce voice only Naomi could hear, "Beauty is found within the broken." With a quick squeeze of Naomi's hand, she placed her hand directly below the title of the painting to be sure Naomi would see it. Before Naomi could react, Luna said, "I would love to take you one day, if you'll let me." Then, Luna rose and walked up the stairs to get ready for the day.

It was days later, and Luna was still confused and conflicted about her feelings toward Naomi. She wanted Naomi's beautiful skin beneath her hands, her mouth on hers, sharing breath. Selfishly, Luna wanted even more than that—she wanted Naomi's compassion and smart mouth to be part of her life. To be able to share art with her, to see her face crinkle in confusion when she looked at a cup of black coffee.

Luna put the sunglasses back on the shelf and turned to find Darin. She couldn't have what she wanted; it didn't matter how badly she wanted it. Luna wasn't even sure Naomi wanted it, either.

As Luna searched for Darin, she came across a small children's paint set, which had eight colors and one small brush. Next to the paint was a set of twelve colored pencils and a small book, no larger than her hand, filled with plain white pages. Luna grabbed all three items and found Darin one aisle over, inspecting a box of chocolate-and-peanut-butter cookies.

Darin looked at her arms, full of art supplies, and asked, "Do I actually want to know?"

Luna smirked. "Probably not, but I'm going to tell you anyway."

Darin sighed, tucked the cookies under his arm, and picked up the two burner holos he had placed on the shelf where the cookies had previously been. He gestured to the front of the store, and with a smile, said, "After you."

They made it back to the farmhouse in thirty minutes, carrying their bags from the general store. Luna had been giddy the whole way home, almost like a child excited for a gift. Her smile faded when she saw Wyatt's maniacal grin as he sat on the porch steps of the farmhouse.

"I was wondering where you got off to!" Wyatt said as he stood, brushing off his pants. He walked toward them as he continued, "We're going to do a test of sorts. I have hidden Naomi somewhere in the woods; she isn't far, but she is well-concealed. Your objective is simple: find her, light a fire, and summon me with the device I have given her."

Luna looked at Darin, who was looking guiltily down at the dirt road, moving around stones with his shoes. "You knew?!"

Darin grinned at her sheepishly.

Luna crossed her arms, the bag swinging with the movement and hitting her in the side. She tried to adjust the bag gracefully, but it had already caught Wyatt's attention. "I don't care what you got at the store, but no supplies." He reached for the bag, which she begrudgingly gave him.

Luna looked to the woods, then to where the sun was dipping toward the horizon. She would only have two hours tops until nightfall.

Wyatt watched her with assessing eyes.

Luna realized he was making sure she was ready and could do this.

With that realization, she straightened and looked Wyatt in the eye, waiting for further instructions.

Wyatt's mouth twitched, revealing the ghost of a smile. "Be back by dark."

Without another word, Luna walked toward the woods.

Before she reached the tree line, Wyatt yelled, "Oh! By the way. She can't see."

Darin stifled a chuckle as the pair made their way into the farmhouse.

Wyatt had shown Luna how to track over the last five days, and while she was still getting the hang of it, this was as good a way as any to demonstrate her new skill. Eager to prove herself, she sank deeper into the forest, her path in her mind clear.

27

NAOMI

NAOMI WAS NOT SURE what sick fascination Wyatt had with putting bags over strangers' heads, but she was *over* it. She had been resting in her room, poring over the art book Acadia and Wyatt had given her, when he knocked on the door. When she told him to come in, he pounced on her and put a bag over her head.

She flung the bag off in irritation, making Wyatt laugh, but he picked up the bag and held it out to her again, asking her to take it. She felt her face crinkle with disgust as she looked from the bag to Wyatt and then back to the bag. Wyatt rolled his eyes but explained they were going to do a training exercise on top of that; it was meant to challenge Luna's tracking.

Naomi agreed, walking out with Wyatt to the woods—thankfully *without* the bag on her head. He only secured the bag once he had tucked her into the hollow of a large oak tree, half of which was missing from a lightning storm. Its upper canopy was broken and bent at odd angles, but it had the perfect opening for a small person to fit.

Then, Wyatt handed her a small plastic square with a button in the middle.

"Okay, once she finds you, you have to make a fire. Once you do that, press this, and I will come get you," Wyatt said as he walked away, his voice sounding farther with each word.

Naomi shouted back, hoping he would hear, "How am I supposed to see with the bag?" but was met with silence.

It felt like hours had passed since Wyatt had helped her into the hollow of the tree. A light drizzle turned into a downpour, and while Naomi had suffered worse, she did not want to be out in the cold and wet much longer, if at all. She knew she could always press the button, but she knew that would not be fair to Luna and her training. She wanted Luna to have a chance, but Wyatt had not taken her that far into the woods, and Naomi was confident Luna should have found her by now.

Naomi's worry grew worse with each passing minute. *Where is she?*

She wasn't going to wait another moment; something was wrong.

Naomi uncovered her face and crept out of the hollow. All she could hear was the rain pelting and hitting the leaves and tree branches around her. Naomi's panic crept along her skin; she clenched her fists five times before allowing herself to move on. She needed to be present to properly track Luna. Naomi had done this so many times, trying to catch small animals in the slums; she was not always successful, but occasionally, she got lucky. So, Naomi closed her eyes and listened.

She listened to the rustle of the new leaves above her. She listened to the steady beat of the rain against the forest floor. Naomi took a slow inhale, letting her mind settle and her body still. She smelled the decay of leaves beneath her boots, the sweet scent of fresh spring rain mingling with the chill of winter. Then, she smelled the floral aroma of Luna's shampoo. It smelled of honeysuckles and strawberries. It was faint, but she could still smell it.

Opening her eyes, she turned toward the smell and started walking. After about two minutes, she paused, grounded herself again, and listened.

Sobbing.

She could hear sobbing just in front of her on the left. Naomi's eyes popped open, and she went as quickly through the dark as possible.

The crying grew louder, but as she got closer, she realized it was not crying, but hyperventilating. Naomi quickened her pace as much as she could around the branches and twigs that were in her way every time she moved.

Behind a fallen tree, Luna sat with her knees curled into herself, eyes closed, and head down.

Naomi approached her as slowly as she could, "Hey, I'm here," she said gently. "I'm going to sit with you, okay?"

Luna's breathing came even faster now. Naomi genuinely had not thought that would be possible, but now she was worried Luna was going to pass out.

Naomi placed herself squarely in front of Luna, kneeling in the wet leaves and mud. She gently moved Luna's arms away from her body and lifted Luna's face with care. Luna still could not open her eyes. So, Naomi brushed her wet, copper hair away from her face as best as she could.

Luna's breathing hitched.

Naomi needed to disrupt her breathing pattern, so she did the only thing she could think of. The only thing she truly wanted to do. She pulled Luna's face to hers and kissed her deeply. Her fingers gently wove into Luna's soaked curls.

Luna took a shaky inhale and gradually pulled away. Now, only small gasps escaped. Luna looked up at her, and Naomi thought she might ask a question, but instead, Luna said, "Thank you."

Naomi, realizing their proximity and her hands still intertwined in Luna's hair, slowly backed up to let go, but she was caught by surprise.

Luna leaned her cheek into the touch of Naomi's palm, enjoying the small contact between them. Her breath was still coming in short gasps, but nothing like before.

Naomi sat next to her, in the rain, and put her head on Luna's shoulder while she made slow circles on her lower back.

Several minutes later, they realized Wyatt had not given either of them a match or a lighter. Even though it had stopped raining, the wood around them was thoroughly soaked. So, cursing his name in every way they could think of, they walked back to the Farmhouse hand in hand, their fingers intertwining together.

It only took about ten minutes to find the main path where they could also see the farmhouse through the trees.

Before they stepped onto the path, Naomi, still fiercely holding Luna's hand, stopped them. "Maybe we tell Wyatt to eat dirt?" She dropped Luna's hand.

Luna snorted and then caught herself, eyeing Naomi out of the corner of her eye. "Sorry, I don't know the last time I did that."

Naomi smiled. "I'm just glad someone thinks I'm funny."

Luna snorted again, causing them both to break down in laughter.

They continued walking down the path toward the farmhouse, talking the entire time, and Naomi felt the long-lost feelings of joy, hope, and possibility bubble up in her chest.

About fifty feet from the farmhouse, Luna's eyes suddenly went wide. "Wait right here! I forgot I have something for you."

Naomi waited, bewildered, in her soaking-wet clothes. It was not long before Luna came back out with a small brown bag.

Acadia peered out into the darkness from the screen door, and Darin from the farmhouse windows.

Damn Nosey Nellies.

Luna turned to see what Naomi was looking at and flipped them off, then turned back to Naomi and handed her the bag. "I didn't have time to wrap it, but I thought you might like it because of—well, you'll see," Luna said giddily.

Naomi didn't know what to say. She had only ever gotten a handful of gifts her entire life; no one ever bought her something purely because they thought of her. It had always been for a birthday or a celebration. Naomi tentatively looked in the bag and couldn't help but inhale in excitement. She looked up at Luna, not sure what to do, but Luna wrapped her arms around Naomi in a quick embrace. "I can't believe you did this for me," Naomi said when they released each other. "Thank you."

Luna shrugged, brushing off her comment.

Naomi grabbed her hand and gave it a quick squeeze. "Really, Luna. No one has ever done something like this for me. It means more than you realize." She watched a blush creep over Luna's cheeks.

Luna let Naomi's hand go before they both turned to walk inside. "I want you to be happy," Luna said.

Naomi felt a beautiful ache bloom in her heart and knew she was falling headfirst with no way to stop it—and she did not care.

28

LUNA

LUNA LAY ON THE warm grass, exhausted from how much Wyatt pushed her shielding this morning.

To train, they needed to be at least one hundred feet from the farmhouse, outside the frequency interference. He had just gone inside for some water, but as she lay looking at the sky, trying to catch her breath, she could feel the sun, deliciously hot on her skin. Omphalos was usually warm, but this felt like the first truly hot day this year, and Luna appreciated the heat.

It had been two weeks since Wyatt had begun Luna's training, and at first, she had hated it. Now she felt a calmness that came with it. The part of her mind that used to run around in circles, now more placid inside of her.

It wasn't just physical activity, though. After the night in the woods when Luna failed to find Naomi in the oak tree, the two spent more time together. Every morning, they discussed art over coffee, and then again after her training with Wyatt.

Sometimes, during their fleeting time together, they would play tic-tac-toe, or Naomi would show her a few of her drawings, which were stunning. She didn't try to replicate exact, realistic features of those around her, but she caught the feeling of the moment. Every detail was recognizable, from the large trees to the tiny flowers. Luna's favorite had been Naomi's first one—the one of the beach.

After Luna had given Naomi the colored pencils, paint, and paper, she didn't touch them for two days. Luna wondered if she had made a mistake with the gift, but on the third day, when Luna's alarm went off to meet Naomi for coffee, she found Naomi sitting on the steps of the porch looking out over the ocean.

Luna approached quietly so as not to disturb her, but Naomi smelled the coffee Luna had made for them. "Careful when you sit down," she'd said, "it's a little wet from the dew."

Luna had shrugged. "I don't mind; I'd rather talk to you."

Naomi nodded, not rudely, but because she was so focused on capturing the sunrise over the ocean.

Luna only caught a glance before asking, "Can I see it?" Naomi's cheeks flushed a pale pink, which filled Luna's stomach with butterflies. She second-guessed herself. "Sorry, I don't need to, I mean— It's your stuff, so whatever is fine."

Naomi looked at her and smiled, which made Luna's heart beat even faster. Naomi turned the page toward Luna so she could see it. The picture was a perfect representation of the chill in the air, the salty breeze off the water, and the sweet scent of spring. Naomi had then grasped Luna's hand, their fingers intertwining, and said, "Thank you for this. I never thought I would have something like this, so I'd like you to have this first one, if that's okay?" Naomi gently tore the page out of the book, handing Luna the beautiful drawing.

Luna didn't know what to say, so instead, she put her head on Naomi's shoulder, folded the drawing gently, and tucked it into the pocket of her sweatpants. She handed Naomi a coffee mug, and they sat in silence, enjoying each other's company. Luna hadn't had many happy memories over the last decade, and she already cherished that one.

When Luna finally felt her heart rate had slowed enough, she opened her eyes and looked at the sky. She brought her hand over her face to shield against the sun and gazed at the clouds slowly floating by. She closed her eyes again, taking slow, steady breaths. Naomi was teaching her to control her anxiety and recently started meditation to control her breath, as well as her heart rate. On her third round of breathwork, she felt something solid hit her stomach with a *thump*.

"Oof!" Then Luna started laughing when she realized it was Marcella whipping a book at her from the porch. "What was that for?" Luna asked with a smile.

"You looked too relaxed. I had to fix it," Marcella quipped with a smile.

Luna tossed the book as far as she could, which sent it almost to the porch stairs. As Marcella walked down to retrieve it, Luna threw up her middle finger for good measure.

"Yeah, yeah. Don't lie there too long, you'll fall asleep!" With that, Marcella walked back into the house.

Luna wrapped her arms around herself and closed her eyes again, taking in the familiar scents and sounds, and refocusing on her breathing. On her third breath in, she realized she was no longer alone—the smell of lavender permeated the air, which meant Naomi was near. Luna tried to lie to herself, but the smell was intoxicating. Luna took a large breath, partly to clear the fog from her mind that Naomi seemed to create, but also to take in as much of that smell as possible.

"Can I sit with you?" Naomi asked quietly.

Luna opened her eyes slightly and propped herself on her elbows. "Seriously?"

Naomi chuckled and sat next to Luna.

Her buzz cut reminded Luna that Naomi willingly went to the testing center at the lab every day so they could conduct tests on her blood and brain waves. She even let Acadia and Marcella shave her beautiful, long silver hair so they could get a better read of the brain waves. Luna remembered Naomi's tears running down her face the entire time; it made Luna's heart ache all over again. Luna had held her hand the whole time.

Luna rolled her head to the right and watched Naomi close her eyes and sigh. "How much longer do we have?"

"Probably ten minutes if we're lucky."

This was their daily routine for the last three weeks. When Naomi finished testing, and Luna was done with training, they would sit together and just... be. Sometimes they talked, sometimes they didn't. It didn't matter, but they kept each other company for that moment. Luna wasn't sure why Naomi had asked on the first day, and she wasn't even sure why she had said yes. She inwardly cursed at herself—she knew exactly why she said yes. She couldn't get Naomi out of her mind. Luna thought about her constantly, and it was worse when they were close. She wanted to touch her all the time and tell her how stunning she was.

Luna wanted to have the space to get to know each other normally, not like this. The problem was that this was all the time they ever had, and while it was something, it was still only a few minutes, and that wasn't enough. Their time was precious but fleeting, and Luna wanted more. So much more. Luna closed her eyes and took a deep breath. She had been waiting for the right time to bring this up; now seemed as good a time as any. When she opened her eyes, she shielded them from the sun and sat up, facing Naomi. "I've been thinking..."

Naomi turned to Luna, her eyes full of worry.

"I don't think we should split up at the state building."

Naomi looked shocked at Luna's request. "There is no way we can search both offices in that amount of time if we don't separate," Naomi said firmly.

"I know, I know," said Luna. How could she explain this in any way that made sense? *Hey, I have a new ability I have been training, but it is still foggy. I don't want you to get hurt, because I keep having this horrible sense that if we split up, we will start down a path we cannot stop.* Luna would sound crazy, and she knew it.

Luna rubbed her hands on her thighs. She was sweating now.

Wonderful, fantastic, she thought.

"I... I don't know, I have this weird feeling, and I really don't think it is a good idea," she finally spat out. *Why had that been so damn hard?*

"Lu, I can't do that. There are too many people counting on us to get this right. Beyond that, our mission is tomorrow night. We don't have time to plan this out differently," Naomi said with a shade of irritation.

Luna wanted to say, "*If you aren't here at the end of this, I don't want to have to find you again,*" but she didn't. Luna just nodded, picking at the new spring grass.

Naomi seemed to realize Luna's genuine concern. She grabbed Luna's hand and said softly, "We stick to the plan, and if something feels off or goes wrong, I will come find you."

Luna nodded, but she felt it settle in her gut. Something was wrong. Something was going to go wrong. She knew it, she could sense it. It was a change in the air, and it made the hair on the back of her neck stand up.

Naomi pinched her features in confusion and pulled her hand back, staring at her palm.

"You good?" Luna asked. Not that Naomi needed a reason to pull away, but it was so sudden.

"Yeah, fine. My hand felt... I don't know. Something felt different, I guess." Naomi shook her head, and then she laughed—a truly unbothered sound full of light, which Luna had never heard from her before. It was infectious.

Luna's own mouth pulled into a broad grin. "What?" she asked.

Naomi looked at Luna and smiled brighter than Luna had ever seen. "I feel happy. I have hope. And for the first time in a long time, I feel that there could be more in my life than what I have had. I don't know if I have ever felt all those things together at once."

Luna tilted her head, waiting for more information, but Naomi didn't give any.

She gave Luna's hand a tight squeeze and stood, brushing off her loose green pants. Then, she strode back to the farmhouse and didn't look back.

29

<u>NAOMI</u>

As Naomi strode into the kitchen, she had the biggest grin plastered on her face, and she didn't care. Naomi felt something akin to the warmth of a light come from Luna's hand—it was warm, electric, and it tingled her palm. She couldn't explain it. It was nothing she could see, taste, or smell, but she felt it in her core.

Naomi started grabbing plates and silverware to set up lunch when Acadia walked around the corner.

Upon seeing Naomi's face, Acadia stopped, turned around, and said, "Well, you seem happy. I don't know if I've ever seen a smile that big on your face before. Are we happy? Or are we planning someone's untimely demise?"

Naomi's grin was going to split her face in two if she continued this way. "Stop!" she said, giggling even harder. "Acadia, you are making my face hurt." She pressed her hands to her cheeks. She still hadn't gotten used to having no hair. She hadn't realized how much she used her hair to cover the sides of her face, but now, as she felt her cheeks blush, there was no hiding it.

Acadia came over, giving her hip a gentle nudge as she opened the refrigerator to grab lunch meat and salad items. As she turned back around, she looked at Naomi and almost whispered, "Are you guys...?"

The shock on Naomi's face must have been easy to read as Acadia threw her hands up in surrender. "Sorry! Sorry! You know. You guys are cute together. And I—" She paused, looking at Naomi, her eyebrows so high they could have been part of her hairline before she said with a shrug, "Maybe?"

Naomi's face must have been the color of a tomato at this point. Naomi couldn't believe Acadia asked her that, but Naomi wasn't entirely surprised, either.

Naomi chuckled but didn't answer.

Acadia then bumped her with her hip again, giving her a knowing look.

Thankfully, Cora ran into the farmhouse's front room toward Luna, who was coming in through the front door.

Naomi felt a sense of joy as Luna entered the house. Naomi had cherished her time with Luna these last few weeks. Even though she had tried to keep her at a distance at first, Naomi couldn't help but gravitate toward Luna.

It stung knowing they could never be anything beyond what they were here. Naomi didn't even know what they were—friends? No, she didn't think she could call Luna a friend. Friend wasn't enough, but also too much. She could never be Luna's friend. She could never be Luna's anything.

Naomi had lied. What's more was she was still lying to them, and she knew she would continue to lie to them every day. She could never reveal the truth. What she made Luna do. Naomi was a coward, and she knew it. Yet it never stopped her from being captivated every time Luna entered a room, and disappointed when she left.

Everything was only complicated further with the entire farmhouse knowing how Naomi felt—everyone except Luna. Even though Luna noticed so much more about Naomi than anyone else, she never seemed to see *that*. But what caused the chasm in Naomi's gut was that she hadn't done anything about it these last three weeks. How could she with all the lies she had spun? Even without knowing the lies Naomi had fed them, everyone here was hiding one thing or another from her. She was the outsider, plain and simple, and they shouldn't trust her—even she knew that.

Naomi brought herself back to her task of helping Acadia, but her attention remained on Luna. She could easily see Luna out of the corner of her eye while pretending to be busy.

Luna closed the screen door behind her, before scooping Cora up and tossing her in the air gently. Cora giggled and squealed in the way only children do. "Again! Again!"

Luna indulged her once, twice, and looked like she would go another time, but then suddenly stopped cold. Luna's face had become ashen, almost sickly looking. She was utterly still, still holding Cora, but slightly away from her body, as if she was afraid Cora would bite her.

Cora wore a look of pure confusion, but before the little girl could open her mouth to say something, Luna plastered a smile right back on her face. Naomi was sure she was hoping Cora wouldn't see that something was wrong, but it was too late for that.

Luna gently set Cora down. "Hey, I'm tired. I am going to head upstairs and rest for a minute. Can I play with you later?" Cora nodded excitedly, and Luna gave her a quick kiss on her forehead and watched the little girl run over to play with her brother on the couch.

As soon as Luna knew Cora was distracted, she went straight to the stairs, taking them two at a time, and quietly shut the door to her room.

Naomi craned her neck to see if Luna would come back down the stairs, but she didn't. Acadia gave her a knowing look and mouthed *"Go!"*

Did she want to? Did she want to open whatever this was? There was no happy ending for Naomi. She knew that, but maybe she could be happy for now. That would be fine. Naomi braced herself and ascended the stairs. Halfway up, she heard muffled sobbing coming from Luna and Darin's bedroom, and she stopped dead in her tracks.

What am I doing?

She couldn't do this. Without looking back, Naomi retreated down the stairs, chastising herself the whole way.

When Naomi reentered the kitchen, Acadia looked at her in question. Naomi shrugged, and that was that.

When it was time for dinner, Luna emerged from her room as if nothing had happened. She was happy, smiling, and her usual kind, light-hearted self. No one said anything, no one acknowledged how Luna was absent all afternoon. Or how she had been crying.

Did they not notice?

Naomi then realized Wyatt and Darin had been at the lab most of the day... and Acadia was dealing with the twins. If she wasn't dealing with them, she was listening to music or an audiobook while cleaning.

It was at this very exact moment that Naomi saw Luna's happy exterior crack, and sadness clouded Luna's eyes. It was so slight and so fast that if Naomi hadn't been paying attention, she wouldn't have noticed it.

But she did.

30

LUNA

WHEN LUNA WOKE THE next morning, she couldn't shake the crawling feeling on her skin. She knew yesterday when she picked Cora up that she had sensed this moment before then. She had felt the joy of the child, the happiness she felt with her ability, and even though she never saw Cora's face clearly, she predicted the moment perfectly. As if her ability knew what was happening, she clicked the puzzle pieces together just before she picked Cora up.

While tossing her in the air, Cora's giggles were infectious, and Luna couldn't stop smiling as Cora squealed, "Again! Again!" while her black curls flew up and down around her head.

The moment of joy vanished in an instant. Luna felt an oily sensation push through her body. She tried to ignore it, she tossed Cora up in the air again, but it was as if time suspended for just a moment—her ability took over, and Luna had to fight the urge to scream.

Beautiful, small Cora was suspended in a green, watery substance, giving her perfect caramel skin a sickly yellow hue. Her eyes were closed, while her long, dark eyelashes fanned out over her too-pale cheeks. Her hair looked like swirls of ink as the curls floated above her head in the green, watery substance. On her arms, legs, and torso were dozens of tubes and wires. She had bruises around several of the tubes in her arms, as if she had fought them going in. Luna felt sick to her stomach. She couldn't let this be real—she wouldn't.

Then, like the last three weeks of training meant nothing, she went to her room, locked the door behind her, like a coward, and cried. Because she was a coward. She was hiding in her bedroom as if the door would keep out what her ability had shown her, but it didn't.

Luna sobbed into her pillow on her bed until she couldn't cry anymore. She wanted to speak with someone who understood the Prophet ability, could help her, and change this.

She barely slept, and knowing this morning was what they had been working toward, she no longer felt prepared. She felt a chasm of darkness closing in around the edges, but she didn't know why, why this mission felt so wrong, so futile.

Luna rubbed the heels of her hands against her eyes, trying to banish the images that haunted her.

As Luna worked through her breathing techniques, she ran through their plan. They would drive to the utility door in about an hour or two, allowing them to enter the tunnel around lunchtime and giving them over three and a half hours to get back through the tunnel to the state building. They included a twenty-minute buffer in case their memory of the tunnels wasn't correct. The tunnels hadn't been on any city blueprint they could find, so they had to work from what they knew, which, unfortunately, wasn't much.

Trudging downstairs for coffee and breakfast, Luna realized she was the last one up, and everyone was at the table speaking with a middle-aged man. The man's skin was similar to Darin's, but at least two shades darker, with silver hair and striking, bright, honey-colored eyes with gold flecks.

Darin immediately popped up with a smile and said, "Luna, this is Milo Winton, the Resistance leader."

Luna walked over and politely shook Milo's hand.

Milo returned the shake with a fervor that made her uncomfortable. "Luna, your parents and brother, they were all so amazing. I would not be where I am today without them, truly."

Luna smiled weakly as Milo's eyes darted to Luna's neck, where her mother's necklace was.

Milo looked stunned. "Is that your mothers?"

Luna could only nod. She knew Milo was the Resistance leader, but she hadn't been ready to talk to anyone this early.

Milo went on, either oblivious of her discomfort or uncaring. "Is it resistant as well?"

Luna looked at him with pinched brows. "I don't think s— Wait. What are you talking about?"

Milo looked both confused and concerned. "This is the necklace your mother always wore, right? If so, it has a resistance property. It is not as effective as the frequencies the antennas produce, but it still emits a small frequency that will disrupt a Behtari's use of their ability on you. Your parents—with all their genius—figured out a way the wearer could still use *their* ability on others. The frequency never disrupts the wearer's abilities. It's incredible!"

Luna looked around the room. It was clear that Milo had been the only person with this knowledge. Darin's mouth hung open, realizing at the same time Luna did—this was how she and Kent were able to move at the club when no one else could.

Milo went on, "It's never been replicated, truly a one-of-a-kind—apart from your father's bracelet, of course. Your parents were such gifted scientists. I am so sorry for the loss of them and your brother. I am glad you are here with us now. Truly, if there is anything I can do, or any questions I can answer for you, please feel free," Milo said with a grin.

Luna smiled politely, said her thanks, and excused herself to get coffee. She needed way more caffeine to deal with this right now.

Thankfully, Milo went back to speaking with everyone at the table.

While Luna poured out her coffee, she mulled over what Milo Winton said about her parents' gold jewelry.

The jewelry emitted a frequency that protected her. How had she not realized? She and Kent were both wearing the jewelry the night of the explosion, allowing them to move. She looked down at the necklace she now rarely took off—the necklace that kept her alive that night. Luna was furious; she carelessly left the bracelet in her apartment in Solles, not knowing what it did. She should have put the pieces together.

Milo made it seem like the necklace and bracelet were common knowledge. Luna couldn't wrap her head around the idea that it was common knowledge, since no one else in the front room of the farmhouse seemed to be aware of it. Maybe it had been in the New Republic's possession for the last ten years? Which begs the question: why would the First Citizen give them to her? Surely the First Citizen knew what they were. Or maybe the

New Republic never tested the necklace and bracelet for resistant properties? That didn't sit right with Luna either. The First Citizen was anything but stupid. Luna imagined that she would have explored every avenue as to what the jewelry could do, especially over the course of ten years.

Luna poured extra cream and sugar into her large coffee mug, wrapping her hands around its warm edges. She felt that prickling along her skin again, but nothing more.

Something wasn't adding up, and she needed to figure it out fast.

The morning dragged on as everyone went about their business. Milo left, wishing them all luck and saying he looked forward to their report afterward.

When it was time to get ready, she went to her room, quickly taking off her oversized sweatshirt, but leaving her black tank top underneath. She turned to latch the door before changing her sweatpants, but right before she was able to lock the door, a firm knock stopped her.

"Can I come in?" Naomi's voice filtered through the door.

Luna swallowed the lump in her throat. "Yeah, sure." As Luna opened the door, she fiddled with the end of her necklace. She did not want to deal with this now.

Naomi entered and pinned Luna with a stern, cold glare.

Luna threw her shoulders and arms up as she scoffed. "Oh, we're not doing—" Luna gestured back and forth between them. "—whatever-this-is now, right?"

Naomi stared at her. "I am not here to talk about that. I am counting on you tonight. I know you have something going on. Don't deny it, I see it, you know I do. I saw it when you looked at Cora."

Luna went still, too still. In that moment, she knew she had given herself away.

Naomi grinned like a cat with a cornered mouse.

Luna said nothing; she knew if she opened her mouth, she would say something she shouldn't. If she said nothing, then it couldn't get worse.

Naomi stepped closer to Luna, and Luna felt like she was on fire. "What are you hiding from them, Luna?" Naomi whispered. "I can't help you if you don't tell me. My job is to find my brother and sister, which begins with gathering any available information. Can you for one minute think of someone else but yourself?"

Luna felt that fire of wanting to reach out and touch her, but the desire combusted to a white-hot rage that coursed through her body. *How dare she? How fucking dare she?* Naomi had no idea how it felt to know there was something inside herself that she could not control. It is terrifying.

But Luna didn't say that. If Naomi wanted to push her, Luna would push back. Luna moved even closer to Naomi, feeling the tension between them pull taut. "You're right. *I* am dealing with it—no one else. I will protect you to the best of my ability. No, this will not be a concern during our mission. So there's no need for all these *dramatics*." Luna gestured to Naomi, still leaning against the door, head cocked to the side. A pose Luna always assumed was anger. She loved the way Naomi looked when she was angry.

Luna wanted to increase the tension between them even more. Approaching Naomi with a deliberate slowness. Luna watched as Naomi's chest rose and fell at a faster rate, her pupils dilating.

Luna was getting under her skin, and she liked it, getting a small thrill of the pure anger and panic on Naomi's face, but just below that, something else only Luna could sense—lust. Naomi's feelings were about to run away with her. So, Luna pushed just a little more.

She took one more step toward Naomi, so they were almost touching, and gently leaned into Naomi's neck. She exhaled, watching the skin on Naomi's neck prickle. Luna brought her mouth up to Naomi's ear, gently brushing her lips against it as she said, "You could have asked nicely."

When Luna pulled away, she let her lips brush Naomi's ear once more.

Naomi's cheeks flushed, her breathing turning ragged.

Luna caught the quick, hungry flick of Naomi's gaze to her mouth. That was all it took.

"Fuck it." Luna grabbed Naomi's face and pulled her in, crushing their mouths together.

Their bodies met with a rush of heat. Luna felt her own desire course through her veins. At the same time, she sensed Naomi's craving for more. The feeling was intoxicating.

Luna tilted Naomi's head and forced her back against the door, firmly shut behind them. She was not gentle; she bit Naomi's lower lip, hungry for anything—everything—Naomi was willing to give.

Naomi returned the favor by slipping her hands under Luna's tank top. Her fingers were cool, raising goosebumps along Luna's skin as she teased her way upward, nearing Luna's oversensitive breasts.

Luna shivered, inhaling sharply when Naomi touched her peaked nipples. Naomi applied gentle pressure, twisting slowly, and a whimper escaped Luna before she could stop it.

Luna felt a faint smile play on Naomi's lips at the sound. Heat pooled low in her core. She had craved this longer than she cared to admit. She reached for Naomi's waist, trying to work her out of her skin-tight leggings. She wanted this. Now—

Knock. Knock.

"You two aren't as quiet as you think you are." Luna could hear Darin's mocking smile through the door. "As much fun as I'm sure you're having, we need to get our gear and go." Mercifully, Darin didn't say anything more, and they listened to his footsteps recede down the hall.

This was going to have to wait. As much as Luna wanted to tear off Naomi's leggings and feel her, taste her, make her shatter again and again, she couldn't. Not now. They would have time. She would make sure of it.

Luna leaned down, nipping Naomi's neck. "You need to get ready," she whispered.

Naomi leaned into her with a soft sigh, and Luna savored the press of their bodies for one last moment before pulling back.

She turned to the bed, grabbed her discarded sweatshirt, and pulled it on before moving toward the door.

As Luna reached for the handle, Naomi placed a hand on her waist, stopping her. Luna lifted her gaze to meet Naomi's warm mahogany eyes, and for that moment, this was all they were—no difference between them, no mission, nothing pulling them apart.

Naomi brought both hands to Luna's face and kissed her, slow and intimate. When she pulled back, she whispered into Luna's ear, "Meet me after?"

It was a question—an invitation—and Luna couldn't help the smile that bloomed across her face. Naomi, clearly satisfied with the response, kissed her once more, then slipped out without another word.

As Luna shut the door, another flash hit her—small clips and images rolling through her mind.

She was reaching for someone, screaming out of sadness and heartache. The sound was so loud Luna felt her vocal cords sting with pain.

She was back in the tunnels again, but they weren't quite the same.

She was in a black room with a soft drip, drip, drip *in the background, but her shoulder was in so much pain.*

Cora suspended in green water.

Luna jolted upright and realized she was on the floor. She realized she must have completely blacked out. Luna turned to look at the clock between the beds. It had only been thirty minutes since breakfast, so she hadn't been on the floor long.

Luna stood, peering out her door to ensure no one had heard anything. She exhaled in relief that it was empty.

She was so screwed.

She had no control over her Prophet ability. She should have asked Milo about it, but she hadn't wanted to expose her greatest vulnerability to someone she didn't know—even if he seemed to know her all too well.

She shivered, trying to forget the feel of his fingers on her hand, clutching so hard it hurt. She knew Darin trusted him, and that should be enough, but why wasn't it this time? She had no way even to sense what would happen over the next forty-eight hours; her ability was too unpredictable. Luna, in her fear and self-deprecation, had lied to the only person who gave her comfort, who understood her. Luna hated herself at this moment. She knew she would never be enough for Naomi, no matter what Naomi thought.

She sat on the bed, her head in her hands. For the first time in weeks, Luna felt totally and completely alone.

31

LUNA

THE RIDE WAS EERILY quiet, not only because of everything between Luna and Naomi, but because of what lay ahead of the four of them. Wyatt agreed to drive Marcella, Darin, Luna, and Naomi to the utility door, or at least as close as he could get them, before going back to Omphalos.

Wyatt dropped them off in the wooded area, but they were still about a mile from the utility door.

Marcella was the first out, opening the trunk and handing each teammate their backpack.

When Luna walked around to take her backpack from Marcella, she tilted her head toward Naomi in question. Luna couldn't hide her embarrassment, immediately breaking eye contact and shaking her head once. She turned away from Marcella as her cheeks flooded with heat. It seemed everyone had noticed Luna and Naomi slowly drifting toward each other these last few weeks.

Luna couldn't help but be surprised at Marcella's observation, but the more she thought about it, the more she realized she was a fool. Of course, they had noticed. Naomi had been the only one to understand her grief and help her through her anxiety.

Luna felt that same chasm within her darken, and she inwardly worried that this feeling wasn't just a feeling. She did not want to interfere with the mission, so whatever this was would have to wait.

They each said goodbye to Wyatt and walked into the forest. Luna paused at the edge of the tree line to watch Wyatt speed away.

Navigating the woods was much faster this time. Once they approached the utility door, they conducted last-minute bag checks and secured additional weapons. Darin had Luna and Naomi practice shooting daily in the Omphalos armory. The armory was on the other side of the lab within the old school. Although the shooting range wasn't extensive, it was sufficient.

Darin ensured everyone had been fitted with tactical gear designed explicitly for this mission. Omphalos was a haven, but the people who lived there were practical as well. The armory was well-stocked with weapons, yes, but also boots, black shirts, cargo pants, and bulletproof tactical vests.

Luna knew the most exciting piece was the tech Darin installed into the hoods of their tactical gear. The hood, before Darin got to it, was nothing fancy—it had a soft interior with little structure, and the exterior was waterproof. To enhance the hoods, Darin installed a headset with a holo-ocular system in each. So, when she put the hood up, the headset settled by her ear, and the ocular system engaged, coming to life as a visor before her eyes. The visor was like a portable interface program and emitted a faint pale blue light. Within the system itself, Darin programmed an integrated map complete with blueprints of the state building, GPS, a scope, and a thermal camera.

After they opened the utility hatch and conducted exterior and interior safety checks, Marcella took point as the mission leader. She tested their equipment one last time before engaging all their ocular systems for their walk through the tunnels. She turned around, looking at each of them, but Luna watched as her gaze fixed on Naomi, and a smile bloomed on her face. "Ready?" she asked. "Let's fuck shit up." Then, Marcella descended into the tunnel.

Luna felt that it didn't take them long to navigate the tunnels, but Darin assured her it was two hours and forty-five minutes. Luna's heart beat rapidly as they approached the door she knew led to the junction in the sewer system. She knew the plan. They would go through the door, navigating the sewers to the state building.

Luna knew this was coming; she had prepared for this for weeks, but her nerves were overwhelming. She could feel that energy again—that threat she might tumble out of her mind and into what might be. Still, Luna didn't understand how she could have developed this ability. She was so afraid to admit what it was, but she knew. In her heart, she knew exactly what was happening to her. If she didn't get control of it soon, she was going to die or go mad.

The brain could only handle the higher frequency for so long with Luna's lack of control. She had been training with Darin, but it wasn't enough. Darin didn't know enough about how the ability worked to help her through the frequency spikes. The high-frequency oscillation spikes happened when the ability took over, forcing the frequency in her brain higher, to a point where Luna could no longer control it.

She needed another Prophet to teach her, and the only one she trusted was dead. If she didn't learn how to control it, she would have a seizure so significant that it would cause permanent brain damage or kill her. She took a deep breath. This was not the time or place for this problem.

She tried to concentrate on her breathing, which Naomi had helped her with over the past three weeks.

In. One, two, three. Out. One, two, three. Again. In. One, two, three. Out. One, two, three. Again. Again. Again.

Anything to keep her mind at bay for a time. She needed a little more time, that was all. She hadn't been there when Kent's ability broke through, but she knew he was around nine or ten, which was early for a Prophet—most showed their ability closer to adolescence—but not unheard of.

When Kent's ability surfaced, Luna's mother had been terrified. She knew precisely what Kent was and understood his significance to the New Republic—particularly to the First Citizen. Thankfully, Kent's Infliction ability set in early, too. Kent used his ability to force their father into a laughing fit, prompting the rest of them to join in. It was one of Luna's earliest and happiest memories of them as children.

After Kent's Prophet ability manifested, their parents withdrew him until he could control it. They wouldn't risk anyone learning about his ability. Publicly, their parents claimed Kent was going through some mental health issues and left it at that. Mental health was not only accepted in their society but also valued. If a Behtari's mental health wasn't up to par, their ability was dangerous to themselves and others.

It took Kent months to learn how to control his ability. Luna didn't have months. Luna only realized something was different right around Kent's death. She had only been training with it for three weeks. Darin tried to help her, but neither of them ever heard Kent talk or vent about how he dealt with his Prophet ability. Luna and Darin moaned and groaned about what they could and couldn't do, what they had and hadn't accomplished, and Kent let them talk, laughing and smiling along, but he never shared his own troubles. Luna mentally kicked herself. She could have done more. Tears silently fell down Luna's face. She could have done something—anything—to learn more about him, to be closer to him.

Out of the darkness of the dim tunnel, there was a hand on her forearm. Luna looked up and caught Naomi's mahogany eyes, full of worry and kindness—a kindness Luna felt she didn't deserve.

"Don't do that to yourself," Naomi said softly. "You are loved here. You no longer need to bear the guilt you carry. There is nothing you could have done differently. For what it's worth, thank you for saving my life. I know you thought I knew to get out, but... I didn't. They told me I would be far enough away. If you hadn't covered me, I wouldn't be here. I will never forget that." Naomi gave Luna's arm a slight squeeze. "I am grateful to have met you, Luna." Before Naomi turned away, she paused, as if debating whether she should say more.

After a moment, their eyes met again, and Naomi said, strong and steady,

"You can be more than the cards you were dealt. But *you* must make that choice. No one else can make it for you." Naomi then kissed Luna tenderly on the mouth and turned, rejoining the others.

For a moment, Luna just stood, alone in the dark tunnel.

32

NAOMI

NAOMI WAS SURPRISED BY how long it took to get into the city. Now she wished she had trained harder during her time at Omphalos; she was exhausted. When they finally stopped, Darin and Luna took out their blueprint maps to assess their location.

Naomi's muscles ached—she was relieved to take a break; her legs were on fire.

Marcella stepped closer while Darin and Luna conferred. "Eat something, trust me."

Naomi didn't have to be told twice. She reached into her pack for one of the meal bars they made at the farmhouse. They included a protein supplement, oats, white chocolate chips, dried cranberries, and some honey.

Naomi realized Marcella had done the same. They stood in silence while they chewed. It wasn't the best thing Naomi had tasted in these last few weeks, but it was better than anything they received on the ground level.

Darin and Luna bickered while they finished their meal bars.

Naomi's mind kept returning to the moment in the tunnels with Luna. Not when Naomi told Luna she could be more if she chose to. Not when she reached out to touch her, feeling that electric burn again as soon as her fingers met Luna's perfect skin. Before that, as they were walking. Luna was behind her, but ever so slowly falling behind.

Naomi had watched from the corner of her eye as Luna fell, back, and back, and back... Naomi could feel Luna's grief thick in the air, growing more intense the longer they went. Naomi knew grief; she knew it from the deepest part of herself. Her parents had been taken from her, and she had to watch her brother's and sister's hearts break over it. She remembered holding them in her arms the night their parents were taken. Ethan curled up on her right side, Ella on her left. Ella had fallen asleep, but Ethan still had silent tears flowing down his cheeks.

Earlier that evening, their mother had been using the wash bin to wash and dry their dinner dishes, which consisted of rice and canned black beans. She was still wearing her gray uniform, a stark contrast to her deep, soulful brown eyes, which matched Naomi's. While Naomi inherited her silver hair from her father, her mother had jet-black hair, the kind of black that absorbed all the light around it.

Her mother added chili powder to their dinner that night, having bartered a tablespoon from their neighbor who asked for some rice. The chili flavor lingered in Naomi's mouth long after the meal. It was rare to have spices for cooking, especially those with intense flavors. Her mother had only used a tiny bit for the meal, but it made it worlds better.

Naomi's mother walked into their small kitchen and tucked the spice into the one large cupboard. They usually only had refrigerated food in the winter; it was too hard to keep in the summer without a refrigerator.

After the spices were stored, her mother returned to the wash bin when the metal door flew in. The door, truly, wasn't a door, simply a thin sheet of metal that barely kept out the wind. It didn't stand a chance against the LEO leading the charge, larger than the rest with dark auburn hair that fell in waves around his face. Six LEOs burst into the small apartment. Naomi couldn't see their faces; they all wore riot armor, complete with face masks.

It only took seconds for all six to enter, and once inside, they wasted no time. Her mother stood, wiping her hands on her apron, and with downcast eyes asked, "How can we be of service?"

Without a word, a LEO toward the back of the group walked toward her, swiftly whacking a night stick across her mother's face. Naomi heard the crunch of bones the strike met her mother's face. She fell to the dirt floor of their home, unmoving.

Her father, with the same silver hair as Naomi, came out of the back room—which they all shared as a bedroom—and looked at his wife, then fell to his knees. Tears streamed down his face as he begged the LEOs not to take her. He begged them. He could have fought, he could have screamed, he could have done anything, but he didn't.

Naomi had resented him until she found herself in the same position with Ethan and Ella. Everything she had done was for them—the torture she endured, the nefarious tasks the First Citizen had made her execute, and the experiments they subjected her to. Her brother and sister were always threatened if she didn't follow through. She longed to see them again, to make sure they were okay, even if she knew they wouldn't be the same innocent children she had left. That burden she felt, that weight she carried, it was sometimes too much.

She knew Luna felt that, too. That constant question *Why couldn't I save them?* broke Naomi's heart every time her head went to that place. Luna was heading down that same path, and it was unacceptable. Naomi stood by before; she didn't fight before, but she would now. She cared for Luna enough that it scared her—enough that she was willing to try. So, she tried; she repaired her half of what was broken. Now, it was up to Luna.

It took about fifteen minutes for Darin and Luna to locate multiple openings to the city streets that would serve as their exit. However, since it was a sewer, most of them were in high-visibility areas. They wanted to be accurate about which sewer grate they would emerge from, so they placed themselves correctly. Everything about this mission was so specific and detailed; they planned it perfectly, incorporating multiple backup plans in case of unforeseen circumstances.

Once Darin and Luna finally agreed on an exit point, they let the night settle in. Before leaving the sewer, Luna covered everyone except Naomi in a shield.

Darin went first. As an Illusionist, he could throw off anyone who walked by. Naomi went next. Darin couldn't put an illusion *on* Naomi, but he could put something in front of her. Then Marcella and finally Luna.

Once they were out, Naomi, Marcella, and Luna headed to the state building. The trio remained in back alleys and shadows as much as they could. Luna used her shields on Marcella and herself. Naomi tried to be as quiet as possible. Which now seemed impossible when she was next to two soundless Behtari.

Darin said he covered himself in an illusion before going to the cafe about three blocks from the state building, although Naomi couldn't see it. The coffee shop—according to Darin—was next door to another building run by the New Republic. He claimed the building housed research files dating back to before the New Republic was established. How Darin knew this, Naomi didn't know, but apparently, it was well-guarded internally and had the most intense security in Solles, outside of the cells within the belly of the state building. So, Darin would hack the security system there. He said he had no concerns about his task because he had accomplished it before, but wouldn't say when or why he'd done it previously. Naomi found this incredibly annoying, and when she told Darin as much, he seemed to be even more pleased.

Once Darin was in the state building's security system, he would send each of them a message via the ocular system the moment the power was down. The more specific part was that he had to send a virus through the system to knock out all LEO communication and render MAVs useless. Once the power was out and the links were down, Luna and Naomi had ten minutes before the backup power system would eat through Darin's virus and repower the building.

Naomi watched the street while Luna and Marcella put on the ocular systems. She had so much energy building inside her that she was shifting side to side. She could do this. Sure, she had never done anything like this before, but she could *do* this.

Naomi tried to pretend like this wasn't a massive violation of every agreement she had ever made to the First

Citizen, or the senators. She closed her eyes so hard it almost hurt. If she still had long hair, she might have even put her hands to her scalp and pulled at the back of her hair to bring her back to center.

Marcella noticed the change in Naomi. "Hey, you can do this. I will be out here keeping watch to ensure you get out safely. If things go tits up, I'll make sure we can get you."

"That is not extremely comforting," Naomi said, looking at the floor out of habit, which she quickly corrected, meeting Marcella's brown, gold-flecked eyes.

Naomi didn't mind the gold so much now that she had friends with gold flecks in their eyes—people she cared about.

When Luna turned, Naomi saw the same fear in her own gaze reflected in Luna's. It was the fear of losing someone who started to matter. Naomi could feel the possibilities she had dreamed of with Luna slipping through her fingers, like sand through an hourglass—slow and inevitable.

Naomi quickly turned. She could not deal with this right now. They had sixty seconds before they made their move.

She needed to focus.

33

LUNA

LUNA AND NAOMI FLEW through the hallways of the state building. Luna could feel the gold necklace inside her shirt sway with her movements. Both the Behtari and the human were so familiar with this building that it was easy to navigate together. Their time spent training paid off. They worked seamlessly as a unit, able to anticipate what the other would do and adapt.

Wyatt ensured they spent extensive time together after the failed mission in the woods. He made them help each other through childish games, such as a three-legged race, but instead of a sprint, it was a mile. Or, when they were tasked with lighting a fire, one was blindfolded, and the other didn't have use of their hands. That had been the most frustrating for Luna, relinquishing control entirely and having to describe precisely what Naomi needed to do.

There was a sense of vulnerability every time they did the fire exercise. One must trust implicitly, while the other must learn to communicate well. Wyatt was diabolical once he realized that it was their most challenging task. He assigned it almost daily, but sometimes they would be in a room where he would turn up the heat to the point they would both have sweat dripping from their brow, and gave them matches instead of a lighter.

Or when he made them do it in the rain, the only cover was a jacket that Naomi was wearing as she instructed Luna on the tools they had and what she needed to do—that time, he gave them flint. It took Luna two hours to light the fire, but it only stayed lit for fifteen seconds. She had wanted to punch Wyatt in his stupid, smug face after that. Now she wanted to give him a bear hug and thank him.

They entered the building through the back entrance, used exclusively for humans—which meant no LEOs. Getting through the backdoor system was easy. There were two security checks: a retinal scan and a fingerprint. Darin made sure both were disabled before giving Luna and Naomi the green light to enter.

As they rounded each corner, they would take turns being each other's six. Luna would round the corner with Naomi walking backward, watching for any threats. Then, once they secured the area, they would switch. Naomi now taking point, and Luna watching her six.

Naomi and Luna had worked together so much over the past few weeks that it felt seamless. They avoided two LEOs using the thermal camera in the ocular system. However, the third LEO they came across was unavoidable.

Luna waited around the corner for the LEO to get farther away before making her move. Once she could barely hear his footsteps, she engaged her shield, becoming virtually silent.

After Naomi gave her a quick, sly smile, Luna didn't waste another moment. She sprinted silently down the hallway, came up behind him, and, with a swift jab in the neck, she inserted the needle containing the sedative. She had to silence him before the sedative took effect. So, before the LEO even had a chance to react, Luna had her right arm around his neck, his chin resting just above her elbow, and her hand holding onto her left upper arm. Simultaneously, with her left arm, she pinned her right hand to her bicep and pulled up, completely cutting off blood flow and his air passages. The LEO crumpled to the floor in less than a minute.

Luna felt the thrill, but also a sense of pride in herself. She never imagined herself being strong enough to take out a LEO, and she liked it.

Naomi came up behind Luna after the LEO's body hit the floor to help Luna move the body into a side alcove. They also took his holo, com link, and keys, which Luna watched Naomi zip into her tactile vest, giving Luna a nod to confirm they were secure. Darin could wipe them all later and dump them.

Luna then pulled up her hood, activating the ocular system so she and Naomi could communicate efficiently, and took off toward the stairs. As they rounded to the third floor where Kent's office was, Luna gave Naomi a quick nod.

Naomi returned it before heading up one more flight to Senator Yeo's office.

As Luna ran down the corridor, careful to keep her shield in place. Tears pricked her eyes upon reaching for the door handle of Kent's office. As one tear rolled down her cheeks, she closed her eyes and thought to herself, *One grain of sand*. Then, she opened the door, stepped inside, and closed it behind her.

Luna quickly said into the headset, "N: I am in."

"Copy, L," was the only reply she received.

Luna immediately realized this was no longer Kent's office. She suspected this, but it didn't hurt any less. However, as Luna took in the office space, she wondered who had moved in.

The office was absolute anarchy—papers lined the four walls, stretching ten feet to the ceiling, as if someone had hired an interior decorator from her nightmares.

Crunch.

Luna stilled and closed her eyes in frustration.

How could anyone possibly work in this?

As she opened her eyes and removed her boot, she realized the overflowing waste bin spilled into the room as if it were on vines. Luna then realized with panic and clarity in equal measure that she was screwed. This was going to take a lot longer than the time she had left—which was approximately four and a half minutes.

Luna moved different pieces of paper from one place to another on the desk. She knew she should make it look like no one was here, but if she moved the slightest paper, it caused four more to move. So, Luna moved on to opening the drawers, but nothing. She then felt under the desk, nothing. The chair, nothing.

Luna looked around frantically; she was running out of time. She'd known this was a long shot. It had been almost sixty days since Kent's death. The New Republic had no reason to keep his office intact. She decided, as a last-ditch effort, to go through the filing cabinet by the large windows.

She opened the top drawer of the filing cabinet and sifted through the files. The cabinet was anything but organized; it was a heap of papers and notes, like the rest of the office. Time was coming down to the wire, and Luna knew it—she needed to leave. She watched the time tick down on the upper-left corner of the blue interface visor. Luna had thirty seconds before she had to leave, and she was going to make it count.

An envelope caught her eye. It was formal documentation addressed to Senator Asher Dawson...

Why would formal documentation be kept here for the Senator?

She realized with startling clarity that not only was this no longer Kent's office... This was Senator Dawson's office. *Why does he now have an office at Kellmont?* Something was wrong. "Senator Dawson's office is here," Luna reported into her headpiece. "Something is wrong."

Marcella's voice came through first. "Repeat to confirm, L."

"M: Senator Asher Dawson's office is here. I repeat, Senator Asher Dawson's office is Kent's old office." When Luna stopped speaking, all she heard was crackling. She needed to get out of here immediately.

As she passed the desk, a name caught her attention.

Governor Derek Seymour

Luna's palms were slick with sweat as she reached for the paper,

Oh, no, no, no. Please, no.

Luna picked up the paper quickly and scanned its contents.

Governor Derek Seymour
Status – Captured, Living
Whereabouts – Classified

Sector/Classification – Project 800
Other Known...

Her eyes felt slow, heavy, and fell away from the paper. Belatedly, Luna realized there had been a tiny prick at the base of her ear on her neck.

Odd.

She didn't remember that before just now, or did it just happen? The floor seemed to be falling toward her in slow motion as she fell to her knees, giggling, thinking this might be the silliest thing she had ever been a part of. Then, her body fell to the floor, her eyes were fuzzy, and so very tired. She closed them as she heard footsteps approaching. She knew she should care, but couldn't remember why.

Then, everything fell away.

34

<u>NAOMI</u>

AFTER NAOMI LEFT LUNA, she snuck behind an access panel designed for humans, reached the back stairway, and went to Senator Yeo's office as quickly as possible.

They all assumed that Kent's office would have been processed, but then the question arose: If someone had seen something, who would they bring it to? Where would it be stored? They all agreed that if anyone had known about the ghost drive and protected it, it would have been Senator Yeo. So that was where Naomi went.

Naomi knew Senator Yeo was extremely particular. In addition, she had a love of the delta lily. She had several dipped in resin and placed in a vase on top of her black desk, but the flowers didn't stop there. The walls featured paintings of the delta flower, and the senator had even decorated the office to match the color scheme. Looking around the room, all Naomi could think about was the art set Luna had given her, and how she had tried to capture the delta lily's likeness but hadn't gotten it quite right.

They had fought before they left, and then Luna had kissed her. She slowly brought her fingers to her lips, lost in the moment again. The second kiss had been so different from the first, which had been of necessity, or even tenderness. This one had not been tender—she had

been hot with rage. The way Luna had drifted toward her
in anger, in that moment, Naomi couldn't breathe. When
Luna's lips crashed into hers, there had been nothing
tender about it. Luna pulled at the base of Naomi's skull,
bringing their entire bodies flush together. She had felt the
intensity build between them like electricity, she couldn't
stop thinking about it.

Naomi mentally scolded herself. What was she doing?
She needed to be moving quickly.

She opened and closed drawers, one after another.

Nothing.

Nothing.

Nothing.

She then reached under the desk, and on the
right-hand side, there was a small lip. When Naomi
reached up a little farther, she could feel something that
was taped. She pulled, and there it was: a tiny ghost drive
of whatever Kent deemed a good idea to collect and store.
Naomi quickly zipped it into the interior pocket of her
tactile vest, ensuring it couldn't fall out. Then, she bolted.

They agreed that Naomi and Luna would not meet
back up again to get out. Once the drive was secured,
the finder would report to the group. Her message would
prompt Luna to leave as well, but as Naomi came out of
the office, she heard voices coming up the stairs. Naomi
froze in panic, unsure of what to do or where to go. That
was when it occurred to her that she probably knew a lot
more about this building than whoever was coming up
the stairs. So then, on instinct, she found the closest access
door for the humans and slipped away.

She was terrified they would find her and catch her.
She had to move, faster, faster. Her legs burned as she

pushed herself. She just had to make it to Marcella; that was all she needed to do. If she didn't make it there, she shouldn't think about that now; she needed to be forward-thinking. Fear will get her captured. She would rather be dead than captured, forced to be a slave again. So, she sprinted onward.

Outside, Marcella waved her over from across the street.

Naomi disengaged the ocular system before crossing the street to Marcella.

"Did you get it?" Marcella asked.

Naomi couldn't help the wide grin that came across her face as she responded, "Actually, yeah, I think I did." Naomi pulled out the ghost drive and showed it to Marcella.

Marcella looked at the ghost drive in amazement. "Okay, put that away. If Luna isn't out here in ten seconds, we have to leave."

Before realizing what she was saying, Naomi answered, "No."

Marcella took a step in front of Naomi to get the best view of the back of the state building, then turned, pointing her finger in Naomi's face. "Listen, I like you. I do. I think you are in a fucked up situation and you aren't telling us everything, but neither are we. So do not, for one damn second, think I am stupid. Because I am anything but. I understand you have feelings for her."

Naomi opened her mouth to speak, but Marcella put her hand up to cut her off.

"Do not make me waste the air in my lungs or yours if you are going to try to deny that. Now that bit is cleared up, let me make this very clear. Number one, I am in charge of this mission, not you. Therefore, you will follow my orders, or you will not be permitted to serve in future missions. Number two, Luna matters to me, too. I am standing here, telling you that yes, we will leave her. We will also come back for her." Marcella's voice softened by the end.

Naomi knew they had to go, but her gut wrenched at not knowing if she was okay or simply running late.

Marcella let them stay a few extra moments, then made the call.

They planned to meet in the alley where they had come out of the sewer, but since Luna was not with them, Naomi knew their plans would have to change.

Marcella was typing frantically on her holo before stopping suddenly, almost causing Naomi to run into her. Marcella sighed. "Well, change of plans. Looks like we might stay for a minute."

Naomi couldn't help herself before she said, "Where? We can't stay in the sewer, right?"

Marcella went wide-eyed. She must have hated that idea as much as she did. "Absolutely not. I would rather eat a bowl of dirt. Literally. We are going to Darin's. His place is on the other side of the city, so it will be a bit of a walk. Are you okay for a while longer?"

Naomi nodded. As much as she wanted to curl up and sleep, Naomi knew she needed to get to safety first. It was odd that she found herself feeling safe around the Behtari. She hated so many of them for so long. Even the ones she hadn't hated, she hadn't *liked*. There had been no positive Behtari in her life until now. And Naomi could honestly say she felt her life was better for it.

After walking for what felt like over an hour, Naomi could see the palest light shining on the horizon. It was going to be dawn soon, and all Naomi could think about was Luna. She hadn't contacted any of them. Although they had not met up with Darin yet, Marcella was messaging him the entire time, and he was responding.

Finally, they turned down an alley to Darin's, and Naomi was immediately concerned with the buildings. They were all run-down, missing windows, and a few had broken-down doors. The house they were heading for had a hole right in the center of the roof. Naomi didn't want to complain, but she certainly wanted to ask Marcella how he lived here. To Naomi, Darin always seemed well-kept and put together. Not like he would live in a house with a hole in the ceiling.

Marcella climbed the three steps quickly, but Naomi took her time, certain one of the three dilapidated stairs would cave in on her. When Naomi passed through the threshold, she felt a pulse through her body. She turned to see what had caused it, and saw the slightly blueish cast outside the door.

Naomi realized Darin had placed an Illusion on the outside of the house because the inside was stunning.

That's when Naomi realized Darin's illusion ability had been used on her—and it worked. She had never been so afraid in her entire life.

35

LUNA

LUNA BLINKED BUT QUICKLY realized it was too dark to see anything.

Drip, drip, drip.

The soft sound of leaking water came from somewhere behind her. Luna tried to move her arms, but they were above her head, bound at the wrist, and her left shoulder was in so much pain it felt like it was on fire. She tried to move her arms, but she could no longer feel her hands, numb from being bound above her head with rope. Luna could feel the tiny burrs from the rope digging into her skin around her wrists.

Recollection struck her. She had seen this before, sensing this moment with her Prophet ability. Luna wasn't sure that meant anything, but at least she knew what she had sensed before was real. Unfortunately, that meant the rest of her visions were real, too. She hoped that when she was tossing Cora into the air, it was some coincidence, but she should have known better.

Where was she? Luna tried to work backward to the last thing she remembered. She had been in Kent's old office. Luna shook her head as if that was going to clear the cobwebs from her mind. She had been in the office that used to be Kent's; she was looking for a ghost drive but hadn't found it.

As Luna's mind spun, she realized she must be in a cell beneath the state building, with no windows or lights—she was surrounded by darkness. She had no idea how long she had been down here. It could have been minutes or days. *How long have I been out for?* Luna remembered the tiny prick she felt at the base of her ear, but then nothing. The only idea she could come up with was that a MAV must have stung her, injecting her with something to subdue her. Anger flared in Luna's chest. How had she been so careless? She'd known she was pushing her time limit, but she stayed anyway.

Luna tried to ignore the constant agony burning in her left shoulder. She knew her joints could not handle this kind of pressure, and if her arms stayed bound like this for much longer, her shoulder would eventually dislocate.

She tried to engage her Prophet ability to sense if there was anything that would help her right now, but it wasn't there. Her panic rose as she tried to engage her shielding ability, but that was also gone. Luna's anger rose again when she realized she must have been given the same suppressant that was used in the museum, rendering her abilities useless.

Luna's mind already felt too taxed from even the small amount of effort she had put forth. She tried to fight her body, to force herself to stay awake, but it was useless. Luna relented, letting her head loll to the side as nothingness consumed her again.

This time, when Luna regained consciousness, she was drenched in ice-cold water and shivering. A blinding light shone in her face, which caused her to slam her eyes shut. Someone had also moved her; she was now sitting with her arms bound behind her back. She was thankful for the slight relief after having her arms bound above her, even if it was brief.

The water came over her head again.

She coughed and sputtered, trying not to inhale, but she couldn't help it. Her lungs burned. Her copper hair clung to her face; her clothes were completely soaked, freezing against her skin.

Luna tried to open her eyes, slowly this time, and made out a pair of boots a few feet in front of her. LEO boots—the same that Kent used to wear as part of his New Republic-issued uniform.

Luna tried to look up, but the damn light was so bright she could barely look past this person's knees.

Luna heard footsteps slowly coming toward her. The steps were slow and purposeful, as if whoever this was enjoyed her suffering and was savoring it.

Then, a voice accompanied the footsteps, saying, "Leave us."

Luna recognized the deep voice but couldn't quite place it.

The LEO who was in front of Luna hesitated. She had a spark of hope they might help her, but it was extinguished when the voice spoke again.

"Need I remind you what happened last time?"

Luna's stomach dropped. Something about this person was so familiar, Luna strained to look up again, hoping to see the individual even with the blinding light in her face, but it was no use. The person positioned themselves perfectly in line with the light, so all she could see was a vague outline.

When the LEO finally exited, the cell door shut behind him.

Smack!

Luna heard the slap against her cheek before she felt its sting. Blood pooled in her mouth as they hit her again.

Smack!

And again.

Smack!

And again.

Smack!

She could barely hold her head up, blood freely flowing from her mouth, but they didn't stop.

Smack!

Her cheek split open.

Smack!

The room began to spin.

Smack!

Finally, unconsciousness claimed her.

36

DARIN

DARIN WAS SO DAMN tired. He slept only a few hours before dragging himself out of bed to start working on the ghost drive Naomi found in Senator Yeo's desk. Darin threw on a light blue hoodie—with the hood up over his curly dark hair—and his favorite pair of black sweats and ambled down the stairs. Darin felt like a shadow of his former self. Sure, the mission was successful, but Luna wasn't here. That realization was like a thorn in Darin's brain, constantly applying pressure and pain.

As Darin came down the black metal spiral staircase, he could already smell coffee brewing in the kitchen. No doubt Marcella would already be awake—she was always an early riser. In fact, Darin wondered if Marcella slept at all last night. As he walked through the living space and rounded the corner into the kitchen, he could tell from the bags under her eyes that she hadn't slept. Marcella's dark hair was tied messily on top of her head. She had on one of Darin's old *Dragon Fight* shirts that was far too large for her. She'd brewed more than one pot of coffee at this point; he was sure of it.

She was so frantically focused on the laptop in front of her, she hadn't even noticed him approaching.

"Good Morning," Darin said as Marcella jumped. Clearly, she hadn't heard him at all. "What are you doing on the interface?" Marcella was excellent with technology and hacking, though not as good as Darin, still quite skilled.

Marcella breathed an enormous sigh. "I figured I would get started on this, and of course, Kent has it encrypted, so I am working through that, but I have only been at it for an hour or two."

Darin nodded and then asked, "Can I see where you are at?"

Marcella turned the laptop toward him without protest.

Darin saw the absolute clusterfuck that was Kent's encryption. Darin rubbed his hand down his face in frustration.

"That's exactly where I am at."

Darin walked to the coffee pot. "Let me get some coffee, and then we can go to my main setup so we can at least work together."

In the living space, they each took an entire couch to themselves, the three large screens in front of them.

When Darin hooked up the laptop, the screens came to life. Darin put the coding on the far left-hand screen, and on the far right, he had his own hacking software program, which he would run on the ghost drive. In the middle, he created a folder to pull the files as soon as the encryption was done.

Marcella had fallen asleep on the couch, and Darin made more coffee and waited.

Darin's hacking software made quick work of Kent's main encryption. About thirty minutes later, Darin heard a *ping!* He pulled open the drive, noting that his software bypassed the main encryption, granting him access to the interior files.

Once Darin was able to access the interior files, he realized this was going to take a lot longer than he had anticipated—potentially too long for them to wait before trying to rescue Luna.

There were over three hundred video files and eight hundred documents, each individually encrypted. Darin sighed. He had known the ghost drive would be encrypted, but he had not realized that each *file* would be.

Darin didn't want to waste any more time. He let Marcella sleep while he set up his hacking program to start with the videos. Each video was expected to take at least an hour to decode, depending on its file size. So, Darin set the program to automatically move to the next video file once the current one finished. Then, with nothing else to do, he grabbed a blanket off the back of the couch and fell asleep.

When Darin woke, it was hours later, and the first video had finished; the hacking system was already on to the following video. Darin looked over at Marcella, who was still sleeping peacefully. He assumed Naomi was sleeping as well since she had not come out of her room.

Darin knew he wanted to watch the video as soon as possible, but he was also starving. He quickly went into the kitchen, grabbing a large mixing bowl, a soup spoon, a box of his favorite chocolate cereal, and the oat milk from the fridge. Darin figured the oat milk would offset the chocolate cereal as he carried the items back to the couch and placed them on the coffee table in front of him. He poured the cereal almost halfway up the mixing bowl, then added the oat milk. He sat back on the couch and played the first video.

The first thing that Darin noticed was that this must have been a clinical observation video. The camera was clearly set up in a lab, and the screen paused on someone standing in a lab coat, their face out of the frame.

As Darin went to press play, he noticed the timestamp in the bottom-left corner of the video.

This can't be right.

It was dated thirty days before the first explosion at the water treatment facility in Ventis, Lembalt. Darin's palms started to sweat. *What had Kent found?* When Darin pressed play, he watched in horror as the First Citizen Kasandra Sanders sat in front of the camera, with plain brown eyes.

<u>**TIMESTAMP:**</u>
<u>**DAY 50 OF THE 1ST QUARTER - YEAR 576 OF THE 2ND AGE.**</u>

MY NAME IS KASANDRA SANDERS. IT IS DAY 75 OF THE 1ST QUARTER, YEAR 576 OF THE 2ND AGE. WE LOST ANOTHER SUBJECT TODAY. THE SEIZURE ONSET WAS APPROXIMATELY AN HOUR; THE SUBJECT DIED WITHIN FOUR MINUTES. THERE HAS BEEN DISAGREEMENT ABOUT HOW TO PROCEED WITH THE SERUM. I AM NOT SURE IF IT WOULD BE BETTER TO TEST IT ON MYSELF OR TO WAIT. ASHER DAWSON HAS RECOMMENDED DILUTING IT IN WATER, AS IT MAY BE TOO POTENT WHEN ADMINISTERED INTRAVENOUSLY. HE HAS AGREED TO BE THE TEST SUBJECT TOMORROW SHOULD THE RATS SURVIVE THE NIGHT.

I WAS HOPEFUL THIS SERUM WOULD CURE MANY DIFFERENT DISEASES, BUT AS THE RATS CONTINUE TO REMAIN UNAFFECTED AND/OR SURVIVE WITH AN ENHANCED WHITE BLOOD CELL COUNT, WE ARE STILL LOSING HUMAN TEST SUBJECTS. I DO NOT WANT

**ASHER TO DO THIS ALONE, BUT I AM AFRAID I HAVE RUN OUT OF
OPTIONS.**

As the video ended, Darin had to force his gaping mouth
shut. Had the First Citizen and Senator Asher Dawson
contaminated the water over one hundred forty-six years
ago? How were they still alive? Behtari had longer lifespans
than humans, but not that long. Darin's mind was reeling
as another soft *ping* came from the hacking system,
signaling the next video finished.

Kasandra was in the paused frame again, but her eyes
were no longer just brown; they were flecked with gold.
Darin wasted no time pressing play.

TIMESTAMP:
DAY 53 OF THE 1ST QUARTER - YEAR 576 OF THE 2ND AGE.

**MY NAME IS KASANDRA SANDERS. IT IS DAY 78 OF THE 1ST
QUARTER, YEAR 576 OF THE 2ND AGE. I AM TWO DAYS PAST
INGESTING THREE DROPS OF SERUM MIXED WITH FOUR CUPS OF
WATER.**

**THE ONSET OF SYMPTOMS WAS SUDDEN AND SEVERE. I WAS
BEDRIDDEN FOR ALMOST EIGHT HOURS AS MY BODY SEIZED ON
AND OFF. THE IMMEDIATE DIFFERENCE IS THAT NOW THERE ARE
LUMINOUS GOLD SPOTS IN THE BROWN OF MY IRIS. NONE OF
THE RATS EVER DEVELOPED THIS TRAIT, AND WE REMAIN UNSURE
OF ITS SIGNIFICANCE. ASHER DAWSON ALSO TOOK THE SERUM
IN THE SAME RATIO AT THE SAME TIME WITH SIMILAR RESULTS.
HOWEVER, HE APPEARS TO HAVE DEVELOPED A SUPERNATURAL
MENTAL ABILITY THAT WAS NOT ANTICIPATED.**

THE ABILITY REQUIRES LITTLE THOUGHT AND CONCENTRATION

FROM ASHER HIMSELF, BUT HE CAN FORCE ANOTHER INDIVIDUAL TO MOVE AT HIS COMMAND. IT IS A VERY INTRIGUING PROSPECT. ONE WE WILL CONTINUE TO STUDY.

AS FAR AS LAB WORK, BOTH OUR WHITE BLOOD CELL COUNTS HAVE INCREASED BY 37%. THIS IS UP 2% FROM YESTERDAY. SO, PROMISING RESULTS SO FAR! WE ARE EXCITED AND HOPEFUL THAT WE WILL BE ABLE TO HELP SO MANY IF THIS CONTINUES TO WORK FOR BOTH OF US.

Darin couldn't let Naomi and Marcella sleep anymore. For the first time in a very long time, Darin didn't know what to do.

37

NAOMI

KNOCK, KNOCK, KNOCK.

Naomi rolled over and called, "Just a second." She looked over at the clock in the room and realized she had already slept most of the day. She was so exhausted in her bones that she collapsed in the first bedroom Darin showed her upstairs. She threw on the gray sweats and plain black shirt Darin left for her and opened the door to find Marcella.

"Hey, I know you're tired, but Darin decoded a few of the videos and wants us to watch them."

Naomi followed Marcella down the spiral staircase and into the living area. Together, they watched the two decoded videos.

Once the second video finished, an eerie silence settled among them—a pit formed in Naomi's stomach.

Marcella spoke first. "Are the other senators involved?"

Darin was standing behind the other couch, watching. He looked at Marcella and shook his head. "I don't know. You've seen as much as I have, but there are over three hundred videos, Marcella. What else is on here? We don't have time to go through every single video and document—which would take days, potentially weeks, to decode—then we would need to sort through it all. We don't have time for that; we need to get Luna and locate Ethan and Ella. Beyond that, if the First Citizen even suspects Luna knows any of this, she will kill Luna."

Naomi asked, "Do we even know where Luna is? They could have easily moved her to another facility by now. I'm not saying I want to wait—because I don't—but we would be going in blind." Naomi couldn't bear the idea of losing Luna, or of the First Citizen torturing Luna like she did to Naomi, but they needed a secure rescue and escape plan; jumping in headfirst was foolish.

Ping!

Without speaking, Marcella grabbed the keyboard and handed the keyboard to Darin. The following video was paused on an image of Kent.

Darin didn't say anything as he leaned over the couch, grabbed his keyboard, and pressed play.

TIMESTAMP:
DAY 51 OF THE 1ST QUARTER - YEAR 156 OF THE NEW REPUBLIC.

MY NAME IS KENT BARDIN. IT IS DAY 51 OF THE 1ST QUARTER - YEAR 156 OF THE NEW REPUBLIC. AND, WELL, THIS SUCKS, BECAUSE IF YOU'RE WATCHING THIS. I'M DEAD.

LUNA, SELFISHLY, I HOPE YOU FIND THIS FIRST, BECAUSE I WANT YOU TO HEAR THIS FROM ME, NOT SOMEONE ELSE. THERE IS SO

MUCH OUR PARENTS KEPT FROM BOTH OF US, BUT EVEN MORE THEY KEPT FROM YOU, SIMPLY BECAUSE YOU DID NOT CHOOSE THIS. THEY WANTED YOU TO MAKE YOUR OWN CHOICE. PLEASE BE AWARE THAT THIS REMAINS YOUR CHOICE—EVEN WITH ALL THE INFORMATION I'M ABOUT TO SHARE—YOU GET TO DECIDE WHETHER YOU WANT TO BE PART OF THIS FIGHT. AND IF YOU DO NOT, PLEASE ENSURE THIS DRIVE REACHES DARIN. I DON'T HAVE THE SKILLS TO DECODE MOST OF WHAT IS ON THE DRIVE. WHAT I HAVE BEEN ABLE TO DO HAS RAISED MORE QUESTIONS THAN IT HAS ANSWERED.

MOST IMPORTANTLY, THE FIRST CITIZEN IS NOT WHO YOU THINK SHE IS. SHE WAS PART OF A GROUP OF HUMAN SCIENTISTS TRYING TO CREATE A GENETIC ENHANCEMENT THAT WOULD NOT ONLY CURE TERMINAL AILMENTS BUT ALSO PREVENT FUTURE DISEASES.

OUR PARENTS WERE PART OF THIS GROUP OF SCIENTISTS; THEY WORKED DIRECTLY WITH THE FIRST CITIZEN TO CREATE THE SERUM. YES, THEY LIED TO US. THEY WERE SIGNIFICANTLY OLDER THAN WE THOUGHT. THEY WERE NOT HIRED WITHIN THE LAST FIFTY YEARS TO WORK AS SCIENTISTS FOR THE NEW REPUBLIC—THEY WERE SOME OF ITS FOUNDING MEMBERS. I AM NOT SURE WHY OR WHEN THEY DEFECTED; I ONLY KNOW THAT THEY DID, EVENTUALLY HELPING THE RESISTANCE FROM INSIDE THE NEW REPUBLIC.

AS FAR AS THE ACTUAL GENETIC ENHANCEMENT, THE DETAILS ARE LIMITED, BUT WHAT I DO KNOW IS, THE SCIENTISTS, WHICH INCLUDED OUR PARENTS, WERE EVENTUALLY SUCCESSFUL AFTER TESTING IT ON THEMSELVES.

AFTER ITS SUCCESS, THEY IMMEDIATELY PRESENTED THEIR FINDINGS TO THE DEMOCRACY OF ARELIA'S RULING BODY, REQUESTING A WIDESPREAD AND RAPID RELEASE, AS IT COULD POTENTIALLY HEAL MANY. THE RULING BODY VOTED, AND IN A RARE OCCURRENCE, IT WAS A UNANIMOUS 'NO'. THE RULING BODY BELIEVED THE SERUM WAS RUSHED AND THAT MORE HUMAN TRIALS WERE NEEDED.

THE SCIENTISTS BELIEVED THEY KNEW BETTER.

THEY PLANNED THE EXPLOSION AND CONTAMINATION OF THE WATER SUPPLY AT EACH WATER TREATMENT FACILITY. WHEN THE DEMOCRACY OF ARELIA CRUMPLED, KASANDRA SANDERS APPOINTED HERSELF FIRST CITIZEN AND SENATOR ASHER DAWSON AS HER SECOND. THEY CREATED A NEW GOVERNMENT, THEY BELIEVED WOULD BE BETTER.

THOSE WHO REMAINED HUMAN REVOLTED, AS YOU KNOW. WHEN THE FIRST CITIZEN AND SENATOR DAWSON REALIZED THE HUMANS WOULD NOT BE CONTROLLED, WOULD NOT WILLINGLY ALLOW THE WATER TO REMAIN CONTAMINATED, AND WOULD FIGHT EVERY STEP OF THE WAY, THE FIRST CITIZEN DECIDED TO ENSLAVE THEM, ENSURING THE GENETICALLY ENHANCED BEHTARI WOULD ALWAYS EXIST.

I AM NOT SURE WHO ELSE WAS IN THE GROUP, BUT THOSE FOUR HAVE BEEN CONFIRMED ON MULTIPLE DOCUMENTS. I HAVE BEEN TRYING TO PERFORM ADDITIONAL RESEARCH, BUT IT HAS PUT ME IN JEOPARDY, AND I NEED TO ACT QUICKLY.

THERE ARE TWO OTHER THINGS I HAVE TO TELL YOU. AND TWO THINGS I NEED YOU TO DO FOR ME, PLEASE.

FIRST, THE ORIGINAL GROUP OF SCIENTISTS ALL HAVE UNNATURALLY LONG LIFESPANS DUE TO THE HIGH CONCENTRATION OF CONTAMINATION THEY INGESTED DURING THEIR TRIAL. THIS IS THE REASON THE FIRST CITIZEN HAS HELD ONTO HER POWER FOR SO LONG.

I DON'T KNOW HOW LONG THEY COULD LIVE, BUT I KNOW THE FIRST CITIZEN IS AT LEAST ONE HUNDRED NINETY-SIX YEARS OLD, ACCORDING TO THE NOTES I HAVE FOUND, WHICH ARE INCLUDED IN THIS DRIVE. THE FIRST CITIZEN WAS IN HER EARLY FORTIES WHEN

THE CONTAMINATION HAPPENED.

SENATOR ASHER DAWSON IS NOT QUITE THAT OLD, HOWEVER, I'VE DEDUCED HE MUST BE OVER ONE HUNDRED SEVENTY, SINCE HE HELPED ESTABLISH THE NEW REPUBLIC, WHICH WOULD MEAN OUR PARENTS FALL SOMEWHERE BETWEEN THOSE AGES.

SECOND, YOU AND I HAVE STRONGER ABILITIES BECAUSE OF THE SERUM DOSAGE OUR PARENTS TOOK. OUR PARENTS STARTED TO RESEARCH IT, BUT THE STUDY WAS NEVER FINISHED BEFORE THEY DIED.

THIRD, TAKE EVERYTHING OUT OF YOUR APARTMENT THAT COULD BE REMOTELY TRACED BACK TO MOM AND DAD'S SCIENTIFIC WORK. IT ISN'T SAFE THERE. THE NEW REPUBLIC IS ACTIVELY LOOKING FOR THE ITEMS THEY WORKED ON—SPECIFICALLY, THE GOLD NECKLACE AND BRACELET THEY WORE.

FOURTH, THERE IS SOMETHING CALLED THE '800 PROJECT.' I CANNOT GO INTO TOO MUCH DETAIL, BUT YOU MUST EXPOSE IT. PLEASE. THE FACILITY WHERE THE 800 PROJECT INFORMATION IS BEING KEPT IS AN UNNAMED ISLAND NORTH OF ZUROS. ON THE GOVERNMENT MAPS, IT IS LABELED WITH A GAMMA RAY SYMBOL. TAKE DARIN, MARCELLA, AND WYATT. YOU WILL NEED THEM. YOU NEED TO GATHER AS MUCH INFORMATION AS POSSIBLE FROM THAT LOCATION AND EXPOSE WHAT THE NEW REPUBLIC IS DOING. MY UNDERSTANDING IS THAT IS WHERE THE PROPHET CHILDREN ARE HELD, BUT I CANNOT CONFIRM THAT.

LUNA, I LOVE YOU MORE THAN ALL THE STARS, MOON BUG. I AM SORRY I AM NOT THERE.

When the video stopped playing, Naomi realized she had tears rolling down her face, not from pity or sadness, but from a writhing pure rage. She couldn't begin to process the magnitude of this video. Everything she knew was built on lies. The First Citizen and the Senators were power-hungry snakes. They had created this entire government around themselves and a living hell for those who were deemed *less*, so they could elevate their own status. She felt like she was going to vomit.

Darin and Marcella were both frozen with shock. Darin looked like he might be sick. He was still staring at the screen wide-eyed and said, "Did you know?" Naomi wasn't sure if he was talking to her or Marcella, but she answered first, her voice filled with malice. "No. I didn't." Then, she asked, "Did you?"

Marcella still said nothing as Darin turned to look at Naomi. His face was almost contorted in anger. She could see the whites of his knuckles as he gripped the back of the couch and said, "No."

When Marcella finally spoke, her voice caught just enough that she had to restart and gain her composure. "Wh—Why did he keep this from us? Why not just tell us?"

Darin looked back at the screen, his eyes heavy with what looked almost like regret. "I don't know."

38

LUNA

LUNA TOOK A SHARP inhale.

She dozed off again. Time felt endless in this small black space. She was so exhausted, she felt it in her bones; she was also filthy and was sure she smelled of sweat and grime. At least they left her in the chair, which meant she finally had feeling back in her arms. She groaned, and she flexed her fingers, even though she was stiff and the ropes rubbed at her sore wrists, she couldn't deny that having the ability to move her hands easily felt wonderful. A stark contrast to how Luna's face felt.

Her left eye was swollen shut, and she knew she was bleeding inside her mouth, but she was pretty sure whoever had beaten her had split her cheek at some point, too, and she felt dried blood on her skin. She couldn't be sure how long it had gone on. The person who beat Luna never asked any questions. It seemed they found joy watching her cry out in pain, only wanting to hurt her.

Luna's body trembled with fear at the idea of his return. She forced herself to breathe, think logically. She knew he would come back; it was inevitable. She just needed to know what she would do when he arrived. She needed a way out—if she didn't, she knew he would kill her.

She tried to flex her ability again, testing whether she could feel anything. There was nothing; it felt almost as if there was a piece of her that was paralyzed, like a missing limb. She couldn't move, couldn't adjust, her clothes she had worn for three days, or was it two? She didn't care; she needed to get out. Her anxiety was going to crush her in this small space.

Panic.

She felt the old nemesis settling in. It came from the center of her chest and radiated outward, like a cancer, but she couldn't rid herself of it. At first, it felt like that part of her body was a boiling oil, so hot and painful, but spreading like liquid over her body.

Breathe... Breathe... Breathe...

In, one, two, three. Out, one, two, three. In one, two, three. Out, one, two, three.

She was almost chanting the word in her head, *breathe,* while she tried to count her breaths. She needed a plan, and to create any reliable plan, she needed all her strength, even if it was only scraps, to make something that would work. She just needed an opening so she could get out of this hellhole.

Before Luna had time to come up with a plan, she heard the cell door open.

Two figures entered. One went around the back of the chair, and, without warning, a black bag was put over her head. The second figure unbound her ankles from the chair, only to replace the bindings with new shackles that were connected, but far enough apart she could walk. They did the same with her hands, unbinding them from behind her back, only to put them in front of her and replace the bindings with new shackles.

They stood her up roughly, and her knees almost gave out. How long had she been sitting here? A few hours? A day? Did it matter at this point?

As they led her from the cell, Luna did her best to follow, but it was almost impossible without her vision. She could see some light through the bag, but nowhere near enough to be helpful.

After a few minutes, they came to an abrupt stop. One turned Luna roughly and pushed her into a wall. Luna could hear as they were moving her chains around again, the clanking so loud above the silence.

When they finally stopped touching the chains, Luna assumed they were going to walk again and tried to move her feet. Luna quickly realized that she was going nowhere. She had no give in her hands or her feet. They were secured in front of her, with an inch or two of movement allowed in either direction.

She did not like being in this position: facing a wall, with her hands and feet shackled to the wall in front of her.

When the bag was finally taken off Luna's head, she blinked several times to let her eyes adjust. It took longer than she anticipated, after being in the dark for so long. Once Luna finally had her bearings, she was able to see the white tiles of the wall in front of her. She looked down at her hands and feet. There were brackets screwed into the wall, each with a circle attached to it that her chains were now connected to. She was literally not moving from this wall unless she could physically rip out these brackets.

Before she even attempted to pull on the brackets, Luna turned over her right shoulder to see where the two guards were, but she saw a human instead.

The human was in their full uniform, including their mask. As they approached Luna, their eyes were downcast. They carried scissors in their right hand.

Luna's heart raced, beating out of her chest. She whispered to the human, "Please."

The human made eye contact for the briefest moment before looking in the corner of the room.

Luna was no longer thinking clearly. Of course, there would be cameras everywhere. She would be foolish to attempt anything right now. Luna let her forehead rest against the tiles, no longer caring who was listening, and said, "Please. Do it."

They gently touched her forearm as they cut her mission clothing off her. She didn't even know if her friends found what they were looking for.

Was she the only one captured? Or was it everyone? She didn't know and had no way to find out. The human cut each article of clothing off with as much care and dignity as they could give Luna. When Luna looked at her soiled clothes in a heap on the floor, all she felt was shame.

She let her head drop to her bare chest, closing her eyes, but right before they were fully shut, Luna realized her necklace was gone. Her eyes flew back open, and panic overcame her immediately. She was not surprised the necklace was gone—of course it was gone. Someone must know it has resistant properties.

Then, Luna paused. The First Citizen gave her the necklace. Why would she give Luna the necklace if she knew it allowed the wearer to be resistant? Why, take it from her again now?

Luna allowed her mind to mull everything over while the human wiped her with a rough cloth dunked in ice-cold water. Luna knew the human was being as gentle as possible. They went carefully around Luna's wrists, ankles, and especially the left side of her face. She watched the human focus, trying to be thorough.

Luna was dried, then placed into a navy blue jumpsuit, with footwear of the same color but with rubber soles. While the human put her in the jumpsuit, the LEOs had to assist, so Luna was never completely unshackled from the wall. All the while, she continued to turn over her confusion with the necklace.

She hadn't known what it could do—maybe the First Citizen didn't either? So, giving it back to her wouldn't be completely unrealistic; it just made the First Citizen a bigger bitch than she already was. Still, Luna knew she was missing something.

They didn't bother with a bag as they walked Luna through the hallways. She must be going to a different area, or it was just a scare tactic. Luna made mental notes of their path—cracked tiles or identifying marks, a light with a blue paint dot on the frame's ring. She hoped it might be helpful to her plan, which didn't exist.

When they finally turned, the guards pulled her sharply to the left. One of them almost stepped on her foot, although he didn't seem to care. Once they rounded the corner, Luna took one step and stopped. Standing directly in front of her was Kasandra Sanders, the First Citizen of Arelia.

Luna froze, dread twisting a knot in her stomach, but she held the First Citizen's stare. The First Citizen wore a loose, flowing gray pantsuit with a dark green blouse underneath. Luna thought she looked thinner than the last time she saw her, but Luna was grateful she and her friends might be causing the First Citizen some stress. She worried what the First Citizen would do if she looked away from her glowing gold eyes.

She hadn't realized it at first glance, and even now, Luna was sure she must be seeing things. She blinked, hoping it was a trick of the eye, or some Illusion being used on her, but it wasn't. When she looked into the First Citizen's eyes again, Luna almost gasped, catching herself at the last moment. Her entire eye was gold—no pupil, no white. All. Gold.

What happened to her?

Inwardly, Luna was terrified; the First Citizen looked almost feral. Luna could sense the emotion behind them, though they held no depth.

Luna was not going to break eye contact with the First Citizen. She would not appear weak. Luna was immovable steel on the outside, but controlling her breathing was a battle within. This time, Luna was winning. She wasn't dissolving into panicked breathing; she didn't feel like she was dying. Was she scared? Absolutely. But Luna was in control of it—it was not in control of her. With that realization, she felt like she might have stood a little taller.

The First Citizen looked Luna up and down as her golden eyes took on a faint glow. A sneer crossed her face before she looked to the LEOs and said, "You are relieved. I will escort her back to her cell."

The LEO holding Luna's left shoulder replied formally. "We have been given direct orders to move her to a different location."

What are they talking about?

The First Citizen stared them down as her eyes somehow glowed with even more ferocity than before, all charm lost. Simply put, she was terrifying.

She hissed, "You can tell him that he does not give me orders." When the two LEOs didn't release Luna, the First Citizen said, "I assure you, she was properly injected this morning. Her ability is properly suppressed. She cannot harm me." Then the First Citizen shooed them away as if there were stray cats—an annoyance, but not an obstacle.

Luna wasn't quite sure why they hadn't obeyed her the first time. She ruled Arelia, and Behtari looked to her for guidance, ensuring human obedience.

Finally, the LEOs handed Luna's chains to the First Citizen as they walked past her and down the hallway, disappearing from view.

Luna listened as their steps receded and waited for the First Citizen to do something, but she didn't move; she stood there, listening. Her eyes were fixed ahead, as if she were waiting for something. Finally, the First Citizen yanked Luna's chains so hard she almost toppled over.

They were on the move. Almost like an afterthought, she looked at Luna and said, "Let's go." She pulled Luna along the hallways with urgency until they rounded a corner next to a darkened stairwell.

Luna did not want to know where it led, but before they took another step, the First Citizen stopped. She turned and looked at Luna, panic in her eyes. "You have to get out; you have to leave. I promised Daphne, I promised her. I tried, I did, but I can't do this anymore."

Luna tried to back away from the First Citizen; she was frantic, unhinged.

The First Citizen clutched Luna's hands, squeezing so hard that Luna was sure she would draw blood. Tears were rolling down her cheeks. "I promised her I would keep you safe, but I ran out of time. It wasn't supposed to go this far," she said, and her lip wobbled.

Luna flinched, trying to avoid the First Citizen's deranged expression.

"Look. At. Me." The First Citizen's tone was stern.

Luna did as she was asked, but when her eyes met the First Citizen's, she knew she had made a mistake. The First Citizen stared blankly past Luna, at nothing, with a maniacal grin on her face. She was partially slumped, but then, as she grabbed at her hair, which was barely long enough to grasp, she pulled it out in large chunks. In many places, she pulled so hard she began to bleed.

Then, the First Citizen stood up straight, turned, and walked straight to Luna, standing only inches from her.

Luna's heart pounded.

The First Citizen gripped Luna's chin, tilting her face to look at her. The longer the First Citizen's hand remained in contact with Luna's chin, the harder she squeezed. Soon, she was forcing Luna to move with her as she backed Luna into the wall. There was nowhere to go.

She stopped only a few inches from Luna and removed her jacket as if she were a snake, shedding its skin. She groaned in frustration, unable to free her arms from her coat. Her lips pulled back as she seethed through her teeth, still trying to wrench her arms from her jacket. Finally, she pulled out her too-thin and too-long arms, as if something had changed her on a biological level. "He used me, told me I was going to be the first, the best."

Tears streamed from her eyes, which were now glowing in earnest. She was truly a horror. Her chest cavity seemed to have shrunk to accommodate the longer limbs, but it appeared her limbs had also grown slightly in length.

At such an odd proportion, Luna wasn't sure how she hadn't noticed the First Citizen's neck was too long and her ribcage too round.

Her eyes were so bright now that they hurt to look at. The First Citizen looked down at Luna's neck, tracing her skinny, long finger along Luna's collarbone. Her finger felt like it was made of ice. It was so cold, it almost felt as if she were burning.

Then, without warning, the First Citizen grabbed Luna's neck with her hand. Her palm was smaller now too, to accommodate longer fingers. She didn't even need a second hand to envelop Luna's neck fully. The First Citizen squeezed while she whispered, "He took it, he knew. I tried to get it away from him, told him it was lost. He didn't believe me."

Luna finally could barely breathe as she choked out, "What are you talking about?"

The First Citizen, now sobbing, released Luna, but was no longer able to control her volume.

"Don't you get it? This wasn't me!" she gestured to her eyes, her arms. "I didn't do this! I was his test subject. I was willing at first, but when I started changing, I refused. He forced me over, and over, and over again." Then, as if the stars aligned, Luna saw over the First Citizen's shoulder, Milo Winton, the Resistance Leader, peering out from the stairwell, his finger to his lips, asking Luna to be quiet.

His silver hair hung in his face, a stark contrast against his deep amber skin, his honey-colored eyes bright and alert. He was utterly silent as he crept around the doorframe. The First Citizen was so loud as she spoke, she didn't hear him approaching.

"LOOK AT ME!!" the First Citizen screamed in Luna's face again.

Luna could have gotten herself and Milo killed if the First Citizen had realized he was here.

She couldn't bring herself to do it; Luna couldn't look at the First Citizen. She couldn't look at the distorted limbs, glowing eyes, and rounded ribcage. With her gaze averted, she could still see Milo growing closer out of the corner of her eye. He was dressed in a dark green and black uniform, which stood out against his silver hair. He was only a few paces away now. Luna just needed a little more time.

The First Citizen, distracted within her own misery, was still oblivious to Milo's presence. Her hands shook as she pet Luna's face while saying, "I'm so sorry. I tried to protect you. I tried to help you. I never wanted this. I wanted—" With a bone-splintering *crack*, Milo Winton snapped First Citizen Kasandra Sanders's neck.

Milo did not give the Former First Citizen a second glance before stepping over the body. Luna briefly glanced down at her body, her neck turned at a grotesque angle, her eyes and mouth still open.

Milo then said, "That was a little too close for my taste." Without breaking Luna's gaze, a strange smile crossed his face. He looked like a child who had a secret he was excited to share. "Luna Bardin, I would like you to meet some dear friends of mine. You can come out now."

His smile turned to pure mirth as the two LEOs who were originally escorting her emerged from the same stairwell. "Now, will you please escort Ms. Luna Bardin to her new cell?" Milo asked them.

They nodded before striding toward Luna and picking up her shackles.

Luna didn't understand. Milo was helping her; he was going to get her out. When she opened her mouth to speak, Milo bent down to whisper against her ear, "Oh, that reminds me. Luna, you seem to be healing well from our last session." Milo traced the left side of her face with his eyes, following the bruises. Then, he softly touched her cheek with the back of his hand.

She flinched. Luna tried to control herself, but she was shaking. Milo pulled away from her ear, but now he had boxed her in. One arm was on either side of her, and his face was only inches from hers when he continued. "It seems that we have a bit to discuss. I look forward to seeing you soon. Do enjoy your new accommodations, the view is stunning."

Luna's blood turned to ice. Everything she knew was a lie.

Milo Winton, leader of the Resistance, had been controlling the entirety of Arelia from the shadows.

He was the leader of the Resistance for three decades. How much of that time had the First Citizen been under his thumb?

Luna's mind tumbled over itself. The First Citizen knew her mother and had promised Daphne she would try to protect her daughter. The First Citizen had given her the gold necklace and bracelet. She had to have known intimate details about the explosion and was trying to protect Luna and Kent because of the promise she made to her mother. Luna was struck with the love and sadness that filled her. How had someone, like this, been so close to her mother to make this promise?

More puzzle pieces clicked into place. Milo was aware of the mission to the state building. They fed him every single detail of their plan and likely ran multiple scenario plans by him. He had ideas and countermeasures for everything. Probably so he could plan exactly what to do. That was how she got caught; they knew she was coming, and they were prepared for her.

As the LEOs escorted her to her new cell, they ascended two flights of stairs to what had previously been a lobby, and smelled of the ocean. Where was she? This wasn't the state building. As the LEOs guided her through the space, she looked out the windows as soon as she could see more clearly. As she looked out the glass windows, all she could see was miles and miles of ocean.

39

DARIN

DARIN WOKE THE NEXT morning feeling groggy and emotionally hungover. Kent's video was almost too much to bear, too much to process after everything that happened. Darin's entire world had turned upside down.

After the video finished, Marcella, Naomi, and he agreed to reach out to Milo to determine the best course of action. They couldn't stay in Darin's house in Solles. It was minimally protected, and they were lucky that no one had found them yet, but Darin knew it was a matter of time.

As Darin slowly walked downstairs, he found a spare burner holo in the junk drawer in his kitchen. Darin quickly booted it, connected it to his encrypted server, and messaged Milo to call him. The message would go straight to Milo's holo, but through the encrypted server, no one would be able to trace it.

Milo didn't answer the first, second, or third time Darin messaged that morning, which was unlike him, but Darin figured he was busy. Darin concluded that this was a situation where Darin would need to ask for forgiveness later. He already wasted the morning waiting for Milo; he couldn't waste any more time.

Darin already spoke to Marcella and Naomi about his plan for today. The next step was to go to Luna's apartment and get everything he possibly could that was related to her parents and the group of original scientists who created the serum.

They all agreed Darin would go to Luna's apartment alone. Even though it was risky, Darin was the only one who could project an Illusion over himself, distorting his features enough not to be recognized.

Darin took the underrail directly to Luna's, avoiding cameras at any cost. He dressed in dark jeans, a black hoodie, and wore a black backpack. Darin also made sure the hoodie was drawn up over his head the entire time, to obscure his face as much as possible. It was a little warm to be so covered, but Darin couldn't risk it.

As Darin arrived at Luna's apartment building, he made sure no one was around to see him pick the lock to the back door. Darin knew that the door would not be the issue; it was rarely guarded, but always locked, and the lock was a simple mechanism that took Darin approximately thirty seconds to unlock.

Inside the building, Darin locked the door behind him and made his way to the elevator. He pressed the button for the sixth floor, leading to Luna's apartment. Darin had only been in her apartment a handful of times over the last few weeks, and while he knew the layout, he didn't know where she kept anything that would be putting off a frequency. So Darin had been up most of the night creating a spectrum analyzer, which was now in the backpack he carried.

The analyzer wasn't anything fancy—more like a metal detector that would beep when held near something giving off a frequency. Darin would have loved to create a more accurate spectrum analyzer capable of detecting frequency levels, but there wasn't enough time. The only other thing in the backpack was Darin's specialty lock pick kit, especially since he hadn't picked *this* door before.

Once Darin was outside Luna's door, he slung off his backpack, took the lockpick out, and went to work. The lock wasn't complicated, but Darin was nervous, and his palms were sweating. When the lock finally gave, Darin let himself into the apartment, locking the door behind him. He only had a few minutes before he would need to leave. He took all the necessary precautions—turning off cameras in the apartment building, but they would soon come back on. He didn't need any LEOs tailing him.

Darin set the backpack on the kitchen counter, grabbed the spectrum analyzer, and set to work. Looking around the apartment, he suddenly felt his plan deflate. Luna was very organized and tidy, but Darin didn't realize how many small decorations she had placed around the house. This was going to take more time than he had.

As Darin scanned the kitchen, he quickly found a gold cat with a moving paw that set off the spectrum analyzer so loudly that he frantically turned it off, fearing someone in the building would hear it. Darin gently wrapped the cat in one of Luna's dish towels—he didn't think she would mind—and placed it in his backpack before swinging the bag back onto his shoulder.

Next, Darin moved to the bedroom, he turned on the spectrum analyzer again, only to be met with the loud beeping again. "Son of a biscuit!" Darin mumbled under his breath; he hadn't installed a volume control on the damn analyzer. He covered the speaker from which the beeping was coming, attempting to muffle it while he searched for the item causing the analyzer's overzealous beeping. Darin located it on Luna's bedside table—a white crystal pyramid, which was quickly secured in the backpack.

Once Darin was done in the bedroom, he turned to leave. For the cubes to work, they had to be triangulated, so he knew the third item wouldn't be in her bedroom. When he was almost ready to switch the analyzer off, it gave off one beep, paused, and then gave another.

Something else was in this room. Darin opened the drawer of Luna's bedside table and found nothing. He threw back the covers on the bed, but no luck. Darin sighed in frustration, letting the analyzer rest at his side. As soon as the analyzer was pointed at the floor, the beeping became frantic.

Darin looked at the carpet-covered floor. Darin quickly got to his knees, pulling the rug away from the floor. Clearly, someone had done this before.

Under the rug was a small door with a notch large enough to put a finger in and open it. Darin opened the door to a black duffel bag. Placed gently on top was the matching gold bracelet to Luna's necklace.

Darin didn't waste any more time. He grabbed the bracelet and the duffel, swinging it over his shoulder next to his backpack. Darin was immediately shocked at how heavy the duffel was, but he didn't have time to go through it. Next, Darin put the bracelet on his left wrist, hoping not to set off the analyzer, and ran out to the living room to search for the last item that would hold the third cube.

With extreme reluctance, Darin turned the analyzer back on and swept it around the living space. The analyzer went wild at a pear-shaped river rock on Luna's yellow table. Darin turned the analyzer away to stop its incessant beeping.

This thing is worse than my last boyfriend.

When he picked up the pear and couldn't help but smile, he had gotten everything he came for and more. He went to turn off the analyzer, but it started beeping frantically again. Darin cursed loudly, switching the damn thing off and looking around the room. Finding nothing of interest, he sighed, cursing every deity he could think of, and with extreme reluctance switched the analyzer back on.

The analyzer was eerily silent as he slowly scanned the living space.

EEEEEEEEEE!

When he reached the faded yellow coffee table again, the tone became constant. Darin quickly turned the analyzer off before approaching the table.

A vase sat on the yellow coffee table, holding a delta lily dipped in resin to preserve it. Darin looked back at the analyzer with a crease forming in his brows. Why did it go berserk over the flower? As much as Darin wanted to open that can of mice, he didn't want to waste more time.

He didn't allow himself to relish his success. He quickly left the apartment, locking the door with a spare key he found in a bowl in the kitchen. Only once he was back in his own house did he breathe a sigh of relief.

40

LUNA

LUNA HADN'T SEEN MILO in days. She knew he would come for her, but the waiting, not knowing when, was a mental torture she hadn't known existed before. Every time her cell door opened, fear coiled in her being, and her adrenaline spiked. Every time a LEO took her somewhere, there was an underlying fear that she was being taken to Milo.

Usually, when she was forced to leave her cell, she would be brought to have her blood drawn or a new scan of her brain. No one talked much around here, but when they did, she overheard, "...because she's Signalborn," and "She's of the Originals." Luna knew she was Signalborn; every Behtari in her generation was, but she'd never been called an Original before. It didn't matter—she wanted to scream every time someone talked about her as if she were not there. As if she were not breathing in front of them. She was a personal lab rat for whatever purpose Milo deemed fit.

When Luna was brought in for another blood draw, she stopped resisting. It was pointless to resist the LEOs and medical personnel. Anytime Luna attempted to resist, they would sedate her, and she woke up in her cell with a bandage on her arm. So she went willingly, learning the building's hallway network and trying to figure out a way out.

Her chains clattered against the floor as they walked past an open window that overlooked the ocean. Luna paused, savoring the smell of salt over the sterile smell of this place. She closed her eyes only briefly, hearing the angry crash of waves against the cliff face on which the building stood. Only to get a shove in the back—an order to keep moving, which she obeyed.

Back in her cell, she curled against the wall. She was able to see out through the plate-glass window to the ocean below. She knew the building was sitting atop the cliff, but from Luna's cell, she could see only the waves below.

Luna then lay on the cold metal slab, meant to be a bed, and waited. Waited for sleep to take her or to be summoned again.

Click.

Her cell door. It was being opened. She stood immediately.

Another thing she learned was that the LEOs hated dealing with an unwilling specimen. So instead of being beaten, she knew it would be better to stand. Better to learn. Better to play the part, pretend, go along until she could have the upper hand.

One grain of sand.

She only needed to wait till she had the upper hand, even for a moment. That was not going to be today.

Ice filled her veins when Milo came into view.

Milo swept into the room, oozing charm that didn't meet his eyes. He wore a black t-shirt, and perfectly pressed black pants, with black shoes and a black belt.

She remained in her navy blue jumpsuit and matching footwear.

Luna felt frozen in place; she couldn't move. She knew this was coming but didn't know when.

Milo looked at Luna then and tutted. "Luna, darling, I am here to negotiate." Milo then waved to the door as a very reluctant chef came in with a cart that was, in fact, a table set for two.

A LEO followed directly behind, bringing Milo a chair to sit in.

As Milo sat, he said to Luna, "Please, no need to stand. Sit." He gestured to the metal slab behind her, a cruel smile twisting across his lips.

Luna knew better than to disobey right now; she needed to outsmart him, she had to beat him at his own game. So, if he believed her amiable for now, she would have a better shot, and she knew it.

The chef uncovered both plates, revealing a beautiful pasta dish with Alfredo sauce, chicken, and spinach, accompanied by buttered garlic bread on the side—one of Luna's favorite dishes. She did not take her eyes off the food as water was poured for them.

Milo dismissed the staff.

They did not close the door. Two LEOs blocked the doorway; should she even attempt to escape.

Milo did not wait for Luna before he took a bite of his own food. Then, with a wink, he reached across the small space to grab a bite off her own plate. "See?" he asked as if she were a picky child who needed to be convinced to eat. "Nothing wrong with it at all—I am not trying to poison you; there are much easier ways to do that. As I said before, I am here to negotiate."

Luna said nothing.

"Let's play a game, shall we?" Milo suggested. "You ask me a question, I will answer truthfully, and in turn, I will ask you a question, which you will answer truthfully."

Luna remained silent. How was she going to play this? She felt as if she didn't have any sensitive information Milo didn't already know, but clearly that wasn't the case if he was here. He thought she knew something.

One grain of sand.

She could be the grain of sand if she could point him in the wrong direction or even delay him in finding Naomi or her friends, it would be worth it. So, Luna played the game. She took her fork and slowly twirled the pasta around her fork before placing it in her mouth.

Milo's eyes watched her every move. "You first."

"Am I going to leave here alive?" Luna asked.

Milo's eyes betrayed a slight hint of annoyance before he sighed. "It is unlikely, but please, be more specific with your questions, child. Now, where is your father's gold bracelet?"

Luna blinked. *That's what this is about? The bracelet?* "In my apartment," she answered softly. She wondered if she could get away with vagueness. The tension between them pulled tight, as if it were a rope fraying in the middle.

Milo's anger visibly spiked, but he steeled himself before saying, "What is interesting is that I have been to your apartment, and it seems someone has already collected that item, amongst others. I would like to know where it is *now*."

It was Luna's turn to blink in surprise. "I don't know," she said softly.

Milo slammed his hands on the table. His eyes were glowing, just as the First Citizen's used to. It was only a second before they returned to normal. Then, he wiped his hands off with the napkin placed on the table. "Apologies, sometimes my temper gets the best of me these days. Of course, you wouldn't know. You have been here." He gestured to the area around them.

"Where is 'here'?" Luna asked, just as Milo was about to put another bite of pasta in his mouth.

He stopped. As his eyes met Luna's, he said, "This is Gamma Island, off the coast of Zuros. It is where the New Republic's—well, let's call them scientific endeavors—take place."

Luna knew at that moment that she would never leave this place. She was on an island off the coast, and there was no way she would ever leave without his consent. Before Milo could ask another question, one of the LEOs came in and whispered something into Milo's ear.

Milo nodded in understanding, while the LEO retreated to the doorway. Milo then looked at Luna and said, "Well, it appears this must be cut short. And while you have been cooperative, you haven't been helpful, which is a shame." Without warning, Milo took the serrated knife on the left side of his plate and drove it into the flesh of Luna's right thigh.

Luna screamed in agony.

"Now," Milo continued, "I do hope you will realize that next time: Cooperation does not only mean honesty, but it also means helpfulness." As he turned to exit the room, he said to the LEOs standing guard. "Take the cart and the knife," as he gestured to the knife in Luna's thigh.

"Be sure it does not become infected; if that is a possibility, handle it."

Luna clutched her thigh; the knife was buried to the hilt. Tears fell down her face from the sheer agony, and when the LEO walked over to Luna—a feral grin on his face—she knew what was coming next.

The LEO bent down, gripping the knife—still lodged in her thigh—roughly, and twisted before removing it from her thigh.

She screamed again before she passed out.

Four Days Later

Luna's leg still throbbed occasionally from the stab wound she received four days ago. Milo sent someone to stitch her leg several hours after he stabbed her. Luna knew the stitches hadn't been for her benefit, but to ensure she could still function as their lab rat and the wound would not become infected.

As Luna sat, curled into herself on the metal slab of a bed, she saw something out of the corner of her eye from her window. Luna sprang up to check she wasn't imagining things.

A small boat bobbed up and down in the water. It was located off the coastline, near the cliffs. The person piloting the vessel must have entered the bay to escape the waves. Luna saw boats come and go from the facility before, bringing goods or shipping things out, but those were usually larger. This vessel was significantly smaller.

Luna was about to walk away from the window when she saw someone come out of the cockpit. A woman with short silver hair, then two others, both with dark hair, one male and one female.

Naomi, Darin, and Marcella. Luna raised her fists to the plate glass, banging and screaming. Screaming for them to leave, to go. Her screams were so full of sadness and heartache that she felt as if she was being ripped in two. Her vocal cords were on fire as she tried and tried to get their attention, but she was too far away; they couldn't hear her or see her.

The tears came then, in a hot flood down her face. Luna didn't want them here—they were in so much danger and clearly didn't know what they were doing.

Without warning, a hand gripped Luna's left shoulder.

Luna stiffened, fear coursing through her body. Tears continued to stream down her face.

Milo Winton stood behind her. He was so close she could feel heat coming from his body. Milo then bent down so his mouth was next to Luna's ear and whispered. "My dear, you are lucky no one is here. You would have disturbed the others." He then looked out the window and saw the vessel, cocking his head slightly so he was almost touching Luna. "Oh, I have been waiting for them, Luna. You see, I need to eradicate the ants before I have an infestation. You understand, of course."

Then Milo straightened. He grabbed Luna's arm roughly as he led her out of the cell. "Let's go watch the show, shall we?"

Milo put shackles on Luna's hands, securing them in front of her body, but not her feet. He worked quickly, careful not to dirty his gray slacks or white button-down shirt. He led Luna to a part of the building she had never been in before.

As they walked through the various hallways, she realized there were no additional staff. No LEOs, doctors, or administrative personnel. She wanted to ask Milo about it, but fearful of the answer and his rage, she kept her mouth shut.

Milo led her down into a tunnel system that reminded her of the tunnel that led out of Solles, but they weren't quite the same. The floor was stone instead of metal, but it had the same lighting and similar wiring as the one that led out of Solles.

Luna felt the temperature drop the further they descended into the tunnel. She didn't know where Milo was taking her, but she knew she was too valuable for Milo to kill. Despite that, it didn't mean he wouldn't try to break her.

They made a couple of turns before he led them to a room full of monitors. There were cameras across the property. A few were turned off or not functioning, but most were up and producing a live feed.

Luna realized Milo could see everything that happened in the building and on the island. One screen in particular caught Luna's attention. It looked like a room full of large tubes, each big enough to fit a person, and down the center were *hundreds* of delta lilies.

Milo noticed her interest. "Ah, yes. That is my favorite room. It was one of mine and Kasandra's best ideas together, if I do say so myself. Unfortunately, most of those subjects didn't survive, which was truly a pity. We have expanded the operation, of course. Before the First Citizen's untimely demise, she was the prototype for the chip at the base of the spine, for compliance. Of course, that is only for the enslaved who refuse to bend, but you know all about that, don't you?" Milo was enamored with himself, looking around the vacant space.

Luna spoke before she could stop herself. "What are you talking about?"

Milo's reflection in one of the unused screens darkened as a sinister smile crept across his lips. "Oh, you don't know about this little project, do you? How much did Kent truly keep from you?"

Before Luna could even think of how to answer, Milo waved her off.

"This is where the 800 Project started. I was one of the original test subjects. At the time, I was human and had been administered enough serum to force the body to accept the gamma waves and become Behtari. The original idea was to force the brain to gamma waves of 800Hz, but it was quickly realized that it could be so much more than that. Even Behtari themselves can become better, become more. The Prophets' children are the best specimens. Their brains are still so malleable. The enslaved children are the test subjects now. After we had too many willing test subjects die, we went about things a bit differently, more discreetly. What you see here is the first version. We now have a better facility, capable of doing so much more. Of course, who wouldn't want to be superior? To have more abilities?"

Milo had such pride, but Luna thought she might be sick.

He turned to her, caressing her still slightly bruised cheek. Luna had to fight not to flinch from his touch. When he spoke next, his voice was low and rough—it made Luna's skin crawl. "If that is something you want, I could give it to you. You would only have to ask."

Luna turned to face him, watching a smug satisfaction cross his features, when she spat in his face. "I am already more than I ever thought possible. Fuck you. You are a monster."

Luna watched Milo intently, waiting for him to do something—anything—but his eyes were fixed on the screen behind her. She turned around slowly and watched as her friends walked into the room with the large tubes, right into the trap Milo set for them.

"Now, for the fun," Milo said with malicious delight, as he flipped a switch on the board in front of her.

Luna watched—panic flooding through her—as white gas flowed out of the vents in the room where her friends now stood.

41

DARIN

DARIN WAS PACING IN the living area of his home. He hadn't slept much over the last few days. He'd finally heard from Milo, but something wasn't right—Milo seemed distracted, off. Stranger still, the First Citizen hadn't been seen publicly in over four days. Darin felt a sense of dread to his core. He knew he didn't have the ability of a Prophet, but he trusted his instincts, and that was enough.

Naomi and Marcella were combing through all the files that had been uploaded over the last few days. There were still over five hundred files to go. Each one took at least an hour, sometimes more, depending on the length.

The most significant lead they had was regarding Naomi's siblings' location. They found Ella and Ethan's names on a document titled, *800 Project*, just as Kent said in the video. Once the document was decoded, it was a list of names and a location: Gamma Island. Darin didn't know where Luna was, so this was the next best plan.

He hoped Luna was too valuable to the New Republic to be discarded. She had not been publicly executed, which was a relief, but not knowing where she was, what was happening to her—Darin couldn't think about it too long.

Luna was brilliant and quick. Darin knew this. She would use every advantage she had. Even in their short time training at Omphalos, she caught on fast. He knew self-preservation would be her top priority, and he was thankful for it.

However, when Naomi, Marcella, and Darin attempted to devise a plan to retrieve Ella and Ethan, the situation became increasingly complicated by the second. They were able to find the island easily enough. Labeled with a Gamma sign on the map of Arelia. But, there was no record of this place, nor was there any information about anyone living on the island. The island seemed to be strictly inhabited by wildlife, not the New Republic.

The other problem was getting to the island. They couldn't get there from Solles. They would have to go to the coast of Omphalos and charter a boat, or travel to Zuros unseen and unnoticed. Both ideas seemed impossible, but as they approached day four in his house in Solles, Darin was going to lose his mind. He couldn't stay here, unable to help, and uncertain of what was happening. He kept having to rationalize with himself.

He needed a plan.

They needed a plan.

Darin knew he could not go in without any information—that would be like showing up to a gun fight with a tranquilizer. They might get lucky, but the odds were stacked against them. He paced in his living space until Naomi approached. Her silver hair was starting to grow out a bit. Her slightly upturned eyes crinkled at the edges as she smiled and then hugged him.

Darin held out his arms as if she were a cactus that might prick her. Was Naomi hugging him? What was going on? Had hell frozen over? Was he dreaming? Darin cleared his throat as he slowly brought his arms down to return the embrace with Naomi. "Um, not sure you know this, but you hate me."

Naomi sighed in irritation. "Sometimes I do hate you, but not always." Naomi held Darin a little tighter as she continued, "I know what it feels like to be lost in your own mind. Feeling like you are following a path to nowhere. When I am lost in my own thoughts, it helps knowing someone else is there. It helps me find my way, guides me out of the darkness, and leads me to the light. Sometimes, that means I need to follow someone else's light to find my own light again."

Darin couldn't help the tightness in his chest or the tears that rolled down his cheeks. This person was enslaved by his kind. This person—who was his friend—had now healed so much of herself that she was able to help him heal.

Darin closed his arms around his friend and wept.

Naomi held him the entire time.

42

NAOMI

NAOMI HELD DARIN WHILE his emotions flowed out of him. Naomi would be his light right now; she would help her friend. Naomi knew if their roles were switched, Darin would do the same for her.

After Darin calmed enough to let Naomi go, Marcella ushered him upstairs to rest.

Naomi let herself collapse on the couch. She could no longer deny her own exhaustion from the past week, feeling as if she could barely process new information at this point.

Even though Naomi was exhausted, she knew they were wasting too much time. They were spending too much energy waiting for the remaining files to be decoded. Something was wrong—Naomi knew it, she sensed it.

Naomi knew they were running out of time for Ella, Ethan, and Luna. Her heart cracked at the idea of never holding her brother or sister again, but Naomi felt it crack even further at the thought of never seeing Luna again. She couldn't explain the connection, the pull between them. Naomi knew it was there, and she knew Luna felt it, too—even if they both made every effort to push each other away in Omphalos.

When Marcella came back downstairs, she flopped on the couch across from Naomi, staring at the ceiling. "We cannot wait any longer. Darin finally agreed with me upstairs. We've waited too long as it is. We have to go and at least try to get Ethan and Ella. Hopefully, we will find more information on Luna once we're on the island, but we are quite certain your brother and sister are there. If nothing else, this is the same island Kent spoke of in the video. The 800 Project, Ethan, and Ella are the priority at this point. We cannot continue sitting here; we are sitting ducks for the New Republic."

Naomi felt her chest fill with a mix of relief and dread. She didn't know where this path would lead, but at least they all finally agreed to do something.

Marcella and Naomi let Darin rest the remainder of the day into the next morning, ensuring they both got a good night's rest as well. The three of them didn't have time to spare, but they also needed to be at their best.

When Naomi came down the stairs the next morning, the sun was not even up, but Darin had already powered up all three screens and was sifting through more documents that had been decoded the night before. Marcella had a steaming cup of coffee and was sitting on the floor in the living area. The coffee table was pushed to the side as Marcella stared at a map of Arelia on the floor, next to larger maps of Solles and Zuros.

Naomi went to the kitchen to pour herself a cup of coffee with cream and extra sugar, the same way Luna made it for her at the farmhouse. Her worry for Luna was so vast, at times she had trouble controlling it. Though it had only been days, it felt like a lifetime since they had seen each other, touched each other. Naomi closed her eyes, remembering how Luna's skin felt beneath her fingertips.

Stop it! Focus.

Naomi snapped her eyes open. She needed to stop her wandering mind. Her worry and longing would not fix this, and she knew it. She sipped the coffee, hot and sweet, hoping it would give her a little boost to help her friends come up with a plan.

Naomi returned to the living space and sat next to Marcella, waiting patiently for her to finish what she was doing before Naomi asked what the next steps were.

Once Marcella finished placing three more green dots on the map of Zuros, she pointed to them. "These are the three marinas in Zuros we could rent a boat from discreetly to get to the island. The island isn't far from Zuros, but it will take at least two hours to get there, depending on how choppy the waves are."

Naomi nodded, excitement rushing through her veins as she realized they were doing this.

Marcella then looked at Darin. "Any luck?"

Darin's face was pinched in concentration. "Don't talk to me, I'm focused."

Marcella rolled her eyes. "Darin, I need to know if I should wait for you or move to a different task."

Darin put in a few more keystrokes of code, then said, "That should do it." With that, the hacking system went to work.

Naomi looked between them. Confusion must have been written all over her face, because Darin gestured to the screens.

"This is hopefully going to give us access to a map of Gamma Island. Anything I found through the New Republic was encrypted." Darin shrugged. "I am not sure if it will work, but having a map of the island, even if we do not know the specific buildings, would be better than nothing. It will also help us to know where we should dock the boat."

Naomi nodded as she looked back at the maps. "How are we going to get to Zuros undetected?"

Marcella and Darin's features both dropped. "Honestly, we don't know," Marcella answered. "We are trying to figure out the best course of action, but we're going to need some help."

An idea came to Naomi. "What if we took the boat from Omphalos, sticking to the coast and then went across the Gamma Strait? I know they don't have an active port in Omphalos, but I am sure we could figure something out. The boating would take a lot longer, though, maybe a day? At least we wouldn't be unnecessarily exposed in Zuros?"

Darin's face broke into a grin. He looked at Marcella and said, "See? I knew she would help!"

Marcella threw her pen at Darin. "I never said she *wouldn't* help! I said she might not have a solution. Turn on your hearing aid, grandpa."

Darin smiled even wider now. Naomi knew Darin loved getting a rise out of Marcella; it seemed to be a strange hobby of his and Wyatt's. Darin clicked away at his keyboard again before saying, "Well, you know. The chicken in the bush is worth two eggs in the hand."

Marcella put her face in her hands and groaned loudly. "Darin, for tits' sake, please no more butchered proverbs."

Darin had a sly grin on his face as he shrugged. "No promises."

Marcella rolled her eyes again, handing Naomi another pen from the small pile next to her as they got back to work charting how they would boat to Gamma Island from Omphalos. Once Marcella and Naomi finalized the boat's route, it was time to return to Omphalos.

It hadn't taken long to pack everything. Darin already had an external hard drive for the ghost drive and his hacking software, so they could continue decoding the rest of the files.

Darin had been in touch with Wyatt and Acadia on and off, keeping them updated on their whereabouts and safety. So, when Darin reached out via the encrypted server this morning, asking Wyatt to meet them at the utility door, it was no surprise when a response came back in minutes. *I will be there.*

Although packing hadn't taken long, they were carrying so much more. Between Darin's external hard drive, the duffel bag from Luna's apartment full of bizarre knick-knacks, and each of their backpacks, they were all carrying much more than they came with. Marcella distributed the items from the duffel bag to evenly distribute the weight. As Marcella handed them out, Naomi noticed a toy cube puzzle in which all the colors had to match on a single side. Curiosity got the best of her. Naomi asked, "What are all of these?"

Marcella continued her task as she answered, "I won't know until I take them apart, but I am hoping that each contains one of the cubes Luna and Kent's parents made.

They emit a frequency that interferes with a Behtari's ability. Like the antennas at Omphalos, just on a smaller scale."

Naomi picked up the toy cube, immediately feeling a buzzing emanating from it. Not painful, but almost like a static charge. Naomi gently set the cube back down and helped Marcella distribute the remaining items among the three backpacks.

Getting out of Solles was a breeze compared to getting in. There was a sewer entrance almost directly outside of Darin's house, allowing them to reenter the sewer system and the tunnels easily. By the time they reached the utility door, it was after midday, and Wyatt was already waiting through the dense woods a mile away, as promised.

When they reached Omphalos, Wyatt didn't stop at the farmhouse; they went directly to the armory, where Acadia was waiting. Acadia ensured that whatever they hadn't brought back from Solles was replaced. In addition, Acadia set aside several extra knives and compact pistols for each of them, just in case.

Naomi, Darin, and Marcella emptied their backpacks of the knick-knacks from Luna's apartment, only bringing what would be needed to get to the island. Naomi gathered her new weapons and tools, securing them where she could on her body and placing any extra items in her backpack. That's when she overheard Wyatt and

Darin talking about the boat Wyatt secured. Something about how it had been obtained so quickly, and that the Resistance didn't usually have boats to spare. Naomi didn't think much of it—she was grateful they didn't have to wait.

Once everything was packed, it was already dark outside. They said goodbye to Acadia and Wyatt as Marcella started the small vessel's engine, and they rode out to sea.

43

DARIN

DARIN DID NOT LIKE sleeping on the boat. Frankly, Darin didn't like boats to begin with, and the rough waters in the open ocean made it even less enjoyable.

Darin stayed below deck most of the time, only coming up for fresh air when he felt particularly queasy. He was still sorting documents and videos from the ghost drive. He didn't want to risk missing something important, or a map if it had been decrypted.

He'd been unsuccessful in finding a map of Gamma Island, but he did find a blueprint of an old building on site, buried within the archived files of the New Republic. It may be the only building on the island. Once they got closer, Darin planned to release three MAVs he had reprogrammed to get a better idea of the island's layout.

Before they left Omphalos, Darin tried to reach Milo again, hoping he could help with a map, but no luck. Milo's lack of communication was agitating. Usually, when Darin needed Milo, Milo could sense it through his ability, mainly because it directly affected Milo. He didn't always get back to Darin right away, but he did get back to him within a few hours. It was almost as if Milo was deliberately ignoring Darin.

Darin felt even more perturbed when he heard Wyatt had apparently reached Milo earlier in the day to ask about chartering a boat for Darin, Marcella, and Naomi to get to the island. Milo agreed, saying he would have the boat to Omphalos within three hours, which surprised not only Darin but also Wyatt.

Usually, it took *days* for the Resistance to procure something of that nature, but Milo said someone owed him a favor and that the boat would be delivered immediately.

The boat was towed over by another slightly larger boat. Keys were exchanged quickly, and the tower sped off the way it had come. The boat was nothing fancy—a small deck area with a cockpit that contained two chairs. Below deck, there was a small kitchen with a folding table and two cabins toward the bow of the boat, each containing two beds.

Darin set up all his equipment on the small fold-out table and was sifting through files on his portable interface, which his system had finished decoding before they left. Without access to a server, he couldn't decode anything else, but there were plenty of files to read.

The task felt never-ending; most documents were nonsense lists of numbers, which Darin was sure meant something to someone, but without additional information, they meant nothing to him. After about an hour, he came across a document labeled *Test Subject 78: M.W.* As with all the other documents, he opened it to skim through it and see if there was anything worth noting. Darin's eyes went wide as he read.

TEST SUBJECT: ZU-554553-0613-78
NAME: MILO 'WINTON'
SPECIES: ENSLAVED/HUMAN
AGE: 52
DATED:
DAY 80 OF THE 3RD QUARTER—YEAR 28 OF THE NEW REPUBLIC

Darin didn't read any further, jumping up from the table and almost smashing his head on the low ceiling. He ran up to the deck where Marcella was teaching Naomi how to pilot the boat. He must have looked quite disheveled because they both looked at him with concern.

But Darin couldn't find the right words. All that came out was, "I can't—I don't—Fuck! I need you to see this."

Naomi and Marcella exchanged a puzzled glance, but didn't argue. Marcella shut off the engine, allowing the boat to drift along the now calm waves, and followed Darin down the stairs below deck. The three of them crowded around the screen. Marcella gasped, her hand flying to her mouth as they read in silence.

TEST SUBJECT: ZU-554553-0613-78
NAME: MILO 'WINTON'
SPECIES: ENSLAVED/HUMAN
AGE: 52
DATED:
DAY 80 OF THE 3RD QUARTER—YEAR 28 OF THE NEW REPUBLIC
-THE TEST SUBJECT HAS BEEN EXTREMELY WILLING TO PARTAKE IN THE STUDY IN AN ATTEMPT TO BECOME BEHTARI AFTER THE ORIGINAL WATER CONTAMINATION DID NOT AFFECT HIM.
-THE SUBJECT HAS TAKEN TWO ADDITIONAL CONCENTRATED DOSES OF SERUM WITH NO IMPROVEMENT. WE WILL ADMINISTER ANOTHER DOSE TODAY.

DATED:

DAY 82 OF THE 3RD QUARTER—YEAR 28 OF THE NEW REPUBLIC
-THE TEST SUBJECT STILL SHOWS NO CHANGE. WE ARE RELUCTANT TO ADMINISTER ADDITIONAL DOSING AS WE DO NOT KNOW HOW MUCH THE BODY CAN HANDLE.

-THE SUBJECT HAS SHOWN NO SIGNS OF SEIZURE OR FEVER.

DATED:

DAY 83 OF THE 3RD QUARTER—YEAR 28 OF THE NEW REPUBLIC
-THE TEST SUBJECT HAS AGREED TO AN INTRAVENOUS INJECTION OF A SMALLER DOSE OF THE SERUM AND WILL REMAIN ON SITE FOR OBSERVATION.

DATED:

DAY 84 OF THE 3RD QUARTER—YEAR 28 OF THE NEW REPUBLIC
-THE TEST SUBJECT'S HAIR HAS TURNED COMPLETELY SILVER FROM ITS ORIGINAL BROWN HUE. IN ADDITION, THE SUBJECT'S EYES ARE NO LONGER BROWN, BUT HONEY COLORED WITH GOLDEN FLECKS IN THEM.

-THE SUBJECT STILL SHOWS NO SIGNS OF FEVER, SEIZURES, OR BEHTARI ABILITIES.

DATED:

DAY 86 OF THE 3RD QUARTER—YEAR 28 OF THE NEW REPUBLIC
-THE TEST SUBJECT STILL SHOWS NO SIGNS OF FEVER, SEIZURES, OR ABILITIES.

-THE SUBJECT REQUESTED ANOTHER DOSE OF SERUM AND WAS DENIED. THE SUBJECT BECAME COMBATIVE, STRIKING MULTIPLE NURSES, ONE OF WHOM SUFFERED A CONCUSSION. THE SUBJECT HAS BEEN REMOVED FROM THE PROGRAM AND FACILITY.

DATED:

DAY 89 OF THE 3RD QUARTER—YEAR 28 OF THE NEW REPUBLIC
-OUR LABS WERE BROKEN INTO LAST NIGHT, SEVERAL BOXES OF SERUM ARE GONE, AND FOUR LEOS ARE DEAD. THEIR SKULLS FRACTURED IN MULTIPLE LOCATIONS, CAUSING TOO MUCH BRAIN TRAUMA TO SURVIVE.

-WE HAVE CAMERA FOOTAGE OF THE SUBJECT COMING IN WITH A CART STACKED WITH FOUR EMPTY BOXES. THE SUBJECT WHEELED IT TO THE STORAGE ROOM, WHERE HE FILLED EACH BOX AND THEN

INJECTED HIMSELF WITH THREE ADDITIONAL SERUMS.
-AFTER THE INJECTION, THE SUBJECT'S EYES GLOWED SO BRIGHTLY
THAT THEY BLINDED THE CAMERA BRIEFLY. WHEN THE CAMERAS
CAME BACK ONLINE, THE FOUR LEOs WERE DEAD. THE SUBJECT IS
GONE; WE HAVE NO FURTHER EVIDENCE OF THE SUBJECT.

Naomi slowly touched her short silver hair, eyes wide with dread. "Is that what they did to my parents?"

Marcella, who was still staring at the screen, answered quietly, "I don't know."

Darin didn't know what to say. Everything he knew about the Resistance fractured. He felt his soul fracture with it. His whole life had been built around the Resistance. What was he going to do?

The rest of the boat ride was silent until the island came into view the next morning.

44

NAOMI

DARIN DEPLOYED THE MAVs and concluded that the information they gathered was correct. The boat was steered toward a small opening one of the MAVs had found along a cliff face, directly below the only structure on the island.

As much as Naomi didn't want to admit it, it seemed the island was deserted. The MAVs had not detected a single life form on the island. They each kept their weapons drawn as they navigated the tunnel, but they encountered no guards, LEOs, staff, or anyone else. Naomi felt increasingly uneasy the farther they went.

They came to an open lobby area surrounded by windows that looked out over the cliffside and onto the miles of outstretched ocean. Everything around them seemed to be discarded—tables covered in dust, papers left strewn about on desks—as if someone had left in a hurry and not bothered to do anything before leaving.

Making their way through the building, they came across several open cells and checked each. None looked to have been occupied in some time. They searched the rest of the floor, finding no one. When they reached the other side of the building, they came to a flight of stairs that led down.

Darin took the lead, silently directing Marcella and Naomi to follow him down. As the three of them descended the stairs, they found no other rooms or entry points; instead, there were two large metal double doors at the bottom.

Marcella went first, weapons drawn as she scanned the area. Darin and Naomi followed closely behind, watching her six.

Marcella stopped.

Naomi turned to see what had happened, watching Marcella's hands fall to her sides.

"What is this?" Marcella whispered.

Naomi followed Marcella's gaze. In front of them were sixteen rows of human-sized tubes in the dimly lit room. Each was about eight feet tall and four feet in diameter. Some of the tubes were cracked open—whatever liquid they contained had long since dried—but the glass shards remained. Some still had figures in them. Naomi couldn't call them people, even though they seemed to have once been.

The rows were split down the middle, eight on each side, with two rows of delta flowers between them. The tubes stretched the entire length of the enormous room; they could have easily fit six vehicles side by side and front to back, with room to spare.

Naomi inspected the contents of the tubes again. The distorted features, the limbs that were too thin, too long. Mouths that were too wide. The figures were suspended in a liquid that preserved whatever was left of their bodies. There was no movement.

Naomi walked past Marcella, who seemed to be frozen.

Darin reached out, stopping her. "We don't know what is in the fluid, don't touch it."

Naomi nodded.

Together, Naomi and Darin passed Marcella, but Darin paused to whisper something in her ear.

Marcella nodded and followed behind Naomi, in front of Darin.

Naomi stopped at one of the broken tubes, careful to avoid any traces of the liquid. Peering inside the tube, she saw connections and various sensors, like the ones used on her in Omphalos to measure her brain activity. There was also—or at least what looked to be—a mouthpiece that came from the back of the wall of the tube.

Were people being kept alive in these?

Naomi stopped herself from going down that rabbit hole with her brother and sister. Ethan and Ella were clearly not here—they had been tricked or had outdated information. *Click.*

White gas began seeping into the room through vents around the chamber.

Within seconds of the white gas surrounding them, Darin and Marcella crumpled to the ground. Naomi ran to each of them, checking to ensure they were still breathing, and both had a steady pulse; thankfully, they both were fine.

She kneeled on the ground. The white gas plumed around her as she tried to figure out what to do. She couldn't pick them up, but she couldn't leave them, either.

Tap, tap, tap.

An audio system crackled to life, and the sound reverberated through the space. Behind her, above the double metal doors, a glass booth that lit up from inside. There, overlooking the room, was Milo Winton, holding a gun to Luna's head.

"Well, hello, Naomi. I will say, I was not expecting *you*. You are indeed resistant to the gas. Very interesting."

Naomi stood with purpose, staring back at him. She would not give him the satisfaction of seeing emotion on her face.

"Of course, we made a few modifications since the last time it was tested on you. It is ingenious, isn't it?"

The white gas fell softly through the vents and onto the floor. It completely covered the ground, so much so that Naomi could barely see past her knees. Darin and Marcella were no longer visible. Naomi knew from experience the gas would only be this thick for so long. Once the gas started to dissipate, Milo would have about ninety seconds before Darin and Marcella stirred, and the effects would wear off.

That was if they hadn't changed anything else beyond the sedative aspect. Naomi only needed to wait.

Milo cocked his head. "I am curious, though, Naomi: Why are you here? I have already tried to kill you once, albeit unsuccessfully. Did you think you set the bomb wrong? Or rather, she did?" Milo looked at Luna and pushed the gun harder into Luna's temple, as she winced. "You have already ruined poor Luna's life enough, don't you think?"

Naomi was shaking with rage. Before she could stop herself, she said, "Don't." Naomi regretted the word as soon as it left her lips.

Milo knew it, too. A too-wide, sinister smile stretched across his face. "Oh, Luna doesn't know, does she?"

Naomi was desperate now. "Please, let me—" Milo cut her off. "Let you *what*? Ruin her life, frame her for murder? Use a MAV to drug her with a twilight drug? So she can function, is compliant, but makes no new memories? Give the First Citizen her blood from the cut you reopened on her arm? Although, to be fair, that was for me—not that you knew that at the time."

Naomi's nails bit into her palms so hard she was certain she was drawing blood, the gas still thick, curling around her feet. Naomi saw red. She would kill him. "I didn't have a choice," she spat. "You were going to kill my siblings."

Milo's grin remained as he leaned toward the glass. "Is that what you think we were going to do with them? Interesting. And no choice?" Milo tutted through his teeth. "I don't know that my darling Luna will agree with you. Shall we find out? Because I am fascinated by my prized, resistant Naomi."

He sighed performatively. "What do you think you are going to accomplish? Crush her more than she already has been? Lie to her? Oh. Wait. You have already done all of that. Although I suppose I may have fueled some of the rage—sending Kent a message just the way Darin was supposed to. Alerting him to the fact that the New Republic knew he was a double agent. It gave him just enough stress to render his Prophet ability useless."

Naomi finally met Luna's eyes, and Naomi's heart cracked.

Luna asked, in the most broken tone Naomi had ever heard, "What is he talking about?"

Milo brushed the gun against Luna's copper hair as he pulled her body closer to his. Naomi could do nothing but watch as Milo caressed Luna's neck and inhaled deeply.

Luna did not break eye contact with Naomi, not even as tears ran down her face and her lip wobbled.

Milo was still touching Luna's face and neck as he said, "Oh, Luna, your little side piece—or whatever she is to you—guided *you* to the club the night you lost hours of your life. Naomi helped you install the explosive device. She ensured you hooked everything up just right and that your fingerprints were on everything. In addition, she collected your blood so we could recreate *this*." Milo held up the gold necklace Luna always wore in his hand.

"The only problem was that the First Citizen gave you this damn gold necklace. I suppose I should have thanked her for that before killing her, though. I didn't realize I would need your blood, mixed with the delta flower, to create more—especially because what Naomi initially delivered to the First Citizen wasn't sufficient. Naomi didn't want to hurt you. It's ironic, isn't it?" Milo cocked his head to the side. He was enjoying this.

Naomi watched as Milo confessed what Naomi couldn't. She watched as tears rolled down Luna's face. Naomi knew it would destroy anything she could ever have with Luna. Naomi had been too selfish to give Luna the truth. Now, she was reaping what she had sown from her dishonesty.

Naomi's mind raced into a void of despair she didn't think she would ever escape. A voice came from over her left shoulder, crashing into her spiraling thoughts.

"Well, as riveting as that speech was, you've admitted you won't kill Luna. You need her for more of these, right?"

Naomi's head whipped to her left as she watched Darin appear from behind one of the tubes, aiming his semi-automatic rifle straight at Milo. But what caught Naomi's attention was the gold bracelet that dangled on his left wrist—Luna's father's bracelet.

Milo's own greed betrayed him. He violently shoved Luna away, like he would climb through the glass to get his hands on the bracelet.

Luna fell beneath the glass windows where Naomi could no longer see her.

Milo seethed with rage as he spat, "Where did you get that?"

Darin smiled smugly.

Naomi knew that grin; he was already one step ahead of Milo, and Milo had no idea.

"Sorry, I've had enough new information for today. Thanks." With Luna nowhere in sight, Darin opened fire where Milo stood. The sound echoed in the walls around them, crashing and breaking glass, exploding with each gunshot. Milo tried to take cover, but wasn't fast enough. The scream that emanated from him was nothing short of beastly. His white shirt darkened on his right shoulder with blood.

The noise that flooded the room was beyond anything Naomi had ever heard. Even with her training, she was not prepared for this chaos. She didn't think anyone could adequately prepare for something like this. Naomi covered her ears as she sprinted to Marcella, who was still unconscious on the floor. She dragged her unconscious body toward the left row of tubes to gain some protection from the glass, debris, and bullet casings that shattered around them.

The white gas finally dissipated, and the gunfire had slowed significantly. Naomi could feel her heart thundering in her chest. She needed to find Luna, to keep Milo from her. She rechecked Marcella's pulse—still strong—, and Marcella began to stir.

Naomi needed to move now. She stood, took one step, and suddenly, felt a tug at the base of her skull that crept down her spine. Her vision blurred at the edges as she swayed. She put her hand out to catch herself, but her knees crashed to the floor. As she looked around, trying to figure out what had happened, the sound around her muffled. She wanted to get herself back on her feet, but slowly lost control of her limbs. Her body hit the floor in a heap, as if she were a rag doll.

Before she closed her eyes, she saw Marcella's open.

When Naomi regained consciousness, it seemed only moments had passed, but the entire room was silent—empty. Marcella, Darin, Luna, and Milo were gone.

Naomi got to her feet as quickly as possible, disregarding the broken glass on the floor. As she pushed herself up, she cut open her palm on broken glass. Naomi followed the original path they had taken back out of this godsforsaken place. She needed to find Luna. She needed to find her friends. As soon as Naomi was clear of the lab door, she ran as fast as her feet would take her toward the tunnels.

The tunnels took more time than she wanted, but she pushed her body to its limit. Every muscle ached, every fiber in her legs burned.

When she stepped into the daylight on the small island, she watched the boat she, Darin, and Marcella had come in on speed away in the distance.

Naomi felt everything all at once. She dropped to her knees and felt the ocean air push and pull around her, almost like a cocoon. Her short silver hair stood on end, while her body seethed with rage and fear.

Naomi unleashed a scream so loud that hell itself heard her wrath.

Epilogue

WHILE CHAOS REIGNED WITHIN the building that housed the former 800 Project, no one heard the *ping* from Darin's portable interface on the empty boat tied up in the cove. There was finally enough bandwidth from the island to download a single video. When the download completed, the interface played the video of its own accord, to an empty space.

TIMESTAMP:
DAY 33 OF THE 1ST QUARTER—YEAR 127 OF THE NEW REPUBLIC.

MY NAME IS DAPHNE BARDIN. IT IS DAY 33 OF THE 1ST QUARTER, YEAR 127 OF THE NEW REPUBLIC. I AM 39 WEEKS PREGNANT WITH MY SECOND CHILD, WHO IS ALREADY SHOWING SIGNS OF A POTENTIAL ABILITY IN UTERO.

THE INFORMATION IN THIS VIDEO IS TIME-SENSITIVE, BUT I FEAR I WILL NOT BE ABLE TO GET IT TO THE PROPER PLACES WITHOUT IMPLICATING MYSELF OR MY CHILDREN. I HAVE SAVED IT WITHIN THE NEW REPUBLIC'S ENCRYPTED SYSTEM, IN THE HOPE THAT FIRST CITIZEN KASANDRA SANDERS WILL FIND IT BEFORE MILO IS TOO FAR GONE.

WE HAVE FOUND A WAY TO DISRUPT THE FREQUENCY OF THE GAMMA WAVES THAT THE BEHTARI REQUIRE TO USE THEIR ABILITIES, NOT WITH AN ANTENNA, BUT WITH 'AU'—GOLD, THE DELTA LILY, AND BLOOD

*OF THE ORIGINALS. THE PURE MATTER BETWEEN THE THREE CREATES
AN ELECTROMAGNETIC FIELD THAT I HAVE NEVER SEEN BEFORE. ONCE
COMBINED, THEY CAN BE DEVELOPED INTO JEWELRY, AS YOU CAN SEE
HERE FROM MY GOLD NECKLACE.*

*WHILE THE MATTER DOES NOT IMPAIR THE WEARER'S ABILITY, IT
CREATES WHAT I CAN ONLY DESCRIBE AS AN ELECTROMAGNETIC
BARRIER THAT BLOCKS GAMMA WAVES FROM OTHER BEHTARI.*

*WE ARE STILL IN THE DEVELOPMENT STAGE FOR THIS NEW
TECHNOLOGY. I HOPE TO CREATE MORE TO DISTRIBUTE TO THE
ENSLAVED IN THE COMING MONTHS.*

*ONCE I HAVE MORE DATA, I WILL CREATE INSTRUCTIONS FOR
REPLICATION. UNTIL THEN, THIS NECKLACE THAT I AM WEARING,
ALONG WITH A BRACELET CRAFTED FROM THE EXTRA MATERIAL, IS OUR
FIRST START.*

As Daphne Bardin stood, she lovingly caressed her swollen belly, saying, "I love you more than all the stars, Moon Bug." She then turned off the camera in the lab where she once worked for First Citizen Kasandra Sanders, assembling a small Coven of Resistance *within* the New Republic against Milo Winton.

Acknowledgements

Writing my debut novel started as a dream, became a challenge, and finally a leap of faith into the unknown. There were nights when the words poured out effortlessly, and others when I wondered if I could actually pull this off. Through it all, I was surrounded by an unwavering support system that lifted me up, pushed me forward, and gave me the courage to keep going.

To my editor, **Allison**—thank you for being the guiding light I didn't know I needed. You helped me hone *Golden Resistance* into what it is today. You answered every question or comment I brought to you with kindness and patience—I cannot thank you enough for that. Your feedback was not only kind but also brutally honest, and your encouragement was—most of all—a breath of fresh air. You helped me turn a messy (six-part, yikes!) draft into a world I'm proud to share. I'm endlessly grateful for your work in *Golden Resistance*. Arelia would not be what it is without you.

To my **beta readers, Ellyn, Sarah, Shayden, and Taylor**, thank you for agreeing to my crazy request of, "Hey, I wrote a book you might like... can you read it?" The four of you agreed without question and stepped into Arelia with a passion I could not have imagined.

Your reactions—from cursing my name, to theories, to the occasional text saying—"HOW COULD YOU!"—gave me the drive to keep going. The four of you helped shape these words into a story that became more thrilling than I ever believed possible.

To my **friends and family**, thank you for being my foundation. This has been one of the most exciting and stressful times of my life. You all celebrated every milestone with me, no matter how small. And also forgave me for the many times I prodded you with questions or ghosted you when I went into writing mode. **Mom** and **Dad**, I'm looking at you here!

A special thank you to my friend **Kayleigh**—*Golden Resistance* would not exist without you. Six years ago, you handed me a book that not only brought my love of reading back but also helped me out of spiraling post-partum depression. That moment was the catalyst that led me here, and I cannot find the words to express how thankful I am.

Finally, to my children—thank you to my **Son** for continually asking, "What's going to happen next?" and pushing me further than I thought possible. And thank you to my **Daughters**, who do not yet know it but have given me more courage than I could have fathomed. Thank you for being so patient when I needed "just ten more minutes" and for reminding me that you are never too old to chase big dreams. You three are the best parts of my world. I would not be who I am without you.

Words will never express the thanks I have for your support and love during this.

Three Squeezes

A.O.

About the author

A.O. Garnette is the author of Golden Resistance - Book One of the Signalborn series.

Nestled in Upstate New York, she juggles a full-time job while crafting stories late into the evening with way too many snacks. Her current favorite is the Buldak carbonara ramen.

She is currently working on Book Two of the Signalborn series, and cannot wait to share what happens next.

Love this Book?

Thank you so much for reading *Golden Resistance*!

If you enjoyed Luna's heart, Darin's sass, and Naomi's
drive, please consider leaving an honest review.
Your review helps other readers discover my work and
supports my continued writing efforts.

Thank you! I appreciate you more than you know.

www.ingramcontent.com/pod-product-compliance
Lightning Source LLC
Chambersburg PA
CBHW021957130726
47903CB00014B/1561